TROUBLEMAKER

AND OTHER SAINTS

TROUBLEMAKER

and OTHER SAINTS

CHRISTINA CHIU

G. P. PUTNAM'S SONS | NEW YORK

This is a work of fiction. Names, characters, places, and incidents either are the product of the author's imagination or are used fictitiously, and any resemblance to actual persons, living or dead, business establishments, events, or locales is entirely coincidental.

G. P. PUTNAM'S SONS
Publishers Since 1838
a member of
Penguin Putnam Inc.
375 Hudson Street
New York, NY 10014

"Troublemaker" first appeared, in slightly different form, in *Tin House* magazine.

Library of Congress Cataloging-in-Publication Data

Chiu, Christina.
    Troublemaker and other saints / Christina Chiu.
        p.   cm.
    ISBN 0-399-14715-2
    1. Chinese American families—Fiction. 2. Chinese Americans—
Fiction. 3. United States—Social life and customs—
20th century—Fiction.   I. Title.
PS3553.H536 T76   2001   00-056501
813'.54—dc21

Printed in the United States of America

10 9 8 7 6 5 4 3 2 1

This book is printed on acid-free paper. ∞

Book design by Gretchen Achilles

TO CLIFFORD, MY HERO,

WITH LOVE

I would like to thank the Virginia Center for the Creative Arts, the U Cross Foundation, the Van Lier Foundation, Hedgebrook, the Ragdale Foundation, The Writers Room, and the Asian American Writers' Workshop.

Many thanks to Helen Schulman, Rob Spillman, Elissa Schappell, and the *Tin House* staff, Michael Cunningham, Miriam Cohen, Hal Sirowitz, Nancy Joachim, and Marguerite Bouvard: your support and encouragement have meant everything to me. Thanks to Milda (the Book Doctor), Maggie Tang, and Anna Jardine for reading these stories. Thanks also to my editor, Aimee Taub, and my agent, Jennifer Carlson, who put their heads and hearts into this work. Last but not least, thanks to Kathryn and Mignon.

Something deeply hidden had to be behind things.

—ALBERT EINSTEIN

CONTENTS

N O B O D Y

I T ' S S N O W I N G. My fingers itch from the cold, but still, I can't go in. The house is too quiet, too empty. Without Grandma, it's got that too big, hollow feeling. It's been three whole weeks, but still, whenever I get home from school, there's a part of me that goes, Please be there. When she isn't—when she doesn't call, "Meme-ah? Is that you?"—I feel this hole getting larger inside me, and if I don't watch out, it'll swallow me up.

Grandma once said, "When someone dies, Meme-ah, maybe she becomes a bird or a butterfly." So who knows? I go around to the back of the house, move Grandma's lawn chair to the wall of bushes between our house and the Sheng-Stevensons', and plant my butt in its snowy seat. The lawn is frosty white and full of animal tracks. Birds. Maybe squirrels. They disappear into the woods, where the ground is covered with pine needles.

I take out my book and read—slowly and clearly, the way

Grandma liked—and what comes back is her pruny-mouthed smile and those fogged-up blind eyes. Snowflakes slip into the back of my collar. I shiver.

ROMEO	Tut, I have lost myself, I am not here.
	This is not Romeo, he's some other where.
BENVOLIO	Tell me in sadness who is that you love?
ROMEO	What, shall I groan and tell thee?
BENVOLIO	Groan? Why no, but sadly tell me who.
ROMEO	Bid a sick man in sadness make his will?
	A word ill-urg'd to one that is so ill.
	In sadness, cousin, I do love a woman.

A branch twitches in the woods. A gray squirrel hops into the yard. It sees me and freezes.

"Grandma?"

My voice scares it. The squirrel scurries up a tree. It hops from one to another, and is gone. Snow falls harder, sticking to my lashes. I wait. But no more squirrels. No birds. The sky hangs dusty white. Scattered clouds drift around like sad feelings. Soon it's too dark outside to read. My butt's all wet and frozen, and I'm shaking all over. I know I've gotta go in, but the house is so dark and lonely.

Next door, Sarah, a girl in my English class, comes out on her back porch. Every day it's the same thing. She smokes one Camel Light, finishing it before her mom comes out of her study. Sarah leans against the porch railing and stares at the woods. She listens for the six-o'clock train to pass.

Does she see me? I duck low in the chair and pull the top of my jacket over my mouth.

Sarah puffs and exhales as if the world's this huge problem.

Yeah, right. What problems you got, huh? Sarah's got Chinese eyes but a tall American nose. She streaks her hair blue and paints her nails silver. She wears big turtleneck sweaters with really short mini-kilts. She blasts her music so loud the whole world can hear it, and she doesn't turn it down, not even when her mom yells. Thing about Sarah is that she goes out with this senior, Evan, so she's got a trillion friends.

It isn't like I care or anything. Grandma once said, "One good friend is better than ten bad ones." She also said books were more reliable than people. They could disappoint you, she said, but they never just up and disappeared on you. Not like some people I know.

"Tryouts are Monday," Sarah says.

"Yeah?"

It's a guy's voice, so I think it's Todd, Sarah's brother, who's the biggest jock in the whole school.

I peek through a hole in the back of the chair. *Gross*—it's Evan, not Todd, behind her, kissing her neck. He sticks his hands up the front of her sweater. She squeals.

Gross. I shut my eyes and turn around.

"I'd make a good Juliet, don't you think?" Sarah says.

"Fuck the play," he says. "You've got your Romeo."

Sarah giggles.

"What? Am I not or am I not?" he asks.

Blah, blah, I think, wishing she'd finish her cigarette already.

"Really, Evan," she says. "It'd be so totally phat being up there in front of everyone."

I shouldn't look, I know I shouldn't, but I peek over again. Evan takes a puff from her cigarette. Smoke funnels out his nose. "Hair's a little blue, don't you think?"

"So I'll dye it back."

Evan smooshes her boobs. From the look on Sarah's face, it can't feel good. "I don't know," he tells her. "I don't want some dumbfuck feeling you up onstage."

The six-o'clock train blows by. The rails clink, and all at once it's gone. Sarah puts out her cigarette. They go inside.

Mom and Dad bring takeout for dinner. General Tso's chicken for me, mapo tofu and beef-and-broccoli for them. We eat Chinese style: chopsticks and a bowl of white rice, the dishes in the center of the round table. I've changed into dry jeans and a thick sweatshirt. My toes and fingers still burn from the cold. Dad takes off his tie and jacket and hangs them on the back of his chair. He runs a hand through his hair as though he's got a lot of it. Outside, the sky is black and moonless. My throat feels funny. Maybe I'm going to be sick. Then I'll be stuck at home by myself. No Grandma to collect snow in the frying pan to make red-bean ices. No Grandma to read to.

"What should we do about that Ametex order?" Mom asks Dad. They've got a textile-exporting business, and they love to talk drapes and upholsteries.

"What can we do?" Dad replies. "They want to hold off. See

what happens." He's talking about Hong Kong. Grandma said the British took it from the Chinese and pretty soon they've gotta give it back.

Mom sighs. The strand of white hair she plucked last month is back, the short stub poking in the air. Dad dishes beef onto his plate. He smashes it in his rice and draws his bowl to his mouth. He shoves it all in. "Did you bring home the fax?" he asks, his mouth full.

"What fax? I didn't see a fax."

"Can I get a dog?" I ask.

"No," Mom says, adding broccoli to the beef on Dad's plate. She knows how he sneaks out of eating vegetables. This way, because it's on his plate, he's got to eat it.

"The fax," he snaps. "Asiatex. I gave it to you."

"Please?" I say. "I swear I'll take care of it and walk it and feed it and you won't ever have to do anything."

"I said no," Mom says, spooning tofu onto her rice. It's greasy red from chili sauce. She turns to Dad again. "You never gave me any fax."

"I did."

"Why not?" I demand. "Why can't I? I'm the only one in the whole world who can't have a dog."

"Laurel," Mom warns. "We've talked about this before, and I don't care to bring it up a hundred times. What about Yu? Don't you like it anymore?"

Right. Like a fish and a dog are the same thing?

"If you have so much time on your hands, you should help your mother more," Dad says, pulling a folder from his briefcase.

Blah, blah.

"She shouldn't have to work all day, then worry about making dinner when we get home. Your grandmother wasn't so good at this kind of thing because of her eyes—"

Something catches in my throat, and I cough. Dinner? That all she means to you?

Dad plucks a paper from the folder. "Ah—see?"

I stare at my food and don't feel even a little bit hungry. "May I be excused?" I ask Mom.

"Finish," Dad says, pointing at my bowl with his chopsticks. "Don't waste. One must never waste."

No, I think, I won't finish. I won't, you can't make me.

I chew each piece of chicken twenty-five, twenty-six times before swallowing, and eat my rice one grain at a time. Finally, when he's done with dinner, Dad leaves the table and goes to the living room. The TV switches on.

I look at Mom. Now can I go?

She tips her head: Go, then.

Upstairs in my room, Yu sees me and swims to the surface of the water. She's orange with black spots, and she has one clear eye and one solid black. Her tail fans out behind. "Don't take it personal or anything," I say, feeding her. She sucks a flake into her mouth and spits it out.

The next morning, I wake up sick. My cough's so bad Mom tells me to stay home. After she and Dad leave for work, I get the courage to go into Grandma's room. Incense, Vicks cough drops, dusty books. The smell of her is still there. Maybe it's in the bed or the carpet. Maybe it's the books. I lie down and close my eyes, and for a moment I can almost hear her reading to me. Thing is *almost*. All I've really got of hers are two shelves filled with books and a bureau with a porcelain Guan Yin. There's also a small night table with a framed picture of me on it, and a twin-size bed with my old Pooh comforter.

Before I know it, I've got my jacket on and I'm racing outside. I brush the snow away from the chair and sit down. While I'm reading, my breath comes out in smoky puffs. The cold makes me start coughing, but I don't care. I can't move until Grandma gives me some kind of sign: something, anything.

Later on, the sun starts to go down, but I'm still waiting. An icicle drips from the gutter. Otherwise it's all quiet. So far I've spotted a chipmunk and a couple of black crows. A swallow appears in the dogwood by the back door. I'm eyeing it when Sarah comes out to her porch. She bangs the screen door. The sound scares off my bird.

I watch through the bushes. Evan's there.

Does going out with someone mean you've got to be with him every single minute? I mean, how could you think with someone squeezing your boobs all the time?

Sarah lights a cigarette. "I don't see what the big deal is. It's just a play."

"You my girl or what?" Evan asks. "You want to be my girl?"

"Yeah."

"Well, I need my girl with me," he says, drawing her close. "You know, here by my side."

He kisses her and reaches a hand up the back of her sweater. All of a sudden he jams his fingers into the waist of her skirt.

"Stop," she says, holding his hand. "My mother."

But even *I* know it'd take an earthquake to get Sarah's mom out before six, and so he reaches up her skirt and tugs down her pink panties. She grabs his hand and loses the cigarette. "Evan— cut it out."

"You a tease or something?" he says.

I shrink into the chair. My chest gets that itchy going-to-cough feeling.

"The guys are right," he says. "Maybe you ought to go back to your crib." He hops the porch to the snow-covered lawn and heads down the driveway to the street. I can hear the crunch of his boots in the snow. He gets into his Corvette and screeches away from the curb. Sarah kicks the railing and turns to face the screen door. Maybe she's looking at her reflection, because she says, "It's no fucking big deal. Just let him do it and get it over with, okay?"

Then the worst thing happens. I cough.

"What the hell . . ." she mutters.

I peek over the bushes and wave my book. "I'm, uh, reading?"

Her face gets all scrunched up. She jumps the porch and pushes through the bushes. She comes at me. "You fucking lesbo pervert," she says.

"I wasn't—" I jump to my feet. "I didn't—"

She's shaking she's so mad. Her hand jerks into the air.

She going to hit me? I wonder. Everything goes into slow motion. Her arm swings down. I go for the block and grab her wrist. I hold it there, and she stares. Stunned, she pulls free.

"If anyone finds out, you're dead meat," she says. "Got that?"

I look at her. Yeah—I got that.

"You're a fucking nobody," she says. "A big fat nothing. Know that?"

She retreats into her house. I'm still standing there when the train rushes by. The woods are dark. Somewhere out there, the rails clink like loose keys.

I lie low for a few days. My body's this giant shell ready to crack open. Sarah's right—I *am* a big nobody, a nothing. I'd be better off dead. In English, Mr. A gives another pop quiz. I look at the five questions, and think, Who cares what Mercutio says? How's foreshadowing important in real life? I write my name at the top of the sheet and hand it in. I tell Mr. A that I'm going to the bathroom.

In a locked stall, I sit and try to get my head right. There's a chance that Mr. A has looked at my quiz by now, so I've got to kill time until the bell rings. The stall is green and covered with graffiti: "Wild girls '99." "A.H. + Z.W." "Eric S. is short for shithead." I notice purple marker: "S.S. thinks she's so cool." "S is for SLUT." "For a good time, call Sarah . . ."

The bathroom door bangs open. A bunch of girls pile in. A lighter clicks on. One of them says, "Right there, fucking in the backseat of his car." From the purple boots, I know it's Sarah's friend Diane.

"He told you that?" someone else asks.

"Tells me everything. Says Sarah just lies there. He calls her 'dead fish.'"

"No! That's so gross."

They start laughing, and I'm thinking, They call each other friends? Then, all at once, they go quiet, and I know they see me. I get up and flush. When I come out, they look at me all relieved. Oh, it's only her. They brush their hair and put on more lipstick. Diane takes her cigarette from the edge of the sink and disappears into a stall with a thick purple marker. I wash my hands and hurry out.

Mr. A snags me the second I get into the hallway. The bell rings and everyone in the classroom files out. Sarah meets up with her phony friends. Mr. A motions with the crook of his finger for me to step into the classroom. From the look on his face, I know I'm in deep shit.

After an hourlong "discussion" with Mr. A, Mom and Dad bring me home from school. Dad drives. He clears his throat a trillion times. Mom shakes her head and sniffles. She's got to be thinking about Chrissy, my older cousin, who's so totally perfect and pretty and smart. Neither Mom nor Dad says a word the entire way home. I look out the window and think, Now what?

At the house, Dad loosens his tie. "Sit," he says.

"It's not my fault," I explain.

Mom takes the paper from her purse and shoves it in my face. "Not your fault? Whose? The devil erase everything? He sign your name at the top?"

"It's just a quiz," I say.

"Just a quiz?" Dad retorts.

I shut my trap and cross my arms over my chest.

Mom shakes her head and looks at me: How could you do this to us? "To go and tell your teacher—a stranger!" she says. "Tell him you want to die. To *die*. Imagine. What do they think about us, your parents, uh?"

"I didn't mean it like that," I say. "It's not like they think anything."

"Oh? They think those Chinese parents don't know how to raise a child. They think our daughter's crazy—needs to see jing zeng bing doctor."

"Ungrateful pig," Dad adds, his nostrils flaring large and round. "You know how hard your mom and I work? Morning to night. Think we enjoy to do this? Think we work so hard because we feel like it? We have fun working ourselves to death?"

"No."

"You have it too easy, I tell you."

Mom nods. "Too easy, too easy." She digs leftovers from the fridge and sets them on the table, then sticks yesterday's rice into the microwave. I watch the timer count down from two minutes.

"You don't know," Dad says. "So spoiled. We should send you back to China. Taste bitterness. See how you like it."

So, send me back, see if I care. Hate you, I hate you, I hate you.

"Look at her face," Dad says, waving a finger at me.

Mom shakes her head.

"What?" I say.

"You know exactly what," Dad says, his voice quivering.

That's right—I hate you.

Mom sighs. "Okay, enough. Say you're sorry, Laurel. Say it and promise it won't happen again. Let's eat."

No, I won't eat. I won't. If Grandma were here, she'd give me one of those "Do what your parents say" kind of looks, and then I'd have to. But she's not here, she's not, so I turn to Mom and say, "For what?"

"You dare talk back?" Dad yells. Mom squeezes his shoulder, and he stops.

I know I should say it—that it's an easy one-word solution to a bad thing about to happen—but my jaw clenches, and I just can't.

"Your mother," Dad says to Mom now. "See how she's ruined the girl?"

I jump up. "Don't talk about her like that! You've got no right—"

Dad leaps to his feet and upturns the table. Everything goes flying. I stumble back into my chair. Dishes smack against my chest and crash to the floor. The rounded edge of the table lands in my lap.

This weird numbness fills me up. There was that spanking I got a few years ago—Dad tried to beat the stubbornness out of me— but Grandma put a stop to it. "You want to hit her again, you'll have to strike through me first," she said, shielding me with her body.

Now when I look at Dad, I want to say, Go on, you big jerk, beat me up if it makes you so happy. See if I care.

Mom looks as though she has a trillion things to say all at once, but when she opens her mouth, everything sticks at the back of her throat.

"Just go," Dad snarls at me. "Get out of my sight."

Mom lifts the table enough for me to get up. She thumps the thing to the floor. I take my knapsack and go upstairs. I don't hurry. My legs throb and it hurts to climb each step. A piece of chicken drops from my shirt to the carpet. In my room, I lock the door. As soon as the light goes on, my fish swims out of her castle and turns a quick circle. She rises to the surface of the water. Her fins look silky and soft.

"They'll be sorry," I say. "You'll see." I picture myself at my own funeral. I'm lying in a casket, and Mom and Dad are standing next to me. They cry and cry, and say, If only we hadn't been so mean . . .

The fish's mouth puckers and opens, puckers and opens. Maybe she's trying to say, Love you, love you. I know I should feed her, that those flakes of shrimp food are really what she's looking for, but that empty feeling fills me up again, so I switch off the light, hug my legs to my chest, and listen to Mom and Dad arguing.

In the morning, I'm out of the house before Mom and Dad get downstairs. A yellowish black-and-blue welt cuts across both my legs. It kills me each time my jeans rub against them. In the yard, Grandma's chair lies on its side. My book sits in the snow, its pages crackling in the wind. I head straight into the woods. Twigs crunch under my sneakers. I push past prickly bushes and pines. Branches flick me in the face, but I don't stop until I get to the tracks. The rails shine coppery orange but stink of engine oil and damp rot. They run across the bridge to the other side of the stream, where there's a low bank. The thing that flashes into my head is that Road Runner cartoon. He gets tied to the tracks before an oncoming train. But just in the nick of time he goes free, and instead Wile E. Coyote winds up getting smashed as flat as a pancake. The cartoon used to make me laugh. Like it's so funny?

I step onto the tracks, pebbles crunching under my feet. The sun breaks out from behind a blank sky. I follow the rails to the other side of the bridge. Halfway across, I look at the water gushing over the rocks. It feels too open out here, as though the slightest breeze might knock the whole bridge down. Snowflakes fall and disappear into the water. Sarah's right, I think. You're a big, fat nothing. Nobody cares. Not even Grandma cares anymore. I bang my fists against the steel bridge and yell, "Oh, yeah? Well, I don't care either—I hate you, too!"

The rails clink. I make my way back over the bridge. I'm about to jump off when the ground starts to tremble under my feet. Vibrations run up my ankles into my knees and body. The air sucks in its breath. And then the train appears. It comes around the bend, and it's not what I pictured. It's got a flat face—a dark eye for a window and a bent grate for a mouth. My jacket flutters like a scared bird. The horn blares, and the world shakes under my feet.

I think, One small step. Just one. A tingly, hot feeling runs through me. My heart beats fast and crazy. This is it, this is your chance.

But the horn blows again, and my head gets all scrambled.

What about Yu? Who'll feed her? One step back, and I'm standing next to the tracks, watching the train blow right by. It speeds away and disappears into the thicket.

I'm standing there, shaking all over. My heart's going a trillion miles a minute, and I'm floating above myself. Then it hits me: It's gone, the train is gone, and I'm still here. My sneakers stick in the mud, and I'm me again. All I can think is, Look at you, you're the biggest chicken in the whole universe. Stupid coward. Can't you do anything right?

After a while, I give up. It's quiet when I get home. Too quiet. Mom and Dad have left for work, and the house looks emptier than ever. The snow has melted. The lawn squishes under my feet. The icicle drops from the gutter and smashes on the ground. My body feels like I've fallen into a pond with my clothes on. I set Grandma's chair right and pick up the book. The pages are wet and stuck together.

I sit and peel them apart. My head feels tired and too heavy. The sun melts my eyes shut. I sink into the dark. Somewhere a bird chirps. It flutters in front of my face, its feathers tickling my cheeks. "Hello?" it calls.

"Grandma?" I say.

But she continues to flap her wings. "Hello?" she repeats. From the milky layers at the surface of her eyes, I can tell she's still blind. "What are you doing?" she asks. Before I have the chance to answer, she takes off into the woods. Branches shake like a cheerleader's pom-poms. I open my mouth to scream, I'm reading! but what comes out is a high chirp I can't understand. The sun flickers, waking me.

"No, wait," I stutter.

"Um, okay."

I open my eyes. It's the blue streaks I notice first.

"Huh?"

Sarah stands over me, blocking the sun. "I said, 'What're you doing?'"

The book's on my lap, so I say, "Uh, reading?"

"No, I mean—you're not trying out, are you?"

Since when did she start caring what I do? Then I get it. Does she really think I want to be Juliet?

"Why?" I ask. "Think it'd be too weird for a Chinese Juliet?"

"No," she blurts.

Right—that's exactly what she's thinking.

"Juliet goes beyond a face, you know," I tell her.

"Chill. I was just asking. 'Sides—I'm sort of Chinese, too, you know."

"Sort of."

Sarah winces, and then I feel bad. "Well, it's not like you've got to worry," I say. "I'm just reading."

"Reading?"

"Yeah, just reading—that okay with you?"

She pauses. From the skeptical look on her face, I know she's wondering why I read out loud. "You're weird."

"So I'm weird today, fucking nobody yesterday. Guess that makes me a weird fucking nobody. Yeah, I like the sound of that. Weird fucking nobody."

She kicks at the grass and takes up a clump. A thin blade sticks to her sneaker. "Listen, I'm sorry, okay?"

"Whatever," I say. "Blah, blah."

"No, really," she says. "If there's a weird fucking nobody—it's me."

From up the street, Evan sounds his stupid horn. *Toot, toot-toot, toot-toot—toot-toot!*

"Oh, shit—" She gets all panicky and hurries back to her house.

On Saturday, a rustling sound from Grandma's room wakes me. It's late—my head feels full of Jell-O. I get up and go to Grandma's door. Mom's big butt is sticking out of Grandma's closet. She's rummaging through Grandma's things. Hangers knock against one another. Mom's already got a box of books packed. I storm into the room and return the books to the shelves. I mean, who does she think she is? She can't just come in here and mess things up. "These are mine," I say. "Grandma said I could have them."

Mom sighs. I'm wearing an extra-large T-shirt. She sits on the bed and folds Grandma's favorite cardigan—the red fluffy one—and sets it in a plastic garbage bag. I arrange the books from small at top to large at bottom. "You can't, you can't touch these," I say. When I'm done, I snatch the sweater out of the bag and put it on.

"I know this is a hard time," Mom says, glancing at the bruise on my legs. It's bluish-purplish black and looks worse today than yesterday. I'm glad. She reaches to touch it, but I step away.

She looks at me with sad-lidded eyes. "Your father loses his temper sometimes," she says, "but he loves you."

Blah, blah.

"If he didn't care so much, he wouldn't bother, would he? If it was that wild girl next door, think he would care less?"

I wind Grandma's sweater tight around me, and I want to say, Maybe he could care a little less, then? And I wish I were that girl next door, Sarah, anybody, just not me, definitely not me.

Mom sighs again. "You know, if Grandma were here, she'd be very upset to find out you skipped school yesterday. They called, you know. You're lucky your dad happened to be out of the office."

"If Grandma was here," I say, "she wouldn't have sat there and let him do that."

Mom gulps as though she's trying to get down a hard-boiled egg. She says, "What were you doing all day?"

"Nothing."

I mean, what am I supposed to say, I tried to kill myself but it didn't work out?

"Fine," Mom says, her lips pressed together. She pushes up to her feet and turns back to the closet. "It's nearly noon. Go wash up for lunch. Dad'll be back any minute."

I'm shampooing when I hear the doorbell ring, rinsing when Mom knocks at the bathroom door. I hurry out of the shower and pull on a clean shirt and jeans. I tie Grandma's cardigan around my waist. Mom's still going through the closet. I head to my room, brushing the tangles from my hair, and find Sarah staring at me with big mascara eyes from the other side of the fishbowl. What's *she* doing here?

"Totally bad fish you got," she says. "What's his name?"

"Her," I correct, my brush stuck in a knot. "Yu."

"Yu," she repeats, saying it all wrong. "What's it mean?"

"Fish," I answer, surprised she doesn't know even a little bit of Chinese.

Sarah checks to make sure I'm not joking. When I shrug, thinking, Sounds good enough to me, she cracks up laughing. Watching her, I do, too. When we settle down, she gets all serious. "Listen, can I ask you something? You see, tryouts start Monday, and well, I'm just dying to be Juliet, you know? Well, and I see you out there reading, and I was thinking that maybe, if you didn't mind, I could sort of hang out and read along with you?"

"You mean rehearse or something?"

"Yeah," she says, smiling. "Yeah, something like that."

I don't get it. Why me?

"Yeah, I know it's kind of weird. It's just, I don't know, when you said that thing about Juliet being more than a face? Well, it got me thinking. You were totally *on*. Juliet *is* more than a face. I want to be that Juliet. I want to be more than just . . . this face."

No way. She thinks that?

"I wanted to talk about it with Diane and them," she continues, "but I don't know, they didn't really get it."

Mom pulls a trash bag full of stuff out of Grandma's room and drags it downstairs.

Sarah sits on my bed. "You ever hang out and everyone's having an awesome time, and well, you are, too, I guess, but somehow you still feel sort of alone?"

Mom ascends the stairs with a new bag. She waves it open and returns into Grandma's room. That space inside me aches again. I have to get out of here soon. "You mean lonely?" I ask.

"Yeah, I guess."

I look at her and think, She's got everything and I've got nothing, but Grandma was right—one good friend beats ten rotten ones. "Only, like, every day."

There's the crinkling of plastic bag from Grandma's room.

"I could come over," Sarah says, all hopeful. "We could practice here in your room. Yeah, Yu's a Shakespeare-lover. Aren't you?"

Yu rises for air. Her mouth puckers and opens, puckers and opens.

"See? She loves the idea," Sarah says, tapping the glass. Yu torpedoes around the bowl.

I shake my head, hear the jangle of metal hangers in Grandma's closet. "Can't be here."

"Well, we could do it at my house." She picks at her nail polish. "It's just that Evan comes around all the time now, and well, he's sort of not into me doing this play." Sarah stares at the fish hiding in her castle. She glances up at me. "Well, I guess you sort of heard that part, huh?"

"I didn't mean to . . . I was just . . ."

"I know, I know," she says. "We've been over that, remember? You're a fucking nobody and I'm a big fat nothing."

This makes me smile. "Come on," I say, leading her out of the room. "I know the perfect place."

Outside, it's all weird and too warm. We cross the bridge and get to the other side. The snow's melted, and the bank has turned into a mini-island. We leap over to it. A baby icicle hangs like a stalactite from the bridge. A drop of water dangles at its tip and refuses to let go. We find a scene from the play and start to rehearse. Sarah turns into Juliet, and I am the Nurse.

> JULIET What says he of our marriage? What of that?
> NURSE   Lord, how my head aches! What a head have I:
>   It beats as it would fall in twenty pieces.
>   My back o' t'other side—ah, my back, my back!
>   Beshrew your heart for sending me about
>   To catch my death with jauncing up and down.
> JULIET I'faith I am sorry that thou art not well.
>   Sweet, sweet, sweet Nurse, tell me, what says my
>   love?

Sarah yawns every sentence. Finally I say, "Think you could maybe be a little more—I don't know—in love?"

"In love?"

"Don't look at *me*," I say. "I'm not the one with the boyfriend."

We laugh. The rails make that *chink-chink* sound, and though we can't see it yet, I know the train is coming. "It's like this," I say. "You're all lovey-dovey. He tells you he wants to marry you. So now it's like, does he still feel that way? Does he really love you like he said?"

"Yeah, okay."

"And your grandma's the only one who can help, so you've gotta be really, really nice."

"You mean kiss ass," she says. "Who's Grandma?"

"Huh?"

"You said 'grandma.'" Sarah digs the heel of her shoe into the dirt. The train appears, gets larger and larger. It shakes up the whole world and pounds over the bridge above us—*thump, thump, thump, thump*—the cars bright orange or green. Cold droplets sprinkle over my face. Inside, I get this strange crackling feeling, as if a frosty ice cube got dropped into a cup of hot tea. Then it's like: Grandma's gone.

"Woooieeee!" Sarah screams. Her hair swoops behind her. She kicks her heels into the ground. I join in, yelling and stamping my feet. The train drowns us out. It isn't until it passes that I hear her saying, "Oh, Romeo, Romeo," and I realize she's crying.

It's getting late when we head back. The woods are dark. We hold hands and watch the ground to make sure we won't trip. The air smells of pine. Our feet crunch leaves and ivy and pine needles. Twigs snap. Branches pull at Grandma's sweater. Sarah sucks at a cigarette.

"He's going to kill me," she says, as soon as we step out of the woods.

My foot slips in a patch of mud. I push the last branch out of the way, careful not to let it whip back and hit her. "You mean Evan?" I ask.

"What about Evan?" Evan asks, from Sarah's porch. He gives

us this strange look. We drop hands. Heat rushes into my face. I'm
stuck wondering, What'd we do wrong?

Sarah goes over and hugs him. "Oh, honey—I was just saying
I'd better get back—I had a feeling you'd be by."

"I've been looking for you everywhere," he says.

"Laurel's grandma's got Alzheimer's, and well, we've been
looking for her all day." Sarah turns to me for confirmation.

She does *not*, I want to say. But I say: "Once in a while she goes
for a walk and forgets how to get home."

He glances at me, eyes my sweater, and I feel myself shrinking.
"The guys are hanging out at Diane's," he says. "Told them we'd get
over there. They're doing 'shrooms."

"Yeah? Well, sorry, Laurel. Hope you find her."

"Thanks," I say, backing toward my house. "For all your help."

Just as I turn around, I hear him say, "What's with the
sweater? She a dyke or what?"

"Shut up," Sarah tells him.

I step through the trees. A pine needle sticks me in the eye, but
I keep going.

On Monday, we get a test in English. I finished the book, but I'm all
jumpy on account of the weird blackout last week. Turns out, I answer all the questions—everything including the bonus points.
When class is over, I feel okay to stay and make up the quiz. Mr. A
looks at me: You all right? I'm thinking, Why'd you have to go and
tell my parents? Didn't I say they'd freak out?

On the way out of class, Sarah turns and winks at me. Wish me luck, she mouths. I want to talk with her, ask her about the dyke thing. Questions fly around my head. I mean, he doesn't really think that, does he?

Diane steps out of the bathroom and waits in the hall directly outside the classroom. She notices me winking back at Sarah. Her eyes narrow.

Yeah, I want to say, she's talking to me, and I'm a trillion times better as a friend than you are. Got a problem with that?

Mr. A steps over to my desk and places the quiz facedown on it. He checks his watch and says, "Go." I turn the page over.

At home later that afternoon, I try reading a new book but can't concentrate. Every time I get to the bottom of the page, I stop and go, What was that paragraph about again? I reread it, but the same thing happens. It's blustery out today—loose wisps of hair tickle my cheeks—but the snow's totally melted. How will I know if Grandma's a blade of grass? What if I accidentally step on her? I check my watch. It's almost five o'clock, and I can't help wondering how Sarah's doing. Has she gone yet? Is she nervous? Is she remembering to be more in love? A part of me hopes she'll get to be Juliet. Another part of me thinks, Like she's going to want to be friends after this? She doesn't need you anymore.

That hole inside me gets larger. I stare at the blur of words in front of me until Sarah appears in the yard. She plops on the ground facing my chair. "I made callbacks, I made callbacks," she yips.

"Awesome," I say, forcing a smile. I hate her.

"What's wrong?" she asks.

"Nothing."

"Well," she says, "okay, but . . ."

After a pause that seems to last forever, I say, "I'm not a dyke."

"Oh . . ." She rolls her eyes. "Evan can be such an asshole—"

"And Grandma doesn't have Alzheimer's. She's never had Alzheimer's in her whole life."

"It was the only thing I could think of. Was that bad?"

I feel myself shaking. "She's dead."

"Oh," she says. "Sorry."

Just go away, I think. Leave me alone.

Sarah gets to her feet. Just as I think she's about to take off, she leans over and hugs me real tight, so tight I lose my breath. The world disappears behind a veil of soft blue hair. From the street, there's the sound of Evan's car braking to a stop in front of her house.

"Shit—Diane opened her big mouth," she says, hurrying back to her house.

I go inside and up to my room. As soon as the light flicks on, Yu pokes her head out of the castle.

My windows are shut, but I can hear Evan's muffled yelling. I hate him just as much as I hate the woman up the street who sometimes kicks her dog. Sarah doesn't say anything. I want to go, Stand up for yourself.

"Oh, Juliet," I say. "Wherefore art thou, Juliet?" Yu watches me with her black button eye. Her mouth puckers and opens, puckers and opens.

Outside, everything goes quiet. I hear Evan starting the engine of his car. He roars up the street. Sarah blasts Nirvana from her room. I want to see if she's okay, but somehow I know that she's crying—crying over a jerk who tells her what she can or can't do, and that's just stupid.

I sit at the edge of my bed and take out my book. Yu splashes the water. I start to read—slowly at first, but then quicker and quicker until I'm practically whispering. Yu pokes her nose against the glass. She fans her black-spotted fins. She's listening, really, truly listening.

An hour later, there's the hum of the garage door opening. I haven't done any of my homework, and I don't even care. Dad hasn't said a word since that night. He's waiting for an apology, and the longer he waits, the angrier he gets. Mom gives me the eye, Just apologize. But why should I? He threw the table—not me.

So it ends up like this: The three of us sit down to dinner. Dad eats without saying a word. Mom gives me that crumpled-brow look, Please—do it for me, Laurel.

My bruises ache. I think, Fine, whatever. "Sorry," I say, poking a piece of chicken with a chopstick.

"What was that?" he asks.

"I said, 'Sorry.'"

"Sorry, who?" Dad asks, shoveling rice into his mouth.

I glance at Mom, and think, See? Told you he'd be a jerk about it.

She nudges me under the table with her foot.

"Sorry, *Dad.*"

He puts down his bowl and chopsticks. He chews, swallows.

"Let's get something straight. If you are so unhappy here, feel free to go. No one is forcing you to stay—"

Mom calls out Dad's Chinese name, but he blocks her with a hand.

"No one is forcing you to eat my food or sleep under my roof," he says. "So if you want to die, go ahead, do what pleases you. But never disgrace your mother or me in front of strangers again. Got that?"

I jab my chopsticks into the rice and push the bowl aside. "Got it."

In the bathroom stall, I find new, thick purple marker: "LAUREL DA LESBO."

Diane, I think. God, I've got to find her. I go straight to the cafeteria. My heart is going a trillion miles a minute. All I can think of is smacking her right across her pretty made-up face. The cafeteria stinks of crusty tomato paste and greasy french fries. Rows of rectangular tables fill the room. People's voices bounce all over. Someone chucks an apple into the garbage bin.

Where is she, where is she, where is she?

Then, right there, Diane appears.

How could you? I want to say, but the words refuse to come out.

She looks at me: Now who's got the problem?

"Why are you such a bitch?" I ask.

The entire room quiets. Someone goes, "Oooh." Other people

snicker. Diane steps closer to me, and without meaning to, I step back. She's not bigger than me. Still, I'm afraid.

"Maybe I'm a bitch," she says, smirking. "Beats being a lesbo les-bi-an."

"Stop it," I say. "I'm not, I'm not."

"Les-bi-an," she repeats, all pleased with herself. Everyone starts laughing. I glance at these people who hate me even though they don't know me. I want to say, What did I ever do to you? Then I see Sarah. She doesn't laugh, but she doesn't say anything, either. She cowers and turns away. She doesn't know me. I'm nothing. Nobody.

Right there in front of everyone, I start to cry.

"Poor baby," Diane says. "Boo-hoo."

People laugh. I take off, running all the way home and deep into the woods.

The tracks smell extra bad of engine oil and muddy rot. I picture my funeral again. There'll be flowers—the white kind Mom got for Grandma's wake—and a trillion sad faces. Mom and Dad, and Sarah will be there, too. She'll be there by my casket, reading her stupid lines and crying. Go ahead, cry.

Hate you, I hate you, I hate you.

The ground trembles. I step onto the tracks, and my legs take me to the middle of the bridge. There's the stream and the trees and the tracks. There's the small island Sarah and I rehearsed on, which is nearly underwater now. The sun dives behind a patch of clouds, and the world gets lost in shade. The rails clink, and I feel the train getting closer. I shut my eyes and pray, Help me, Grandma, please help me do this, but when I open them, Sarah's on the tracks. "Laurel," she calls.

"Leave me alone."

She drops her books and comes after me. "I'm sorry, okay?"

"Like it's that easy. 'I'm sorry,' and everything's okay again, right? Wrong."

Sarah catches me by the wrist. "O happy dagger. This is thy sheath. There rust, and let me die." She pretends to stab herself and falls onto the rails.

The train appears from around the bend. The bridge rumbles. We're paralyzed, watching the train coming closer. I look at Sarah, Why? Why didn't you say something? She shakes her head and takes my hand. The horn blares, the sound ripping through me. I pull Sarah to her feet. Without another word, we turn and run for the other side of the bridge. Behind us, books crunch. Papers flutter like little white butterflies, and we still run.

D O C T O R

M Y F I R S T year out of med school, I started working at an eating disorders clinic on the Upper East Side. I was twenty-six, a recovered bulimic, understood the nature of the disorder, and felt that I could make a difference. One of my patients, Laurel, came to us weighing eighty-two pounds. She was five feet, five inches tall, and her sixteenth birthday was in a month. Despite twelve days of treatment, she'd lost another two pounds. Her pulse was down to forty-two beats per minute: her blood pressure 80/50. She had an arrhythmia, which put her at risk for heart failure.

Laurel was my last patient before the weekend. She had come to me through Ma's friend Mary, who was the girl's aunt. I knocked at Laurel's door. "It's Dr. Wong."

"One sec," she called. There was a rustling sound and the sharp squeak of bedsprings. "Okay!"

I opened the door. Laurel's cheeks dipped inward, the bones

protruding against her taut skin. Her face was flushed. Droplets of perspiration showed over her lip and throughout her thinning hair. Her nostrils flared.

Sit-ups again, I thought.

I noticed the fishbowl on the table beside the bed. The bowl contained a lone orange-and-black fish and a miniature white castle. The goldfish circled, searching the glass for a way out.

"Cute fish," I said. "Your mom bring it?"

Laurel shrugged. She was propped against a bunched-up comforter, her legs crossed and a foot bobbing in the air. She was reading *Romeo and Juliet*. The cover of the book was torn, the pages stained and crumpled.

Laurel whispered the sentences quickly, prayerlike, but with a passion that reeked of compulsion. The room's thermostat was set at seventy-eight degrees, and condensation fogged the windows. She wore a red woolly cardigan, a T-shirt, jeans, and thick athletic socks. The sweater hung from her gaunt shoulders.

"Does it have a name?" I asked, looking at the fish.

She gave me an eternally bored expression. "Yu."

I laughed—in Chinese, *yu* means "fish"—and Laurel's eyes darted up at me. There was a moment of recognition: Oh yeah, she's Chinese, too. She smirked; I was on the in. Finally, I thought, a connection.

"So how was the visit with your mom?" I asked, taking her pulse.

She shrugged again, shook her leg. "Same. Worried sick, blah, blah."

"Did you ask for something for your birthday?"

Laurel squinted at the fish. "She'd just say no."

"There's no harm in asking, is there?"

"You don't know Mom."

My nostrils tickled. My attention was suddenly drawn toward a corner of the room. One whiff, another. It was rancid food. Laurel's eyes darted from me to the bureau, then back to me. Her foot went still. "A dog," she stammered. "That's what I want."

I acknowledged her with a nod.

"A German shepherd," she said, clenching my hand. For someone so frail, she caught me off guard with the force of her grip. "But Mom's all like, 'Gain a few pounds first, and then we'll see.'"

I freed myself from her grasp and moved toward the bureau.

"Don't go in there," she said. "It's private." The panic in her voice made me want to take her in my arms, cradle her thinning bones to my body. You have your whole life ahead of you, I wanted to say. A lifetime of experiences to live for. But I could remember the terror. The chaos. Every moment painful and all-consuming.

"I'm sorry, Laurel. You know the rules." I opened the drawer. She quieted as I unraveled a towel filled with carrot bits, biscuit, browning lettuce, and rancid chicken.

"I didn't do it," she said, bolting out of bed. She knocked the table. Water splashed from the fishbowl. Yu banged into the castle and, stunned, drifted in place.

"How many days has this been going on?" I asked.

"I'm being framed. It's Katy. She hates me, the fat cow."

"Hey—come on." I rubbed Laurel's shoulder. She winced and shriveled from my touch. She sat back on the bed.

"Laurel, Dr. Brady's explained what's going on, right?"

She rolled her eyes.

"So you know your body's on the verge of—"

"Yeah, yeah—breaking down my muscles. Blah, blah."

"Internal organs like your heart."

"Blah, blah."

"And liver."

"Blah, blah."

"And brain," I said.

Her body grew stiff, and I knew she must be exerting every ounce of energy not to cry.

"You look scared," I said. "Are you scared?"

She nodded and turned away, and gripped the paperback with both hands. Veins puffed at her knuckles. "Everyone wants to make me fat," she said.

"I don't want that. Neither I nor Dr. Brady is going to let that happen to you."

Her brows creased with suspicion. She shrugged and took up her book. I touched her arm before she could go back to reading. "I'm not going to let your condition get worse without doing something about it, okay?"

She fidgeted, leafing through the book's pages, her foot shaking violently.

"We'll talk more about this on Monday," I said, rolling the towel into a ball. But I knew how it went. As soon as I walked out the door, she'd be counting sit-ups; by the time I got on the Bronx River Parkway, she'd be counting down from one hundred.

———

I exited the highway into town. The defroster cleared the cloudy windshield. My feet felt clammy. They were sweaty yet cold. At the supermarket, I parked the car and headed inside. Wind sneaked down the back of my coat, making me shiver.

The store was brightly lit, and bustling with the after-work commuter crowd. Cashier lines extended all the way into the dairy department. Half-filled metal carts cluttered the aisles, their loose wheels jangling like rusty tambourines. I resisted the urge to leave. Mark has had a long week, I told myself. The least I can do is have dinner ready when he gets home. I hurried up and down the aisles, filling a basket. I felt so hungry that I bit into an apple. Who knows what kinds of pesticides and germs were on it?

I was waiting at the checkout line when my cellular went off. "Hello?" I answered.

"Georgie?" Ma said.

I remembered I was supposed to deliver Uncle's allowance. The envelope of cash was in the zippered pocket of my purse. "Oh, shoot."

"Ah, yah—you forgot?"

"I'm sorry. Things have been crazy lately."

"How could you forget? Uncle has nothing to eat."

I unloaded my groceries onto the belt. "I'll drop off some food. Mark can fix dinner while I'm out."

She quieted the way she always did at the mention of Mark. Neither Dad nor she was all that happy that I'd married a hei ren, but with time, I knew she'd get over it. Taking off for Hong Kong had been Dad's idea. "Mei mien zi," he'd said. "How are we to show our faces?"

This summed up what he'd told my sister, Amy, a born trouble-maker who, after a steady string of F's on her report cards, was caught shoplifting. He'd had her banished to a boarding school in New Hampshire. I felt bad, of course, since some of her problems must have stemmed from me—Ma and Dad constantly compared the two of us. "Georgie made straight A's when she was your age," they'd tell her. "Georgie got a perfect math score on the SAT."

Now, it was me, Georgianna, the one with the grades and scholarships and med school. *I* was the troublemaker.

"Make sure to go up with Carlos," Ma said. Carlos was the super at the St. Martin's. It had been a decent residential hotel when Uncle moved in years before, but now, as one of the few remaining welfare hotels, it had a reputation for crack deals and urine-stained hallways. Ma had tried to move Uncle elsewhere, but he wouldn't have it.

The clerk tallied the groceries. Prewashed salad, a baked chicken, French bread, and a large bag of apples. "When are you coming home?" I asked Ma.

"Ah-yah, I didn't tell you? Your father's buying an apartment."

My stomach bottomed out. They're gone for good, I thought. For good. Most people were leaving Hong Kong in droves, what with all the doubts about the Handover, but not my parents. They couldn't get there fast enough. I finished the last bite of apple, and felt hungrier than ever.

"In Wan Chai," Ma said. "Very nice."

Next to the cashier stood racks with magazines, candy, and

every kind of baked treat you could imagine. Just looking at the Hostess cupcakes—chocolate with the promise of cream in the center—made my stomach growl.

No, I reminded myself. You're not hungry. You're upset.

I handed two packs of sugar-free gum to the cashier and then, after she had rung them up, ripped one open. I stuffed a piece into my mouth. Peppermint soothed my gums.

"There's everything," Ma said. "Any kind of food you like—zong tse or xi tse—just go outside and it's there."

I handed the cashier my credit card.

I heard Dad calling for Ma in the background. "Have to go, now," she whispered. I glanced at the cupcakes and casually tossed a two-pack onto the belt.

Dessert. Everyone needs dessert.

Mark was there when I got home. It was six o'clock and already dark out; I was acutely aware that my patients were sitting down to dinner. From outside our ranch house, I saw the changing light of the television. I entered through the kitchen, and put my purse and keys and the groceries on the counter. Mark had set the dining table with items from our registry: fine china, crystal glasses, silverware, cloth napkins. The lit candles were half melted. On each plate sat a tuna-fish sandwich and a large pickle. He had prepared mine the way I liked: quartered into triangles and with the crusts cut off.

Mark was asleep on the sofa. He'd changed into a T-shirt and sweatpants. Back in school, he'd been so thin—"skinny," he called it—that he used to layer his clothes for bulk. Tonight, however, I noticed his Buddha belly peeking out from under the T-shirt.

I tiptoed to the couch, took a deep breath, and blew on his stomach. It made a loud, farting sound. "Hey," he said, awake now, his eyes pinkish and heavy with sleep. He sat up and yawned. I thought about Laurel, wondered how she was doing with dinner.

"Hey there—you all right?" he asked.

I sat facing him at the edge of the coffee table. "One of my patients . . ."

"Up, up—get your head out of there. We worked last weekend. This one's for us, remember?" He sneaked a finger under his glasses and rubbed his eye. We'd planned to shop for the house (we still needed a television stand and a desk for the study), maybe see a show, possibly dine one night at his favorite French restaurant.

"Agreed," I said. "But—"

"But?" His glasses settled crookedly on his nose.

I leaned my head against his shoulder. "I forgot about Uncle."

He sniffed my hair, which, like my hands, must have smelled of hospital. "Can't it wait? The man's not going to starve, is he?" he asked.

"Hope not."

A vein at his temple pulsed. Even halfway around the globe, Ma and Dad were still plaguing our relationship. He yawned to cover his irritation and pushed himself up from the couch, his knees crunching loudly. He drew me to my feet. "Well, let's do it."

"Honey, thanks, but . . ."

"But?"

"Strangers frighten him."

"Never mind a black man like me, right?" He looked up to the ceiling, sighed, and I could tell he'd spoken before he could stop himself. "Forget I ever said that," he said. "Just go—get this over with already, all right?"

At the St. Martin's I double-parked in front of the building, my haz-ards flashing. I polished off a cupcake. My teeth sank through lay-ers of soft chocolate cake into the cream core. Sweetness filled me up.

I stepped out of the car and wind sucked the crumbs from my coat. The St. Martin's as I'd remembered it was gone. The lobby window was cracked, and boarded on the inside with duct tape. The doorway smelled of urine. In the lobby, chipping paint re-vealed a layer of bluish wallpaper. The furniture consisted of a black imitation-leather ottoman, a desk chair, and a plastic lawn table. The elevator had an "Out of Order" sign. Carlos sat behind the front desk, feet propped on the counter and hands locked be-hind his head. His hair had grayed and thinned. He looked me over and nodded. "Your ma said you'd be comin'."

He labored to get up from the chair, and the springs squeaked under his weight. "Your face just like your ma's," he said. He searched through keys on a ring. When he found the one he was looking for, he locked his TV into a cabinet. We went upstairs. The red carpet stretched to the end of the hall. It was as spotted and matted as a sick tongue. The place reeked of body odor. "I'll wait here," Carlos said, at the stairwell.

"Thanks for waiting with me." I felt for the envelope of fresh bills.

Carlos noticed someone loitering on the landing above. "Eh— you wanna drink, do it in your own room," he said. He didn't take his eye off the guy until the door shut. "I wouldn't have it any other way. Now get going. I gotta get back to the desk soon, eh?"

I stepped to the end of the hall. Today's Chinese newspaper sat outside the door. A dark stain seeped out from beneath. I knocked lightly. "Uncle?"

"Harder," Carlos whispered.

I rapped again, the sound of my knuckles against steel echoing down the hall. "Hello? It's Georgianna."

I waited a moment. "Is he in?" I asked Carlos.

He shrugged and nodded at the foot of the door. "Should be. Paper's still there."

I tried again and again. My knuckles ached. I checked that the hallway was clear, then tried to shove the envelope through the crack under the door, but it snagged and ripped. Air streamed out warm and humid over my hands. It stunk of sour sheets.

"Shoot," I cursed, removing the torn envelope. I returned to the stairwell. "Would you mind?" I attempted a handoff.

Carlos shook his head. "Sorry. Too many kooks in here to be gettin' involved."

Right. I stuffed the envelope into the zippered pocket of my purse. Mark's going to flip, I thought. As if it weren't bad enough, what with the way Ma and Dad had treated him. Now this. I decided I wouldn't tell him. What could I possibly say, any-way? I went to give Uncle money but he refused to open the door? Tonight, when Mark asked, I'd say everything was taken care of.

Carlos cleared his throat. "You called?"

Called?

"Oh, you gotta call," he said. "Your ma always called."

Much too early on a Saturday morning, the phone rang and rang, drawing me out of a convoluted dream. It was about Uncle. He was ringing our doorbell. There were vague bits about sit-ups and cupcakes, sheets of newspaper blowing over the lawn. I remembered opening the door, to have his head roll off into my arms. Mark nudged me awake. He handed me the phone and dropped facedown into the pillow.

It took a moment for me to get my head straight. "Hello?" I said.

It was Nurse Anderson. Laurel had lost another half-pound. "Put her on watch," I said. "Dr. Brady in today?"

"Yes, Doctor."

"Have her meet with Laurel, before you assign staff," I said. "Notify me of any changes."

"Yes, Doctor."

When I hung up, I realized Mark was sprawled over three-quarters of the bed.

"You hog," I said, slapping his rear.

He looked up from the pillow, bleary-eyed: What was that you said?

"I'm sorry about last night." I rubbed his arm. "Strangers really do frighten him."

"Let's drop it." He shifted onto his side. "You're okay, I'm okay, we're okay." He drew me close and tried to wrestle and pin me to the mattress. I went for his underarms and tickled him until he flipped onto his back. "Stop, stop, I give up," he finally said. He was laughing so hard he could barely breathe.

The phone rang again. This time, I was short of breath when I answered.

"I'm so sorry, Doctor." It was Nurse Anderson, stammering with embarrassment. I could picture her going red in the face.

"What's the problem?" I asked.

"Laurel's mother is here. Dr. Brady tried to explain the possibilities of hyperalimentation. Mrs. Tung is adamant that we not perform the procedure. She wants to withdraw Laurel from the clinic."

"I'll be there in half an hour," I said. "Just keep her occupied until I get there."

Mark buried himself under the comforter. I kissed him through the duvet. "We'll do French tonight, okay?" I promised to make it up to him.

At the clinic, I found Mrs. Tung at Laurel's bedside. She was calm, smiling even, and feeding her daughter a spoonful of applesauce. "Choo-choo, choo-choo," she cooed. "Chew-chew for Mommy." Nurse Anderson flashed me this look—Guess who's getting taken for a ride?—then excused herself from the room. Laurel opened her parched lips, her egglike eyes focused on her mother's face. Between bites, she went back to reading out loud, her voice raspy and quick.

Today Mrs. Tung had on a purplish-black top and matching skirt. There was a crease of shriveled skin at the back of her neck. She reminded me of an overripe Chinese eggplant: slender and without sharp features. She heard me enter and turned. We greeted each other politely. Static danced in her hair, and her skin sagged around the eyes and mouth. She had the look of someone who had, as the Chinese say, tasted a bitter life.

"May I speak with you in my office?" I asked her.

"Yes, yes," she said, ready to feed her daughter another spoon of applesauce.

"Don't go, Mommy," Laurel pleaded. The goldfish swam up for air.

"I'll be right back," she said. Laurel started crying. Mrs. Tung glanced at me for reassurance. Should I? Panic showed in her eyes.

"It's just ten minutes," I said.

Mrs. Tung nodded and followed me out the door. "Ten minutes. Ten minutes and I'll be right back."

Laurel cried harder. She threw her book and screamed, "Grandma would never have dumped me in this place! She never would have left me!"

Mrs. Tung froze in the hallway. She shut her eyes, and before Laurel could witness more, I swung the door closed.

"You all right?" I asked, taking Mrs. Tung's arm.

She pulled away. "No tubes or pumps, hear me? Not for my daughter."

"It's a very minor procedure." I tried to keep my voice down. "We don't plan to implement it unless her condition gets worse."

Mrs. Tung shook her head. "My husband says no."

Your husband has yet to show his face, I thought.

I lowered my voice and explained. "Your daughter's very sick."

"She eats every bite," Mrs. Tung said. "Every bite *I* feed her."

I felt like shaking her. Can't you see? Your daughter's dying.

A gasping sound from Laurel's room caught our attention. Mrs. Tung looked at me. I nodded—Go ahead, open it. She stared at the door, took a breath, turned the knob. Laurel was on the floor, struggling with a sit-up, forcing elbows to knees. She shook from the strain. The grimace on her face—lined and weathered like that of a seventy-year-old—made me feel utterly helpless. Laurel's determined to die, I thought, and ultimately there's nothing I can do to stop her.

I found myself at the corner deli two blocks from the St. Martin's. It was close to five p.m. I'd missed breakfast and lunch, and my body was trembling. The store smelled of newspaper and fresh-brewed coffee. The aisles were stocked with colorfully wrapped candies, boxes of assorted baked goods, and bags of snack foods. From the freezer at the back of the store, I grabbed a bottle of diet Coke. I considered an apple for a snack, but then noticed a box of éclairs. In med school, I couldn't stay away from these. Six soft pastries, covered with chocolate and stuffed with creamy vanilla pudding.

One wouldn't hurt.

My cellular sounded, and I nearly jumped into a shelf of Tastykakes. I wondered what I would say if it was Mark. I'd told him I had more to finish up at the clinic, and so we'd meet at the restaurant at seven.

After the third ring, I lost my nerve and answered. There was a staticky, long-distance pause. "Ma?" I said. "Is that you?"

"Georgie?" she whispered. In the background, I could hear Dad's loud, guttural snore.

"What are you doing up?" I asked. "It's six in the morning over there."

"Getting old." I could picture her in her terry-cloth robe, pacing in the dark with a cigarette. "I worry," she said.

"Don't."

She exhaled. I thought of Laurel struggling with her sit-ups— up, down; up, down—and a longing ache stuck at the back of my throat.

"Oh, Ma. Everything's fine. I'm fine."

She sighed. "Uncle all alone in that place. So dangerous. If only we could find him some place in Chinatown."

Who's "we"? I wanted to say.

"He's fine," I told her.

She quieted. "Maybe you should take him out for food sometimes?"

"Never mind dinner," I said. "I can't get him to open the damn door."

"You didn't give him the money?"

"It's not my fault. This is my second time already."

"Ah-yah. You have to call first."

"I know that *now.*" I told her I was, even as we spoke, on my way to the St. Martin's.

"Take good care of Uncle, uh?" she said softly, and from the tone, I knew they weren't coming back.

I called Uncle from the car. After an infinite number of rings, he finally answered the phone. I had just taken a bite of éclair. When I looked up from the wheel, there was a woman in the middle of the road. I braked. The woman dragged her treasures across the street. She turned to me and continued to talk to herself. Circles of rouge dotted her cheeks.

"Hello, hello?" I shouted into the phone.

"Ah?" Uncle stammered.

I swallowed the mouthful of éclair, and it went down like cardboard. "Uncle, it's me. Georgianna."

"Oh my God. Wong Lung Fang-ah?"

"Yes. It's Wong Lung Fang."

"Oh my God."

"I came by yesterday. Didn't you hear me knocking?"

"I was, oh, yes, taking a bath."

"Well, I'm on my way over. In fact, I'm just about there now."

Though it was already growing dark out, you could tell the St. Martin's must have been quite grand in its day. Its façade was covered with soot and streaked with stains, and sections of molding had chipped and cracked, yet the building's French Renaissance–style architecture gave it a certain historic presence. Several floors had wrought-iron balconies, which extended around the building. The windows were framed like doorways.

"Uncle? Hello?"

"Oh my God," he stammered. "Oh my God."

"Open the door, okay?" I said. I double-parked and entered the lobby.

"Ah?" he said. "Sleeping."

Open the door or I'll break it down with my bare hands, I thought, stumbling over an abandoned plastic doll and nearly twisting an ankle. The doll had long hair and open-and-close eyes.

"Uncle?" I repeated into the phone.

There was a click and the line went dead.

I was banging at the door when my phone rang. I kicked Uncle's newspaper aside and answered, "God damn it—hello!"

"Doctor?" Nurse Anderson peeped. "Doctor Wong?"

"Oh, hi," I said. My knuckles burned. "Sorry. I didn't mean to yell at you like that. What's up?"

"It's Laurel—"

I've lost her. Jesus, I've lost her.

"Cardiac arrest, but we were able to resuscitate," she said.

"What are her vitals? No, never mind, I'll be there in a few minutes." I hung up and headed for the stairwell.

"He comes out at night," Carlos told me, as I passed him on the landing.

"Excuse me?"

"Seven. Sometimes eight or nine."

I nodded and raced downstairs. Don't do this to me, Laurel, I prayed. You've got to fight this. In the car, my sugar-coated fingers stuck to the wheel. I raced uptown. Stores and fast-food restaurants blurred past.

At the clinic, I found Laurel in critical but stable condition. Dr. Brady and I discussed the possibility of surgery and the immediate changes in her treatment plan. She was now being fed intravenously at a rate of forty cubic centimeters an hour, which was to be increased gradually within the next two weeks to one hundred sixty cubic centimeters. This would be the equivalent of two thousand calories per day. From X rays, I could tell there was damage to the heart; the right ventricle had thinned to the point of possible hemorrhage. I was keeping Laurel in intensive care, but I knew that if she had another attack, there'd be little we could do to save her.

After meeting with Dr. Brady, I spoke with the cardiologist and then sent X rays to his department. Later I went to look in on Laurel in IC. The curtain was drawn partway around her bed. The cardiomonitor beeped: up, down; up, down. The infusion pump gurgled. IV dripped. An oxygen mask covered Laurel's nose and mouth. The Tungs were already there. Laurel seemed to be asleep, yet her mother was at her side reading out loud from *Romeo and Juliet*. Mrs. Tung held her daughter's hand. Mr. Tung was positioned at the foot of the bed. His briefcase was in one hand, his wife's purse and coat in the other. He looked from his daughter to the IV.

It had taken this to get him here.

Mr. Tung loosened his tie. The knot tipped off center. His eyes were glassy and dazed. It was a look I'd seen before: What did I do so wrong? How has it come to this?

Before I could stop myself, I ducked away, quickly gathered my things from the office, and hurried out of the clinic.

It was a miracle. Uncle was standing outside the St. Martin's when I arrived. The poor guy was staring at a piece of litter skipping over the sidewalk. His back was bent; his hands were tucked deep into his coat pockets. He was smaller than I remembered, overexposed to the elements. I tossed the pastry box into a garbage can. There was only one éclair left. My pants dug into the skin at my waist.

"Uncle?"

He remained still, frozen in his thoughts. I touched his shoulder and he flinched. He looked at me as if I were a ghost. "Si-mong, ah?"

"It's Georgianna, Uncle."

He blinked. "Wong Lung Fang-ah?"

"Yes. Wong Lung Fang. What are you doing out here?"

He scanned the ground at his feet. He seemed to be checking that he hadn't dropped anything.

"Have you eaten?" I asked. "Would you like to get dinner?"

His head rocked forward and back.

"Okay, how about that diner on the corner? I can smell burgers from here." My stomach throbbed painfully. It felt too full, like it might explode.

Uncle's head bobbed from right to left. "Ah," he muttered. His eyes shifted from the space in front of him to the diner. His hands came out of his pockets. He wrung them again and again. They were bloated and leathery, the nails thick and cracked, layered at the tips like eroded sandstone. I wondered if I could get him to a psychiatrist.

"You don't have to get a burger," I said, moving toward the diner. "You could get soup and a sandwich if you like. Or maybe a salad. You like chef salad?" I stepped inside and Uncle followed, pausing in the doorway, checking right and left, right and left.

The diner smelled of grease and burnt coffee.

"Sit and I'll be right back," I said, racing for the bathroom at the rear of the restaurant. There was barely enough time to get the toilet seat up. A mess of chocolatey cream forced its way up my gullet and exploded into the bowl. I hugged my arms around my stomach. Weakness drew me to my knees. When the retching stopped, I stared at the brown mixture swirling around and around, small particles clinging at the water's edge, and thought, It's back.

I flushed the toilet and wiped the tears from around my swollen, red eyes. I rinsed my mouth and spit. A brown spot stained the front of my shirt. I wiped it clean, only to create a large damp circle over my left breast. My knees ached. I glanced in the mirror, fixed a loose strand of hair, and told myself, Under no circumstances may that ever recur.

When I returned to the dining area, I heard the owner yelling out the front door. "What did I say about coming in here, huh?" Through the grease-streaked glass, I could see the curve of Uncle's back outside. His thin frame wavering in the wind.

I rushed to the front of the diner. "Excuse me," I said, tapping the owner on the back. "That man you are yelling at happens to be my uncle."

He looked me up and down. "So?"

"We were planning on dining here this evening."

"We close in fifteen minutes," he said, and slammed the door in my face.

Uncle stared at the spot in front of him on the sidewalk. His hands were low in his pockets.

"I'm so sorry," I told him. "Is there another place you'd like to go?"

We walked a block in silence and entered a Latino restaurant with glittery Formica tables and haggard polyester booths. The radio played a Spanish rendition of "Like a Virgin." At one table, a Latino family of three had started dinner. The woman was heavily made up with foundation and thick black eyeliner; her hair was pulled back into a long braid. Her daughter wore a ruffled pink party dress and had a pink ribbon in her hair.

Uncle and I took the booth closest to the bathroom.

"Chicken and rice? Chocolate milk?" the waitress asked from behind the counter. She had a chipped front tooth.

Uncle nodded. I said, "Just a diet Coke for me."

The waitress stuck her head through the sliding door that led to the kitchen. "Chicken rice, chocolate milk, diet Coke!" she shouted.

I laughed. "I like this place."

"There's music," Uncle said.

On the radio the singer switched into English: "Like a virgin, woh-oh-oh, like a virgin."

"Nice touch." I glanced at my watch. It was six-forty, and I knew I should call Mark.

Uncle's hands slid out of his pockets. He wrung them over the table. "Ah? Where's your ma?"

"Hong Kong," I answered. "I think they want to move back."

"Move? Oh my God." His hands circled around and around.

"It's okay. I'll bring anything you need." I slid the envelope across the table and placed my hand over his. Uncle leaped out of his seat. "Oh my God. Oh my God."

"Jesus," I said.

He glanced helplessly at his hands, wringing them faster.

Somehow I understood. "Here," I said, slipping the envelope into place. He nodded and disappeared into the bathroom. The waitress leaned back into the kitchen. "Keep warm," she yelled. She checked her nails, and reached into her apron pocket for a file.

From the bathroom, I could hear the faucets gushing, water splashing. I pictured Uncle compulsively washing his hands, and wondered whether medication might improve his condition. Would he agree to see a psychiatrist? Likely not.

Minutes passed. Finally I got up and knocked at the door. The waitress looked at me. When Uncle failed to answer, she went back to shaping her nails. I couldn't get Laurel out of my head. Those sit-ups and the expression on her face. Up, down; up, down. A bad feeling came over me.

My phone rang. I pulled the cellular from my purse and watched until it went silent. My hands trembled. I noticed chocolate cake on the counter.

"Do you have any fresh fruit—apples, maybe?" I asked the waitress.

"Fruit?" she said.

"Never mind." I placed the phone on the table. I could hear water splashing onto the floor in the bathroom. I ordered a piece of chocolate cake. Just one bite, I told myself.

After I'd devoured the cake, I knocked again. "Uncle? I have to go soon, okay?" By now the family of three had eaten, paid, and left.

Ten minutes later, Uncle used his feet to kick open the bathroom door. He had the timing down so that he didn't have to touch the door with his hands. The waitress mumbled something in Spanish and shook her head.

Uncle continued to wring his hands. His knuckles were red, almost steaming.

The food arrived. The waitress set Uncle's plate in front of him. She placed the glasses, pinched between her fingers, at the center of the table. Her thumb was in my drink. She dropped a clump of napkins near Uncle's plate.

"Excuse me," I said. "Do you have any utensils?"

"Utensils?"

The wringing stopped. From his pocket, Uncle withdrew a set of wood chopsticks. He fished them through the rice and hovered protectively over his plate.

"Oh," I said.

The woman shot me a look: You're the stranger here.

I excused myself to the bathroom. Everything was wet—toilet

seat, walls, and ceiling. The mirror dripped. Streaks distorted my reflection. "Don't do this," I said. But carefully, so as not to touch anything, I leaned over the toilet and cried.

"You're not hungry?" Uncle asked, glancing up from his dish.

I felt weak all over. "My husband and I are going out for dinner tonight."

"Oh my God."

"It's okay. He'll wait."

"Ni?" You? he said. "Married?"

Great—Ma hadn't even told him. "Yeah. His name is Mark." I dug out a wedding photo.

"Oh my God."

"Yes, he's black."

He stared at the photo the way he had stared at the spot in front of him. "Si-mong," he whispered.

"Excuse me?"

"Ah," Uncle whispered thoughtfully. Suddenly everything seemed to make sense to him. He picked up the last grain of rice with his chopsticks, inserted it into his mouth, chewed patiently. He placed the tips of his chopsticks against the edge of the plate and with one hand pushed one chopstick over the other, over the other.

"Spanish?" he asked.

"Excuse me? Oh, you mean tonight? With Mark?"

"Mm."

"Probably French."

"Oh my God."

"You don't like French food?"

"Expensive," he said. "You should come here—cheap."

Uncle's chopsticks moved one over the other, the wood clicking softly, and I found the motion, the sound, strangely comforting.

M A T R I A R C H

N A M E O F the Father, the Son, the Holy Spirit. Amen. I enter the cemetery equipped with a purse pack of Kleenex, a fresh batch of peonies, and a glass rosary. Despite the rumble of traffic beyond the front gate, it is quiet. The silence lends to a feeling of coolness. Humidity beads the surface of each tombstone. I pass the guardian angel, the grave with the jar containing the handwritten notes, then the tomb of the smiling woman, cracked at the center of her eye. I have to be careful not to brush against them and soil my new outfit.

"Wah, Peony—I've always loved you for your vanity," a voice teases. There is the damp smell of earth and the scent of pipe tobacco; L.Y. is here.

"Husband, good afternoon," I say, exchanging the old flowers with the new. I turn a slow circle in front of his portrait. "Isn't my skirt pretty?"

"Too short."

"But you like it. Marilyn Monroe, you always say."

"That was when I was *alive.*"

His photo stares off into the distance. So handsome in a pin-striped suit. So dignified. By the time it was taken, he was already balding, though his brows were still thick and spiny like treetops. The look on his face is as stern and authoritarian as a headmaster's. A critical eye stares at the ongoing flow of traffic beyond the gate. Cars ascend the hill with audible groans.

I feel for the initial paternoster bead and begin a series of Hail Marys.

"And granddaughter?" L.Y. asks.

"Rai-cho was accepted to university," I answer, pausing between beads. "Can you believe? A fancy one in the United States called Well-es-ley. But such a good girl. She wants to go to school here. Stay and keep me company."

He remains rigid, distant in the black-and-white photo.

"She's turning into such a lovely young lady," I continue. "We went shopping yesterday, and she found a beautiful dress for her graduation party."

His lips refuse to even hint at a smile, and I know he's waiting to hear about Georgianna, the eldest, and the only grandchild he had the chance of knowing before he died. He used to take her everywhere he went, including mah-jongg nights with friends.

"Okay, okay," I acquiesce. "Lucy tells me she's doing fine. Spoke with her just the other day." Heat weighs me down. I dab my brow with a Kleenex. I don't much like to think about Georgie—

married now to a black man. How could I ever tell L.Y. a thing like that?

"Why doesn't my Georgie come to visit?"

"She's so busy—so much work—I told you that. Think she can forget about her patients? Just one, two, three—go on vacation?"

He quiets.

"Don't sulk," I say.

"The children, then. What of them?" L.Y. knows how they can squabble.

"Hahhh . . . Look at me, alone here. What can I do? The children always fighting. You know Esther. So stubborn—just like you, L.Y. And Henry. He said he would take me out to dinner the other night? I was waiting and waiting. Eight o'clock, nine o'clock. Xia si wo le. Finally I called. He forgot, can you imagine? That slothful wife. She's behind it."

"What of Steven?" L.Y. asks, since he is the only grandson.

"I tell Virginia she better find him a wife, but you know that woman—very wu su wei—anything okay, everything okay. Last year, I finally told Esther, I said, 'Esther—you had better do something.' Dear Peter—rest his soul—he'd have a heart attack if he knew his son was still so unsettled."

"Once a heart attack victim," L.Y. says, chortling, "always a heart attack victim."

"How can you say such a thing about your own son?" I feel short of breath.

"Wah—dead man can't have a few laughs?"

"One of these days, L.Y.," I say, close to tears, "I'm going to chi si. So heartbroken. What with Paul and Lucy in Hong Kong now, too ashamed to show face. And our dear son-in-law. The brute—"

Ah Ming, the driver, calls from a distance. "Tai-tai?"

Impertinent fool, I think, and ignore her.

"Wah." L.Y. chuckles. "Loud enough to wake the dead. She must think you've gone deaf."

"They all do. Screaming, screaming into my ear." I don't mention that I've been pretending. Only like this can I hear the gossip. The latest news? Heard the maids chattering about Ah Ming's young nephew. Got caught cheating on a school exam. It's all blood and breeding, as they say. Some rise in the world, others . . . And oh yes—at tea at the Mandarin, those jealous gossips talked lies about Rai-cho. "Easy," they called her. I don't mention this to L.Y., either.

On the rosary, I reach the next decade and recite the next series of prayers. Just outside the gate, Ah Ming leans against the car. When she first started working for me, she was quite skinny. But over the years she's grown fat and tired. She grumbles constantly to herself.

I notice a speck of dirt on L.Y.'s portrait and wipe it with a Kleenex. Soot rubs off. The clean patch only magnifies the dirt coating the rest of the stone. I continue scrubbing. The Kleenex shreds to pieces.

"So dirty," L.Y. complains.

"Quiet, old man," I scold, and place the soiled tissue next to the dead flowers and withdraw a new one from the package. I touch it to my tongue and then proceed to polish, circling my husband's face and continuing to the outer edges of the stone. Tissue by tissue. "Husband-ah? If only you had the opportunity to know your other grandchildren. Your grandson, of course. He looks more and more like our Peter—bless his soul—every day. And yes, my Rai-cho—she is my only sweetness. Last week, I tell her about Ah Fang. I say, 'Sister was like a mother to me. So beautiful—a new dress every day.'"

"You *told* her?"

"Don't talk nonsense," I admonish. Ah Fang hung herself from the ceiling light in my room. Tears sting the back of my eyes. "Think I want my granddaughter to know how wicked I am? That I stole away the man Sister loved?"

"Now, now—must you always go on this way?" L.Y. says. "If there is anyone to blame, it is me. But was it so wrong that I loved you? That I wanted to marry you?"

I dab the tissue over my eyes, then realize I used it to wipe the tombstone.

"So what were we saying?" he asks. "Every day a new dress?"

"Yes, yes—a new dress. Then darling Rai-cho says, 'You're beautiful, too, Grandma.' Like that, L.Y. And the very next day, she went and bought me this pretty outfit. Can you imagine? Her own allowance money."

A tap at my shoulder makes me jump. It's Ah Ming.

"What's the meaning—scaring me to death like this?" I say. Heat rushes to my head, but then my blood pressure falls and I feel chilled, dizzy. Perspiration breaks out over my skin. The sky turns hazy, and for a moment the ground feels unsteady.

Ah Ming takes hold of me at the elbow. "You okay, Tai-tai?" she yells.

I gain my footing. The smell of tobacco is gone. Ah Ming studies my face. Worry dimples the corners of her mouth, and I know she must have heard me talking. No one can accept the fact that, ever since the stroke, L.Y. talks to me.

"I'm sorry if I interrupted," Ah Ming says, collecting the bits of tissue littering the ground. "I was calling and calling. We have to leave now, or I'm going to be late."

"Late picking up whom?" I reprove. "Tell me—who is so important? So important you can interrupt me? Me!"

She puts on her sourpuss face. "Rachel, Tai-tai. She had a dentist appointment."

"Rai-cho?"

Her mouth curves downward at one side. She is supposed to be keeping an eye on the girl while Esther and Philip are away. Lord help the child if she's still meeting that Filipino boy. God knows what her father would do this time. The brute.

Ah Ming picks up the dead flowers. I twist the rosary around my wrist, then hurry toward the gate. Just as I get there, I remember that I've forgotten to pay respects to Ah Fang. From where we are, her urn is nothing more than a yellow dot on the back wall. Ah Fang cries, "Xiao mei," little sister.

"Hai," I say, and pause. "It's me."

Ah Ming walks right into me, nearly knocking me over. "Oi—"

"What's wrong with you, today?" I exhort.

"Terribly sorry, Tai-tai. Were you saying something?"

The yellow jar, lost among all the others on the back wall, awaits me. It can't be farther than fifty yards away, and yet it seems impossibly far. "Never mind," I say, and I sign the cross. Father, Son, Holy Spirit.

An accident just outside Lane Crawford results in a twenty-minute traffic jam. A teenage boy driving a Porsche collided into a Mercedes that had stopped illegally at an undesignated area. Central is busy with after-work commotion. Too many cars; too many people. It makes me dizzy. Ah Ming leaves the car in neutral. The air-conditioning sighs. Only three blocks away. Outside, cars idle in the heat. Exhaust wavers through the air. Finally we turn the corner. The buildings are stately, colonial. The shop windows display upcoming fall fashions.

I finger the rosary between thumb and forefinger. "Hail, Mary, full of grace, the Lord is with thee—"

"You needn't worry, Tai-tai," Ah Ming says. "We're just about there."

I search the sidewalk. Where is she? I fret. There's no reason why Rai-cho wouldn't be outside Landmark by now. We wait and wait, and the longer we wait, the more certain I feel that I should have gone to see Sister. The extra few minutes wouldn't have made a difference, after all.

"Hai—I'll find Rai-cho myself," I say, opening the door.

"Tai-tai!"

The door swings out and with a heavy thud knocks against the Jaguar next to us. Quickly I shut the door and sit back. The chauffeur in the Jaguar rolls down his window, and Ah Ming—

mumbling under her breath—does, too. The chauffeur sticks his head out the window to check for damage. He removes his driver's cap, revealing a head of damp withered hair.

"Terribly sorry," Ah Ming shouts. She cranes her neck to look out the passenger-side window. "Anything?"

The man shakes his head. "Looks fine," he says. They exchange a few words; then the windows scroll shut. Fortunately the Jaguar isn't carrying passengers. I shut my eyes and pretend to have fallen asleep. Ah Ming continues to babble to herself. "As if I don't have enough headaches to worry about," she says.

I want to scream, Who do you think you are?

But I don't. I keep my eyes shut and go on pretending.

In my head, I can hear Ah Fang. "Xiao mei," she calls. Her voice echoes with solitude, and I know that in this small way, I am being punished.

I wake from a doze as Rai-cho ducks into the car. The Filipino boy is with her. He has a broad face and large bulging eyes. Ah Ming catches my eye in the rearview mirror. Now what do we do?

"What took so long?" Rai-cho asks Ah Ming. The stench of sex adheres to her clothes the way smoke does after a fire. I dig a crumpled tissue from my purse and draw it to my nose. My fingers smell of peonies.

"There was an accident," Ah Ming explains. "Took fifteen minutes to turn the corner."

"Where?" Rai-cho asks. "Anyone die?"

"Eh?" I demand.

"Hi, Grandma." Rai-cho kisses me on the cheek and settles over the hump of the seat. The boy sits and shuts the door. He greets me politely. "Hello, Mrs. Wong," he says, but I pretend not to hear.

"Your parents would be very angry," I tell Rai-cho in Chinese. I can't help glaring at the boy. Do you understand the risks you are putting her in? I want to ask him. Last time, Rai-cho got away with stitches—right there over her left brow. The gossips talked about it for weeks. If I hadn't stood between Rai-cho and her father—told him he'd have to beat through me first—the good Lord only knows what he would have done.

"Please don't tell Mom and Dad," Rai-cho replies, speaking Shanghainese. Ah Ming, who understands Shanghainese because she's worked for me all these years, shakes her head. Another big headache.

"You plan to do whatever you want?" I say. "Go wild?"

"Oh, Grandma. Allen and I . . . we're just peng you."

Friends?

The boy glances back and forth, waiting for an explanation.

"Good friends," she says. She checks the condition of her cuticles in order to avoid looking at me.

"Hah." I shake my head. "I thought I raised a lady."

Rai-cho looks down at her lap.

"My mother came from the best family in Shanghai," I say. "Her dowry was a trunk full of gold as large as this car, Rai-cho. This car. And my father. He owned two tigers. Two. Imagine. Gold chains—each link as thick as my fist."

Rai-cho fingers the scar on her forehead.

"We had four tailors," I say. "One for Mama. One for second wife. Two for us."

"A new dress every day," Rai-cho says. She sighs.

The boy raises his brows, indicating to Rai-cho that she should in fact begin translating. He offers me a chocolate. I shake my head no, even though it is my favorite kind. He unwraps it slowly, bending the foil back bit by bit. Rai-cho watches, licks her lip, and says nothing.

"Rai-cho tells me you won a scholarship to university," I say.

He shouts, "Yes, Mrs. Wong. I'm going into medicine."

"Like his father," Rai-cho adds.

"Rai-cho has been accepted to university, also," I say.

"Wellesley's a great school," he says, smiling. "She'll love it."

"Such a good granddaughter she is." I pat her hand. "She wants to stay with Grandma. Go to HKU. Isn't that right, Rai-cho?"

He looks at her, his eyes straining in their sockets. Rai-cho nods and stares at her hands.

"You must be quite bright for your age," I say to him.

"He got into Harvard, Grandma. The best college in the United States."

"In the world," he says. The chocolate balances at the tips of his fingers.

How immodest—and can't he be gentlemanly enough to offer Rai-cho that sweet? Downright rude. Blood and breeding, as they say.

"Never heard of it," I tell him.

"Harvard, Grandma. You know, Georgie went there." At the

mention of her name, Ah Ming's eyes dart at me in the rearview mirror.

"Hush," I admonish.

"But Grandma—"

One look and she silences. She knows: To be forgotten is a terrible thing. Terrible; it could happen to her. She's had fair warning.

We ascend the hill, and Ah Ming switches gears. We pass St. Joseph's and I make the sign of the cross. "Father, Son, Holy Spirit. Amen."

Rai-cho stares out the window at an empty basketball court. The boy offers her the chocolate. She shakes her head no, but he insists, "Come on—I've been saving it for you."

He feeds it to her. I hear the slippery sound of her tongue pressing the chewy candy to the roof of her mouth. I close my eyes and work the rosary through my fingers. All those years, not once did L.Y. feed me chocolates.

The heat penetrates the window. My limbs weigh heavily and I feel myself doze.

Rai-cho whispers, "Allen—stop."

"What?" he says.

I rise out of sleep, and though I'm tempted to put in a few words, I force myself to wait. The odor of sex strikes me like an angry wave.

"Just don't," Rai-cho says.

"Holy shit—kissing's off limits, too?"

That's my granddaughter. See? Those gossips. What do they know? Whispering, always whispering. I hear their lies.

The car growls. The road winds up the mountain. When we finally come to a stop, I know we are at the junction exactly two-thirds of the way there. Ah Ming takes the road to the Peak. The other direction leads toward Happy Valley or Aberdeen.

"I thought we were planning to be together," the boy whispers.

"I don't know," she replies. "She's all alone here. She needs me."

That's right, I think.

"I need you," he says. There's a long pause before he adds, "You know, it isn't like we have to go through with this."

With what?

"Who's 'we'?" she says. "I'm the one in trouble here."

"Whoa. Okay, then—you."

"Me? It's just as much your fault as it is mine."

"But you just said—" he starts. "Oh, never mind."

We ride over a crest of the mountain, and I know we're just two blocks from home. An earthy smell rises into the air. After a brief lag, I can make out the overripe scent of peony. The rosary beads stick against my palm. Hot and cool, then hot again. A prism of light flashes through my head. Then darkness. A tunnel opens and I feel myself slipping through it. At the end, beyond the spirals of dusty yellow light, I can make out my husband's distinct figure. He is a large man, slightly portly. His soul burns like fire. He rocks back on his heels and sucks at his pipe. "Peony," he calls.

Is that you, L.Y.?

From a distance, I hear Rai-cho with the boy. "What are we going to do?" she asks, and he answers, "I don't know, baby. We'll think of something." Their words grow muffled and distant.

"Peony," the voice beckons. "Peony."

Coming, coming. I move toward him. With every step, his image grows steadily larger, older. When I finally get close enough, I see that he is balding and gray, as in his last days. His brows are thick and white. The stern look on his face has given way to a grandfatherly smile. To see him like this surprises me, makes me feel closer. The gap of time between us closes, and yet there is a sense of eternal distance. Twenty years, after all. Look at me: my hair coarse and dyed, my skin soft but loose about the eyes and neck, my breasts like tired sacks.

In his arms, L.Y. holds out a fresh batch of red flowers. So handsome, hai, so handsome.

I reach for him, but just as our fingers touch, a chill rustles through me. I draw back. The skin at his eyes and lips withers; his nose sags and melts away. The red petals fall, dropping from the stems, leaving a gray slippery mass at the center of the bouquet. Cupped within his hands is a human fetus, its skull too large for its frame, its eyes like deep saucers. The skin looks freezer dark.

"Not even a prayer for the dead, Peony?"

I look up and L.Y. is gone, and in his place is Sister. Her skin is fair to the point of translucence, the way it was when she was alive, so carefully shielded from the sun. Her hair falls like thick strands of black silk. Her eyes are more beautiful—mournful and dark, hollowed by longing. She is wearing the robe we found her in. Bright turquoise and embroidered with red flowers. A purplish bruise snakes around her throat; the neck has elongated, making her skull seem disproportionately large.

"Forgive me," I say.

"Forgive those who trespass against us," she replies, kissing the child on the forehead. Ah Fang smells of the sandalwood coffin in which she was cremated. "Isn't that right, little sister?" she asks.

I look at the dead baby. A feeling of dread sticks me in the stomach. "You were with child?"

She laughs. "Why don't be silly. You needn't doubt your darling L.Y. It's the child I've waited for. A gift from your darling. Your darling Rai-cho!"

"No!"

Ah Fang rocks the fetus in her arms. She smiles. "This precious darling will soon breathe the air I breathe. She'll open her eyes and see her mommy." The scent of rot fills the air.

"You can't," I say. "I won't let Rai-cho do it."

She swaddles the child in the long folds of her sleeves. The smile falls from her face. Ah Fang watches me with something like pity. "Either way," she says, "the girl is damned."

A sound jerks me back, sucking me into the tunnel, where I fall through a dusty yellow sky. When I look back, Ah Fang is hanging from the ceiling light, her bluish toes touching the silk sheets of my bed. The whites of her eyes show. Her neck pulls from the weight of her body. I cut her down with a kitchen knife, try to hold her in my arms, but the knuckles of her spine slip from my fingers like a string of pearls.

The rosary drops to the floor. I open my eyes and find the car parked in front of the house. My head swarms with strange sounds. The glare of the whitewashed walls hurts my eyes.

"Grandma, you okay?" Rai-cho asks. She kneels to pick up the rosary. "You're clammy all over."

"She's shaking," Ah Ming says, leaning over the front seat.

"Oh my God—she's having another stroke," Rai-cho says. "Hello, hello? Grandma, can you hear me?"

"Jesus Christ," I hear the boy yell. "Holy shit."

"Tai-tai! We have to get her to the hospital," Ah Ming cries.

"Give me my rosary." I bat their hands away. My body shudders. I look at the boy. "How dare you use the Lord's name in vain?"

"Oh, Grandma," Rai-cho says, a hand to her chest. "You scared us."

I take a long look at my granddaughter. She has large, knowing eyes. The scar from her father's beating extends an inch over her left brow. I touch it gently, feel the stitched texture of skin. In my ears, I can still hear Ah Fang: "Either way—the girl is damned."

"What's wrong, Grandma?" Rai-cho asks.

I shake my head, allow Ah Ming to help me into the house and up to my room. There, I shut the door so everyone will know I'm not to be disturbed. I light all the candles at the altar, illuminating a photo of L.Y.—taken close to his death—and the statuette of the merciful Holy Mother. Shadows fall across the wall. I remove my shoes and kneel before the Madonna.

Just after I've turned away dinner, there's another knock at the door. I continue praying: "Merciful Mother, show us the way." My chest aches. What has become of my family? Hai, first Peter is taken from me. Then I lose Georgianna. Now my Rai-cho, too? The Virgin watches me with a frozen, peaceful smile. All these years— Ah Fang has been waiting for revenge. "So this is to be my punishment," I say.

The door opens and Rai-cho peeks inside. She removes her slippers and kneels next to me at the altar. She places her hands over mine. The light flickers.

Ruined, I think.

"It isn't fair to pretend one thing when you are another," she says.

I start the second series of Hail Marys, feeding the beads through my fingers.

"You mustn't lose the child," I say. "It's a sin. A sin in the eyes of the Lord."

"Oh, Grandma," she says, slumping against the altar.

"You love the boy?" I ask. "You can marry."

Her lips tremble. "What then, Grandma?"

I can't look at her. The scent of sandalwood fills the room. Out of the corner of my eye, just beyond the candlelight, I can see Ah Fang waiting with open arms. The robe shines turquoise, red flowers blooming over the silk like windblown fires. When I look directly at her, she disappears, only to reemerge at the periphery of my vision as soon as I turn back to the altar.

Rai-cho, my one sweetness.

"Wellesley is close to Harvard?" I ask. "You want to go there?"

"Yes. I mean no. Oh, I don't know."

"Your Mama says it's a good school. If it is a good school, you must go."

"But Grandma—don't you want me to stay? You know, come home weekends? Go shopping? Get our hair done?"

Tenderness fills my chest. I touch the scar over her eye. My child, not even I can protect you now.

"You're grown," I say. "Go now. Tomorrow we say good-bye to Grandpa." The candle flickers. I shut my eyes and pray.

Heat radiates off each tombstone. I continue to the back of the cemetery with a plate containing one ripe papaya. Rai-cho follows with a fresh batch of peonies. She's dressed in a black silk shirt and a matching full-length skirt. Perspiration dampens her armpits and collar. At the back wall, I point at the porcelain urn several feet over our heads. "The yellow one," I say.

"Your sister."

"That's right. If only you could have seen her. Such a good sister—"

"Like a mother to you."

"Yes, like a mother."

The smells of moist earth and sandalwood pervade the air, and I know Ah Fang is present. I place the plate on the ground, unfold a Kleenex, then kneel on it. Next to me, Rai-cho does the same, settling beside me. I close my eyes and pray.

"Do you think God is really up there watching over us?" Rai-cho looks at the sky.

"Of course."

"How do you know?"

"One must have faith in the Lord."

Rai-cho gazes at the shelves of urns. "You think I'm going to end up back here?" Forgotten, she means.

"Hush." From my purse I withdraw a cloth bundle, unwrap the knife within, then slice the papaya down the middle. The inside is lush, darker than a ripe peach. I hand Rai-cho the knife and she removes the round black seeds.

"For you, Sister," I say. "Something to assuage your hunger."

Ah Fang refuses to respond.

"Please. Forgive me. You loved him—that I know. I saw how you blushed when he spoke with you." Perspiration trickles into my eye. "I've sinned by coveting your things. Your lovely hair. Those large, dark eyes. That beautiful robe . . ."

Rai-cho watches me with big, sad eyes. I take her hand and cradle it to my cheek. "Ah Fang? I told you about my granddaughter? So beautiful, she is. So good. An old lady's one sweetness in life. See? I brought her for you to see. So much like you, hah?"

Rai-cho gets to her feet. "Come on, let's go, Grandma. Let's get out of here."

"Ni bu dong"—You don't understand—I say. "I must be punished."

"Please," she says. "You're scaring me, Grandma."

Sandalwood thickens in the air. "Smell that?" I say. "She's here. She wants to take the baby."

Rai-cho freezes. "It's got nothing to do with her."

"But it does," I say. "I know it does."

Ah Fang appears before me, her face glowing with bluish phosphorescence. Her apparition fades, and I'm left with a hollow feeling. The papaya lies before me like a cavern that once contained my own heart. "Behold, a virgin shall be with child," a voice whispers.

Wo dong le, I understand. What I've taken from her in life, she is now reclaiming in death. "She's lonely," I say.

Rai-cho checks over my shoulder. "She, Grandma?"

"Ah Fang," I say.

"That's it." Rai-cho removes the Kleenex from the ground, scoops papaya seeds into it, then rolls it up. She helps me to my feet. I think of Ah Fang rocking the fetus in her arms, its purplish skin holding together a fleshy gray bundle.

This is my punishment. My own—damned.

Rai-cho kisses me on the cheek. "It's okay, Grandma," she says. "It's going to be okay."

"You mustn't do it," I say.

"Oh, Grandma."

I turn my back. "Go, then."

She starts toward the gate, but stops first at her grandfather's grave. She crosses herself, says a short prayer, recrosses herself. She watches me for a moment, then turns to leave. I pick up the peonies and make my way to L.Y. His stern face stares back at me. The flowers from yesterday are still in bloom, but I change them anyway. Pipe tobacco lingers in the air.

"That was the quickest prayer I ever heard," he jokes. "One, two, three—she's already gone."

"Don't laugh," I say. "This is no time to make fun."

L.Y. chuckles. "There's always time to make fun when you're dead."

"Hahhh . . . Husband—you left me here alone."

He silences. "She prays you won't be lonely."

"She told you everything?"

"Heard it from the dead," he says. "They talk, too, you know."

Rai-cho hesitates at the gate.

My darling. My Rai-cho.

She steps into her future and, without looking back, disappears down the hill into the throngs of people in Central.

Ah Ming calls for me, but I sit at my husband's grave and dig through my purse for a Kleenex. Humidity weighs at my clothes. I dab my face. "Tai-tai?" Ah Ming calls, hurrying to my side. I allow her to escort me to the car. At the front gate, I turn back to the yellow urn. "Sister," I say, "may you rest in peace now."

In the name of the Father, the Son, the Holy Spirit. Amen.

M A M A

T H E   I C E, ai, the ice. So smooth. So peaceful. One skate after another: one, two, three, four; one, two, three, four. An Italian tenor sings over the loudspeaker. The words—who knows? But from the sound, what else could he be singing of but love? The vibrato of his voice stirs a feeling in me—something tender, slightly tart, something akin to the sensation of a first kiss. Ai—to be young. One, two, three, four . . .

Rockefeller Center has barely woken. The gold statue, like one of God's ethereal beings, seems to drift through layers of the heavens. He smiles, relives his own sweet memories. "Happy New Year," I say. It is the Year of the Ox. Surrounding the rink, flags blow with the wind. Red, yellow, blue, and black; stripes and stars, sickles and moons.

One, two, three, four; one, two, three, four . . .

But ai—so many troubles. Has Chrissy heard from law schools? Please, let it be Harvard. Lucy, my friend since elementary school, her daughter went there; and if Georgie was accepted, there's no reason why Chrissy won't be, too. One, two, three, four. How unfortunate, though, that at school, Georgie didn't meet a Chinese boy—not even a freckle-faced guai lo—but a hei ren. Ai, just think about the children. As the saying goes: Yellow mixed with yellow makes yellow, yellow mixed with white makes light yellow, but black and yellow make dust balls. Poor Lucy. All frozen face the whole wedding. One, two, three, four.

Will Sam's plane arrive on schedule? Should I leave for the airport at eight o'clock?

The Frenchman skates by me. He has a groomed mustache and wears a white silk scarf. He stopped coming last year when his wife fell ill. Today, he skates in circles with her ghost. By the way he holds her, I can almost see her slight dimensions and the red silk scarf knotted neatly at her neck. They face each other, swaying to and fro, circling the rink. The tenor's voice crescendos, cries out passionately, longingly.

I skate past the woman in the corner. She has a head full of gray hair and wears a short pink tutu. Does she think she's turned eighteen again? She practices skating backward. Right hip, left hip. She sees me and stops. She nods at the Frenchman. "Heartbreaking, isn't it?"

"Ai," I reply. "So heartbreak."

One, two . . . Will Chrissy bring her "friend" to the airport? That Elaine—like a man. My skate wobbles, and the world slips out from under me. The wind whistles in my ears; white sprawls outward like a shiny carpet. I smack against the ice. My body slides forward. My hands and knees scrape and burn.

"You okay, Mary?" the attendant asks. Mike, his name is. He lifts me, handling me by the armpits.

"O-kay, o-kay," I say, my legs shaking. In the restaurant next to the rink, a man in a tailored suit coughs up his coffee. Even that statue mocks me with his eternal smile. "Ni xiao shen me?" I ask. What are you laughing at?

There's a giggle from the side of the rink. I don't have to look to know it's Chrissy. Certain things about one's child never change. He-he-he, he-he-he, like a five-year-old. What's she doing here?

"Caught that," Chrissy says. "You told me you made it up to six beats—that was barely four."

I feel myself blushing. "Still warming. Why you come, any-way? What you want?" With Chrissy, there is always some kind of reason.

She bites her lip, her two front teeth jutting out like a rabbit's. "Gosh, Mom. Happy New Year to you, too. Just forget I even came," she says, and starts to leave.

Turning her back to her own Mother. Ai—ever since college, she's become more and more like one of those Americans. No re-spect. Parents here treated like piggy banks. Children shake you only when they want the money inside.

Chrissy stops. "Oh, here," she says, plucking my diamond ear-rings from her ears. She borrowed them for Georgie's wedding months ago and, as with most things of mine, "forgot" to return them. Today, right here in front of every pickpocket in New York City, she decides to give them back to me.

"Ai, ai," I stammer, hurrying toward the guardrail. My blades nick the ice and I almost trip.

"Oops," Chrissy says, realizing her mistake. I shake my head. Since I'm wearing my jade, I tell her to put them back on before they get lost.

Mike circles the rink, skating to a full stop in front of Chrissy. "Mary's daughter, eh?"

Girl or boy, no difference—it's always been like this. When Chrissy was little, strangers would say, "What a lovely child," or "That's one angel you've got there." Even at Georgie's wedding, I heard people saying, "Looks just like Gong Li." Half a dozen of the groom's friends asked her to dance. This kind of attention only gives her the idea that the world owes her, makes her feel more entitled.

Mike introduces himself. Chrissy tucks a strand of hair behind her ear. I sense a spark between them. My heart pinches with hope. Mike's not Chinese, but ai, no need to be picky. Take what I can and run, as Americans say.

Chrissy's nose turns pink. She has dark eyes like me, and high, triangular cheekbones. Her skin is usually smooth and clear, but today pimples protrude from her forehead, forming a T pattern. I look at her, it occurs to me that she isn't as beautiful as I am, or at least as beautiful as I was at her age. "Wah," people would say about me. "Is that Miss Shanghai?"

Ai. I push away from the rail and continue to warm up. One, two . . . Terrible. How could I think such a thing? Of course she is more beautiful. Of course.

. . . three, four . . . Mike offers to fetch Chrissy a pair of skates.

I shake my head no, because I know she'll take advantage, but she accepts. "Cool," she says. Mike smiles, and ai, she smiles back. Something's happening? They disappear into the locker room and return with a pair of rentals. Mike kneels to lace her boots.

. . . five, six . . . Yes, my daughter is more beautiful.

Chrissy rushes onto the ice, turns a full circle around me, then skates backward, her hips swaying to the music. "Wow, I forgot how fun this is," she says. "It's been, sheesh, how many years?"

Show-off. "Where's Mike?" I ask.

She explains he had to take a phone call. "Nice guy."

"Good-looking," I say, even though he's freckle-faced, and, even for a na gua ning, he's only mama who who, only so-so. "Strong, too."

"Ma," she says, and I know she's thinking, Why are you being like that?

"This just his morning job," I say. "He's studying to be a doctor. Okay, vet. But still."

She gives me ba gnie, white eyes. "And Elaine? I don't think she's into threesomes, but I could ask."

"Zu di hu," I scold. A rush of cold snakes under my sweater. After college, Chrissy came home and said, "Mom? Dad? I'm bi." At the time, I thought, Buy what? But soon enough, she said it: "Bisexual."

"Jeez, Ma," she says now, her eyes glassing over. She skates away, circling the rink. Faster, faster still. Ai, such a beautiful girl. If only she met the right man. She'd marry and settle down. Soon there'd be children. Sam and I would give her a wedding to re- member. Better than Georgianna's; much bigger. Yes. The Ritz-

Carlton or the Plaza. Yes, yes, the Plaza. Two hundred people. And flowers everywhere—lush arrangements at every table—and a brass band. A dress. Oh, yes. A dress fit for a queen.

I rest at the railing until Chrissy returns. She takes me by the hand and skates backward, leading me to the middle of the rink. With her other hand she tugs at her earlobe. The diamond makes a rainbow of color. "What'd you think of Georgie's wedding?" she asks. "Pretty elegant, don't you think?"

"Lucy didn't invite anyone," I say. "Too shame."

"Well, I liked it better that way. It was small, intimate, you know? That's what I want when I get married."

"Shows how little you know." I sigh. "Ai, ai—poor Lucy."

"Oh, Ma," she says. "What's with you today?"

"So? That's how I think." It's a free country.

"Lift," she orders. With perfect timing, my back leg rises and I turn. "How can you be so limited?" she says, towing me over the ice.

"Who so limit?" I want to know.

"They love each other. Doesn't that count for anything? I think it's wonderful. I actually have some respect for that girl now. How'd she get so ballsy? She used to be so goody-goody. It was absolutely sickening."

"So waste," I say.

Chrissy speeds over the ice. "I'm going to fall," I say.

"You're fine," she says.

The Frenchman passes, twirling and twirling, reaching for his wife's ghost. Chrissy notices this.

"Wife died last year," I explain. "Cancer."

Chrissy watches the man dip his invisible wife. "They must have been a handsome couple," she says. A finger picks at a pimple on her forehead.

"Don't pick!" I slap her hand. We skate to the edge of the rink and step onto the rubber. "Have you been using the cream I gave you?"

She unties my laces and pulls off my skates. I touch a blackhead on her chin. "So ugly, I tell you. Come to office. I give you facial."

"It's not that bad."

I see Mike standing behind us. He chuckles. "How about a drink sometime?"

She flushes, and I can tell she's deciding whether or not to tell him about Elaine.

"Boyfriend, eh?" he asks.

"You could say that," she says, and I wonder, If she's that "bi" thing, when will she change back?

I tug Chrissy's arm and she waves good-bye.

We walk up Fifth Avenue, passing all the fancy clothing stores. The sidewalks are congested with people on their way to work. Tourists take photos on the steps outside St. Patrick's. Chrissy stops outside a boutique near the salon. "Look," she says, pointing at a batik slip dress with a flower design. Spring line. For the pauper that she is, she has expensive taste. Thank goodness she's planning on becoming a lawyer. Imagine if writing was to become her career. Ai— trouble.

"Not on sale," I say.

"Yeah, but still—isn't it pretty? It would be great on me, don't you think?" Good thing Sam isn't here. Chrissy knows how to get him every time. "Please, Daddy?" she squeaks, poking out her bunny-rabbit teeth, and that's all she has to do. I tell him it's a mistake to indulge her this way. She's already so spoiled.

In the salon, the receptionist says, "Goodness, Chrissy's so grown-up."

"So twenty-three," Chrissy says.

"So ugly," I say, pressing at the blackhead on her forehead.

"You're so mean," Chrissy says.

We walk down the hall, which leads to the rooms at the back. When we are in mine, I switch on the steam machine and spread a towel over the reclining chair. "Be quiet," I order. "Lie down."

Under steam, her pores grow steadily larger. "Go easy, okay?" she says.

"Close your eyes." I dab the moisture from her face. Steam rises to the ceiling. Blackheads press like spider eggs beneath the skin. Dark pillows of fatigue tremble under her eyes.

"You haven't been sleeping," I say.

"Elaine and I had a fight."

Again? Always fighting, those two. They had a big argument the morning of Georgie's wedding.

Steam whistles from the machine. I feel the blackheads with my finger to get a sense of how close they are to the surface. "Some guy called—Esther's 'friend.' He left this weird message on the machine," she says.

I try to swallow my excitement. "Really?"

"What do you mean, 'Really?' You're not in on this?"

"Ai—there you go. Blame Mommy. Always blame Mommy."

"Well, Esther *is* your friend."

"My friend, so I can control what she says . . . what she does?"

She sighs. "Look, Mom. I know it's hard, and it's not like I expect you to go telling the whole world or anything, but Elaine's my girlfriend. She means a lot to me. You know how crazy she got when she heard that message? She's paranoid that I'm going to ditch her and go running off with some guy."

Well, aren't you? I want to say.

"Don't you ever go tell Esther," I warn. "You know how she is. Big mouth."

I massage the skin at her cheeks and forehead. She doesn't say more, and though I want to know about the call—Who was it? What did he say? Will they be going on a date? When?—I don't ask. The muscles in her face relax, and I can sense her drifting to sleep.

"So have you heard from school?" I ask, covering her eyes with wet cotton and turning on the overhead light. I extend the magnifying glass over her face, and with two wet wads of cotton, I squeeze a blackhead. The pore relinquishes the deposit without a fight.

Chrissy jerks back to consciousness. "Yeah."

I clap my hands together. "I knew it," I say. "When do you start?"

"Program starts in September, I guess."

The next pimple isn't ready to be squeezed, so I move on to the next. My fingers move clockwise around her face. Harvard. My daughter got into Harvard. Wait until I tell Lucy. And Esther—her daughter only got into Wellesley.

A blackhead over Chrissy's brow remains clogged. I search through my shelf of supplies to find a sterilized needle. "Daddy and I can drive you—help move everything."

"Well, I should be hearing from Columbia this week," she says.

Columbia? I locate the needle and carefully peel away the wrapper. "Harvard's near to Boston, yes?"

I prick the pore. She clenches her hands together, and a thick vein surfaces at the back of her palm. "To be honest, I'm sort of hoping to stay in New York," she says.

That Elaine—she's the one to blame.

Ai—willing to give up Harvard. Spoiled child. I always knew we shouldn't have spoiled her the way we did. Cooking and cleaning. The best clothes. Best everything. We should have sent her to China when we had the chance. See how she would have liked it. I prick the clogged pore and force out the blackhead. The pore begins to bleed. Chrissy squirms in the chair. "Ow."

"Don't move." I attack a pimple at the temple, pricking again with the needle. Spoiled rotten. I squeeze until the pimple pops.

She kicks her heels. "Ma—go easy."

The receptionist taps at the door, a signal that my next client has arrived and is waiting in the lobby. "Be still," I say. "Have to hurry."

Chrissy presses her lips together until they turn gray. Tears escape from the corners of her shut eyes. She barely breathes until

I'm finished. Her body slips feet first off the chair, and she examines the splotches over her face in the mirror. "Ma?"

"What?" I straighten the counter, prepare fresh wads of cotton and soak them in water.

"You heard what I said about Elaine?"

I remove the towel from the seat and wipe the condensation from the machine. "I don't understand why you can't be just friends. Just friends not good enough?"

She bites her bottom lip, her eyes following me in the mirror.

I shrug and spread a clean towel over the chair. "That is my thinking," I tell her, and though I sense there's more she'd like to say, I dab at the bleeding blackhead and push her out the door. "Be ready when I come to pick you up," I say. "Eight o'clock-ah? Daddy will be tired."

The two of us wait outside customs. People crowd around the barricades. It must have been a 747—full flight. Chrissy takes off her coat. I pretend not to notice the batik dress on her body. All day I've been thinking and thinking. When I was young, half a dozen suitors came to my door. Two of them my father rejected from the outset. One had protruding eyes, which signaled a painful death; the other had open nostrils, which meant he would never be able to keep money from flowing away from him. Of the other four, it was decided that Sam would make the best husband. After all, he came from a good family and had money. What's more, he did not live in excess, which my father felt was a most important trait in a man. What other choice was there, really? With Chrissy, everything is different. All her life she's had too many choices. It's a free country, right? How is it she always chooses the wrong one? I look at her and all I can think is, Spoiled rotten.

The doors slide open and Sam appears. Chrissy waves. "Daddy, Daddy," she yells, jumping up and down. His eyes go big behind his glasses. He seems startled to find his daughter undeniably a grown woman. She runs to him, wraps her arms around his neck, and kisses him on the cheek. "Daddy, Daddy," she repeats, and his grim expression transforms into a smile. He takes her hand and rolls the suitcase toward me. His eyes are pink and watery from exhaustion. He inspects the splotches on Chrissy's face.

"What happened?" he asks.

"Mom did it."

Sam gives me a look as if to say, Zen me yang-ah? Just what have you done, now? He shakes his head. Just wait until he hears about Harvard. This time, I'll let Chrissy tell him herself. She can be the one to break her father's heart.

"How's business?" I ask.

"Same," he says. "Slow."

"Still?"

He nods. We walk to the parking lot. I dig out my keys and get into the driver's seat. Chrissy gets into the back. She leans forward between us. "Emmy bust any ankles lately?"

"That's not nice," I say. Emmy is Sam's longtime secretary. She's an eater—so heavy she broke her ankle stepping off the curb.

Sam removes his glasses, rubs a hand over his eyes, and yawns. He puts his glasses back on. "Actually, she's lost some weight."

"No way," Chrissy says.

"She said twenty-five pounds."

"Twenty-five pounds," I say. "Why—that's a whole roast beef!"
Sam laughs.

"Gross," Chrissy says as we drive out of JFK. She reaches into
my purse for the bag of dried plums, takes one, and pops it into her
mouth. "What happened? She come out of the closet or something? Get some sex finally?"

Sam glances at her over the rims of his glasses. "Have some respect, hah? Sex, sex. She's a very decent, hardworking woman."

I look at Chrissy, as if to say, Didn't I tell you so? and she pouts.

"She had a heart attack," Sam says.

"Oh." Chrissy sucks on the sour plum.

"Why didn't you tell me?" I signal to get into the left lane,
which leads onto the BQE.

"It was a minor one—doctor said it's just a wake-up call."

"Ai," I mutter. "She probably wonders why the boss's wife
doesn't bother to telephone her."

"Bu hui," she won't, Sam says, shutting his eyes for a quick
nap. Behind us, Chrissy sinks back into the seat and stares at the
Manhattan skyline. The buildings stand well defined even in the
dark. Rectangles, pyramids, domes. In the rearview, Chrissy seems
contemplative, almost sad. Maybe that's not such a bad thing—she
could be thinking over what I've said. She could be reassessing op-
tions and making better decisions. Soon, though, I notice Chrissy's
asleep, too, a frown etched on her brow.

I stop in Chinatown. Sam likes to get a bowl of his favorite
noodles when he comes home from a long trip. It's a small place on
Mott Street. "Home isn't home until you've had Shanghai noo-

dles," he says. When I find a parking space, I say, "Wake up, wake up." The two rouse from sleep. "What?" Sam says, droopy-eyed. "Where?"

Chrissy rubs her eyes. "Dead-duck bowling alley, here we come."

"Oh, yes," Sam says, patting his belly. "Good, good."

There's a line outside the restaurant. Mostly guai lo. They huddle in their coats. A gust sweeps a piece of newspaper into the air. In the restaurant window hangs a row of roasted ducks, their necks stiff like coat hangers. I can smell soy sauce and fried lard. In the front window the cook cleaves a duck into sections and with the rectangular blade scoops the pieces into a container. We pass everyone on line and go inside. People complain about us, but after all these years the waitress knows us, so she says to them, "She my cousin. Are you my cousin?" That shuts them up.

"Three?" the waitress asks me.

"Four," Chrissy replies, and a lump comes into my throat. The waitress prepares a back booth for us. The room is narrower than a train car. Five booths to a side, each wall mirrored to make the restaurant seem larger than it is. Sam and I sit facing the kitchen. Chrissy sits across from us. We order Shanghai noodles for Sam, soup dumplings, ni gau, and Chinese spinach.

The soup dumplings arrive and Chrissy jabs her chopsticks into one.

"Not like that," I say, but it's too late. The soup inside leaks onto her plate. Chrissy bites into the dumpling's meaty center.

The door opens and a chill cuts through the restaurant. Maybe it's instinct: I turn to find Elaine walking toward our table. She has one of those lawyer's accordion folders tucked under her arm. She's wearing a gray two-piece suit—trousers, that is—with black laced shoes. Why doesn't she wear the wool skirt and jacket that I bought her for Christmas? And that hair—shorter than Sam's.

"Hi, sweetie!" Chrissy calls, and for a moment, I'm afraid they'll kiss right there in the restaurant. Sam and I duck low into our seats. The cook cleaves another duck breast.

Elaine greets us politely and slides into the seat next to Chrissy. Sam acknowledges her with a forced smile. "So sorry I'm late," she apologizes. She, too, has dark circles under her eyes. "I had to get a contract to the printers."

The Shanghai noodles arrive. Sam gives the bowl his full attention.

Chrissy takes Elaine's briefcase and stores it under her seat. "What's the matter?" Chrissy asks.

Elaine sits. "Just busy," she says, and from the tone, I can tell something is still wrong between them. I nudge Sam's thigh. He sucks noodles into his mouth. Soup spills from the corners of his lips.

"You should wear my suit," I tell Elaine.

"Yeah—" she says.

"Elaine doesn't wear skirts, Ma," Chrissy points out.

Color drains from Elaine's face. "I loved it, I really did."

"Elaine thinks skirts are too feminine," Chrissy says.

Elaine fidgets with her chopsticks and doesn't look up. She purses her lips. Poor thing. Chrissy's going to turn her into a door-mat by the time she's done—she'll stamp her dirty shoes over her and go into the house. She'll leave her alone outside.

"Obviously *you* don't think anything's too feminine." I nod at the batik. "Even in this kind of cold."

Chrissy beams. "I was wondering when you'd notice. Isn't it pretty? I was feeling all yucky when I left the salon, so I decided to splurge a little."

"So small," Sam says. "Like underwear."

"Oh, Daddy—it's the style." Chrissy circles a strand of hair behind an ear. "I think I look sexy."

"Ai-yah," I exclaim. Such thick-skinned arrogance. "You're too much."

Sam guffaws. "Especially with all those marks on your face."

"Her pimples were like this—" I show the tip of a chopstick.

Chrissy picks a piece of lint from her dress. "I am too, sexy. I don't care what you say."

This makes Elaine laugh. "God—you are such a girl."

"That's right—all girl here," Chrissy says. They smirk, sharing some intimate secret.

"Of course she's a girl," I say, chewing a piece of sticky ni gau. These Americans—sometimes I just don't understand them. Elaine laughs and Sam coughs his soup. Chrissy looks at me as if to say, Oh, Ma. Poor Ma.

What? I wonder, feeling myself blush. The rest of the food arrives. I help Sam with a spoonful of ni gau and spinach before serving our guest. "Eat, eat," I say. "More coming."

Chrissy presses up against Elaine. "Admit it," she says. "You love it."

She says this right in front of everyone. I want to disappear.

I want to die. Sam's entire being seems to grow dimmer. Ai. As soon as we get home, he'll be planning his next trip back to Hong Kong.

Elaine turns so pale her skin looks green.

"Come on," Chrissy pushes, "admit it."

Elaine chews with her mouth closed. She swallows and, without looking up from her plate, says, "Will you shut up and eat already?"

A chopstick slips from my hand.

"Are you snapping at me?" Chrissy asks, bewildered.

Perhaps I was wrong about Elaine? She may be one of the few people strong enough to handle my daughter. No one has ever put that girl in her place.

Elaine clips spinach with her chopsticks. "Who's snapping?"

"You are."

The cleaver splinters a fowl, bone and all, once, twice, three times. Our neighbors crouch over their bowls of soup, pretending to suck at their noodles. I swallow too quickly and the ni gau clumps in my chest. Sam pushes his bowl away. Chrissy stuffs her cheeks with noodles but refuses to chew. I sense people's sly looks in the mirrored walls. The door opens again, and the cold rushes angrily back at us. The cleaver bangs against the board. I force down my last bite.

Outside, I zip my coat and pull on my gloves. I fix Sam's scarf snuggly around his neck. Chrissy and Elaine have gone on ahead. The sidewalk is crowded, and Chrissy trails a step behind. They hold hands.

Then a strange thing happens. There's a loud clunk. In front of us, an old man falls from a stoop, knocking right into Elaine. He drops to the ground. His slipper sails past me into the street. We all back away and cover our heads with our hands. We look up at the roof, but nobody is there. The old man lies still. He's bleeding. At first I think he's Lucy's brother. But she told me he lived in midtown. Can't be him.

A na gua ning crouches to check whether he's all right. Sam takes my hand and pulls me toward the car. I reach and grab Chrissy, who tugs Elaine from the crowd.

In the car, with Sam driving, everyone starts to talk at once. In back, Elaine drawls, "Shit. Oh, shit."

"What happen?" I ask.

"Boy," Sam says. "Up on the roof."

"You all right, honey?" Chrissy asks Elaine. "You hurt?"

"I'm fine," she says quietly. Sam turns north onto Bowery.

"Why would a child do such a thing?" I wrap my coat more tightly around myself.

"And to some old guy," Chrissy adds. "The poor thing."

"Yeah, poor thing," Elaine drops her briefcase to the floor. "Thing should have hit me. It was aimed at me."

"No," I tell her.

"Don't be silly," Chrissy says.

"Who's being silly? Antigay violence is up these days. Or haven't you heard?"

"Come on," Chrissy says. "You're being paranoid."

"Will you stop telling me I'm being paranoid?" Elaine exclaims. "The truth is, shit like this happens. It happens all the time."

No one speaks another word.

A couple of weeks later, a phone call wakes me in the middle of the night. I'm dreaming about roast duck served on a platter with onion rings, and I'm thinking, But I don't like onion rings. The duck's head sits on a pile of duck meat. It bites my fingers when I reach for a drumstick. It's maybe the second or third ring that yanks me out of sleep. Sam rolls over. It could be his brother with news about little Laurel. Girl refuses to eat—can you believe?—and has gone into hospital.

But I look at the phone, and I know that it's my baby and that it's going to be bad.

"Hello?" I answer. "Chrissy?"

There's a faint sniffle. Darkness shifts itself into objects. The clock glows red. Midnight, it says. "What's wrong?" I ask. "You hurt?"

Sam rises and clicks on the lamp. "Who is it?" he whispers.

"Chrissy," I say, covering the receiver.

"It's over," Chrissy says, pausing before she starts to sob. The sound reminds me of the Chinese marketplace: the wailing pig that knows it's about to be slaughtered. There's a brashness, an anger couched in her voice, as if to say, It's your fault—now do something.

Sam hears her crying and takes the phone. "What happened?"
He listens and nods. "Uh-huh . . . No, don't talk nonsense, hear?
You'll do no such thing. Hear me?"

I ball the blanket in my fist and try to calm myself. The ice, ai,
the ice. One, two, three, four . . .

"Now listen to Daddy," Sam continues. "Stop crying, okay?"

The murmur of Chrissy's voice makes me feel helpless, the
way I felt when she was little and ran a fever that would not stop
climbing.

"Where are you?" Sam asks.

. . . One, two, three . . .

"What are you doing there?"

I grab the phone from him. "We'll be right there, okay,
Chrissy? Mommy will be right there."

She stops crying and goes silent. I can hear water dripping. "I
love her, Ma. Why can't that be enough?"

"Ai, Chrissy."

"I want a normal wedding like everyone else, you know? Can't
I have one? Why can't I?"

I sigh. "We'll be there soon."

Sam rings the bell while I dig through my purse. His hands are
shaking. I find the keys, and when the door opens, the two of us
stand there stunned. Shattered glass, ripped posters, crushed
books, upturned tables.

"Oh my God," I whisper.

"Chrissy?" Sam calls.

We race from the living room to the bedroom to the bathroom. The door is locked. We call and plead for her to open it. Finally she does. We push our way inside. She's leaning her head against the whirring toilet. I switch the light on and Chrissy squints at us with a sorrowful, confused look. Her face is as puffed as a ready pimple, loose strands of hair sticking to her cheeks. She stares at her hands. They are bruised at the knuckles, crusted with blood.

I pull a towel from the rack and wipe her hands.

"I'm bleeding?" she says. Blood trickles from a cuticle. I notice a purple toothbrush and a pink one on the floor next to the toppled garbage can. A bar of white soap bobs in the toilet bowl. The shower curtain hangs halfway to the floor, ripped along the punched holes of plastic.

"Jesus—get the peroxide," Sam orders, shifting in the doorway. "Use cotton. Over there—there in the cabinet."

The peroxide foams at the cuts, and I blow at them to take away the sting. Chrissy watches as if the hands belonged to someone else. Her eyes are nearly shut from crying, her nose and mouth distorted and swollen. I search the cabinet for bandages.

"No, no," Sam says. "The larger ones, for Christ's sake."

I turn on him. "Please, okay? Go get some ice."

"Ice? Ah, ice." He disappears to the kitchen.

Chrissy giggles. "She's the one with misgivings, not me," she babbles. "Right, Ma?"

I wrap her hands in gauze. "It's going to be all right," I say.

Tears swell from her eyes. "Who says? Who says it's just an experiment? What guy am I going to run back to, huh?"

The stink of peroxide covers my hands. She continues, and the nonsense talk begins to frighten me. "No chances, oh no." She cackles deliriously.

I help her to her feet. She looks at me, shuddering. "Friends," she says. "Elaine wants to be friends. Isn't that nice? Isn't that just peachy, Ma? Isn't it? Huh?"

I feel myself about to cry, but Sam appears in the doorway carrying a bag of ice, and I force the tears back.

"Let's go, baby," I say, getting a hold of myself. "Time to go home."

It's three-thirty in the morning when I get Chrissy settled in bed. She's hugging on to the same stuffed bear she left behind all those years ago. I enter my bedroom, and Sam doesn't say a word until the lights are out and we've each settled into our own sides of the bed. His hand reaches under the blankets for mine. I take it, give it a tight squeeze. "What happened?" he asks.

"Went their separate ways."

"I know that. But what was all that nonsense she was saying?"

"Chrissy wanted to get married."

"Married?"

"I know—as if they could go into church together?"

"Hunh."

"Americans," I say. "They have some really strange notions."

In the bathroom, the toilet whirs. I get out of bed and make my way there. In the dark, I remove the porcelain top from the back of the toilet and put the plug in place. When I return to bed, the water has begun a new, steady rhythm. Filling, filling.

"Think this will change her back?" Sam asks.

I try to sound hopeful. "Ken ding," perhaps. "Elaine seemed to think Chrissy would sooner or later."

He sighs. I close my eyes and feel him shifting closer to me. The tank stops whirring, and suddenly the room seems too quiet.

"What's going to happen to her?" Sam says, and I wonder if he's thinking about Emmy. Alone all these years. Obese, yet perpetually starving.

"Women these days can take care of themselves," I tell him. "Besides, you know your daughter. The child has better luck than she deserves. Spoiled rotten. Maybe now she'll learn."

"Don't be like that," he says.

"It's true. The girl needs to learn. Things come too easily for her. Like Harvard—she wants to throw it away. Just throw it away. Yes, this will be good. She'll learn."

The doorknob turns, and Sam gives my hand a firm squeeze. The two of us watch the door creep open. Chrissy waits like a dark shadow in the doorway.

"Can't you sleep?" I say.

"Can I sleep with you tonight?"

I feel myself stiffen. Does she think she'll squeeze between us as she did when she was five? "But where will your father sleep?" I ask.

"The couch will be fine," Sam says, rising.

"No, that's okay, Daddy." She backs out of the room. "Never mind."

"Chrissy," I call, just as she is about to shut the door. She returns to the doorway.

"Bring your comforter and lay it here by the bed," I say.

"Yes," Sam agrees. "Sleep here on the floor."

She returns to her room and retrieves the bedding. I spread it over the carpet. She lies down and I draw the blanket over her. She sniffles. Her wrapped pawlike hands stick out from the blanket. I kneel, brush the hair from her face and kiss her forehead. My baby, I think, and that helpless ache fills my chest again. I shut the light, slip under the blanket with Chrissy, pull her to my body. In the moonlight I can see the shine of her teary eyes.

"Close," I say, covering her eyes with my palm.

I imagine the wedding I've had planned all these years. The altar filled with flowers. A tall, dark-haired Chinese boy in a tuxedo. My beautiful daughter. "One day," I say, "Daddy and Mommy will give you the best wedding in the whole world."

"The best," Sam chimes in.

"Your gown like Cinderella's."

"Big wedding," Sam says.

"Yes, big," I say.

"How big?" Chrissy asks.

I stretch my arms as wide as I can. The gauze catches on my nails.

"Big enough to invite all your friends," Sam says.

I name all her friends. "Ai, and that girl—what's her name, again? The one with the messy hair? Always sucked her dirty thumb?"

Chrissy laughs. "That girl was from kindergarten, Ma."

"So? You can still invite her."

"Why not?" Sam adds.

"And there'll be flowers," I say, imagining lush rose center-pieces at each table and a single cello playing during dinner.

"Whatever you like," Sam says.

"But what about *your* friends?" Chrissy asks.

The weight of Chrissy settles awkwardly into me, crushing my thoughts, and yet I don't move. Even in the dark, I can sense her two protruding teeth. Sam remains quiet. The three of us lie awake in the dark. I know Sam is thinking we could never invite our own friends. We couldn't. How could we?

An hour before it's time to wake, Sam begins to snore. Chrissy relaxes in my arms, and soon I can feel her slow, steady breath. Ai. All these years, and what comes back to me is how tiny Chrissy was when she was born—smaller than a chicken—and how, from the very start, she had taken to my breast with two hands as if it belonged to her. The thought makes me smile. My chest burns like a scrape over the ice. I stare at the blank ceiling, imagining the wedding again, and in my ears hear the Italian tenor swooning about love. The ice, ai, the ice.

TROUBLEMAKER

"HEAR ME, Eric?" Ma says, turning from the TV. She's got her swollen feet propped on the rim of the tub, which sits dead center in the middle of the kitchen. "I don't want to hear any more complaints from Lao Gong." Ma's got on a new uniform. She's done up her hair with a thick red ribbon and she's even got lipstick on, too. It's New Year's. Big tips tonight, she says.

"Damn cripple," I say, crossing the imaginary line into my room. Moved in two months ago and thinks he owns the place. "The only *ba-la-lang* going on around here's in Lao Gong's ugly fat head."

"Ai." Ma sighs, giving me a look like she's sucking on a pickled plum. She shakes out her apron. "He's old."

"Relax, Mrs. Tsui," Seymour says. He blows a bubble with his gum. "We're just going to hang. I gotta go help at the store later, anyway." Seymour practically runs the place these days. His old man spends most of his time doing these fucked-up paintings. Ma said it's no secret—except to Seymour—that his Ma took off with some Hong Kong rich-ass. His old man would rather tell Seymour she's a missing person—"A bad man took her away"—than dish the truth. Seymour thought some asshole had her tied up somewhere; he wanted to find the bitch. These days, though, Seymour doesn't say much. Thinks after all this time she's dead. Why else wouldn't she have come back for him?

"Eat here," Ma tells Seymour. "I cooked too much. Don't want to waste."

Seymour and I toss our knapsacks on the top bunk and dump ourselves below on my brother Johnnie's. The Asshole would shit if he saw us here.

I give Seymour a look, like, Wish she'd get lost already. With my foot, I kick up the skateboard and catch it in my hands. The wheels spin, ball bearings ticking in the air. The hallway leading to the door's got my name all over it: Skate, go ahead, skate, it tells me. There's a scuff mark from the ollie over the tub; a turned-around S from pretending to thrash a half-pipe.

On TV, Oprah blabs on about all that feel-good garbage Ma likes to hear. "Everyone says they want to be happy," Oprah says. "But when asked, they don't have an image of what that really means to them." Ma nods and mumbles in agreement. She uses her arms to push herself up, then irons an apron. She does this slowly, pressing her weight onto every wrinkle, even the ruffles at the bottom. There's a burn the size of a fingernail. The thing is clean, scrubbed by hand every night in the bathroom sink, but against the new outfit, it isn't white the way it should be. Closer, maybe, to a ratty dishrag. Ma folds it in half, then half again, and irons it to get square creases into it. Like that's going to make it look new?

An hour before the Asshole gets home, I think. Just enough time to get down that flip kick over the tub. "You're going to be late, Ma," I say.

"Ai. Have to hurry." She ties the apron around her waist and pulls on a jacket. It's too thin by itself; she has to wear a coat over it. Seymour and me, we hang on Johnnie's bunk.

Ma heads out the door. She walks like a spider. Quick and soundless.

Skate, go ahead and skate, the hallway calls.

I drop to my knees, dig out the ramp from under the bed, and just to be sure she's gone for good, race to the window. Ma's red ribbon disappears toward Canal. Seymour and I move all the food to the kitchen counter, fold the table, and snake the shower curtain up over the metal rod. I set the ramp against the tub, find some speed metal on the radio, and skate to the end of the hall.

"This is the shit," Seymour says.

With my back against the door, I focus on the space above the rim of the tub and picture myself there: just me and board and air. "Yes," I say, pumping my foot. As I close in on the tub, I kick back, and boom!—flying. Nothing can pull me down.

"Yeah, man. Shred it up!" Seymour says.

Lao Gong bangs his cane again. "Damn cripple," I say.

Seymour races to the end of the hall. "Check this out," he says. "Totally bionic." But the front door opens and in walks Johnnie. Seymour stops mid-step, his sneaker squeaking against the floor. Lao Gong bangs away at his ceiling.

"What the— Didn't Ma say to cut that out?" The Asshole moves toward me until I've got my back against the wall. He tries to stare me down.

"Get out of my face," I say.

"What was that?"

I take a swing but miss, and he catches me in a headlock. I try to wrestle him to the ground, but his hold tightens and I start to choke. Seymour's face is like, Oh, fuck. Johnnie dumps me into the tub. My head bangs against the spout and my knees catch the porcelain edge. I cough and spit, cough and spit. "Get up," he says.

I hope you die, I think. I hope that girl dumps your sorry ass and then you die. Seymour's still got that frozen look on his face. Spit hangs from my mouth. I laugh.

"What's so funny, huh?" Johnnie asks.

I wipe the drool with my arm. "Nothing."

Johnnie jerks his arm, making me flinch. A snarl curls the side of his lip. "Didn't think so."

The Asshole tells us to get lost and we do. First to McDonald's for a couple of Big Macs and fries. Then to the roof, where one of the guys from school sets us up with a bunch of six-packs. The sky seems lower than yesterday, like one of these days it'll fall and we'll be lost inside it. There's the crackling of firecrackers. Once in a while a rocket. Seymour checks out the scene below. "Man, I never knew your brother got so uptight."

"Fucker can't get laid."

The wind cuts through my jacket. I kick a flower pot, and a

bony dead plant topples over. My ear throbs, and I imagine all the ways a chick could dis the Asshole. I gulp my beer. His girl could take off with some other Asshole tonight. Yep. Take off with some Hong Kong kid who owns a Porsche.

Wind sweeps over the rooftops and funnels down the street, lifting a paper napkin into the air. People squeeze slowly past one another. Somewhere in the dark, firecrackers go off like pistols. Smoke rises and drifts. It smells crisp and sour.

"We need a bunch of those," I say.

"Nah, what we *need* are a bunch of bottle rockets. Remember Jimmy Ho? Heard he lit one of those, then threw a stuffed mannequin off the roof. Everyone went nuts."

I crush the beer can between my palms. "Idiot, I was there."

"You were in on that?"

"Sewed the gloves on myself."

"Shit, did that thing really knock some guy unconscious?"

"Nah. That's Jimmy's big mouth. The thing dropped on a truck. But it was still awesome. You should've seen their faces. Everyone ran—thought someone got shot."

"He got the cell for that? Ain't shit."

Just then, Johnnie steps out of the building. A bow tie pokes over the top of his coat. His hair's slicked back, and not even the wind can get to it. He's got one of those Asian parties tonight. Tavern on the Green, he said, like he's some kind of rich-ass. Yo—like he's really going to get one of those yuppie jobs on Wall Street?

"He going to score or what?" Seymour asks.

"With that rich-bitch girlfriend he's got? One look at this place and she'll be making a beeline back to Westchester."

"You seen her?"

"Nah. Just listen to shit he talks on the phone." I squash the aluminum can between my palms. The cold metal sticks to my skin. I could peg the Asshole right now and he wouldn't know what hit him. As if he read my thoughts, Johnnie looks back and gives me the finger.

"Do it," Seymour says.

I shove the can into my pocket. "Nah, too easy."

"Right. Like you would have gotten him? You couldn't get me here, your arm sucks so bad." This gets me laughing. Seymour eggs everyone on like this.

"Shut up," I say, opening a new beer.

A cop appears on the other side of the street. He looks up, and just like that, Seymour and I are eating gravel. Fucking popos. "Did he see?" I ask.

Seymour snorts and breaks out the Chinaman rap he uses at the store. "Wew-come China-tong. Wan buy watchie? Gucci onry ten dolla."

The wind cuts down the neck of my jacket. "Ten dollars?" I say. "Oh, my. So expensive? How about nine?"

"Nine-la, okay-la. And a Happy fucking New Year to you, too, bitch."

We down our last beers. That's when Lao Gong appears. He clutches the rail in one hand, his cane in the other. He's got on the same gray coat he wears all the time. Even from up here, I get that sour old-man stink.

"What's he up to?" Seymour asks.

"Got me. He never leaves the place."

Seymour crushes a can. It folds together like an accordion. "Your chance, man. Get him good."

"Shut up."

"What? Scared?"

"I said shut up."

"Ten bucks says you are."

The guy drags one leg, then the other, down each of the steps. Couldn't miss even if I tried. With a flick of my wrist, the can whirls through the air. At first it seems as though it'll arc past him. But one, two, three, and tock! The thing smacks his ear. A sound that's tinny and flat.

Lao Gong freezes. His fingers splay apart. The cane falls, the handle knocking, knocking, knocking against the concrete. There's a sharp whine before the old man crumbles.

"Oh, shit," Seymour says, and does a hyena laugh. The old man drops, knocks into a passerby, then hits the pavement. A black cloth slipper goes flying into the street. People scatter.

"Bionic, man!" Seymour says.

We nosedive onto the roof before anyone sees us.

I put out my hand. "Ten bucks."

The ambulance catches our attention. The siren squeals, red lights swirling. The old guy's still lying on his side, one leg twisted at a funny angle. The wind flaps a lonely strand of hair.

"He's dead," Seymour says.

"No way. Wasn't any beer in the thing."

The medics move around the body, checking the pulse at his wrist. They lift his eyelids.

"Get up, old man," I whisper. "Get up."

A crowd circles as they put him on a stretcher. Cops appear. We junk the beer and scramble downstairs. The roof door shuts out the screaming horns, and for a second it's dark and quiet.

In the apartment, the lights are out. There's the lamplight from the street. Seymour's got the door, and me, I'm by the window. The ambulance takes Lao Gong up Mott, and the red lights swirl until it turns onto Canal.

Where's the slipper? I wonder.

The cops get to the neighbor's door within the hour. "Mr. Yang no home," Mrs. Yang says. The chain rattles against the door frame.

"May we ask a couple of questions?"

"No home. Mr. Yang no home." The door bangs shut.

Feet appear beneath the door to our apartment. One, two, three solid, even knocks. Seymour looks at me like, *Shit.*

The cop knocks again. One, two, three; one, two, three. They know we're here. Everything stops. It's Jimmy Ho who jumps into my head: "That first night, thought I'd shit my pants," he'd said. Sweat drips down my neck into my jacket. Seymour starts to whisper to himself. I'm like, Shut up already. He's praying. The guy doesn't even go to church and he's praying.

The feet finally step away from the door. The boards creak under their weight.

"Shit," Seymour groans. "Oh, man."

Neither of us says another word until the cops are gone.

Outside, the street's beginning to empty out. Wind sweeps down Mott, making a low flute sound. Johnnie shows, head tucked low into his coat, walking straight into the wind. I knew the sucker wouldn't score.

Just as he enters the building, the cops appear. One of them speaks, his voice low and muffled, and I can hear Johnnie slurring, "Yes, Officer . . . No, Officer." He lights a cigarette and adds, "Jesus, who'd be sick enough to do a thing like that?"

Just like that, I know that he knows.

"Gotta take off," I tell Seymour, grabbing my board. "Asshole's back."

Seymour blocks the door. "Got fried brain in the head or something? Can't go out there."

Then it's too late. A key twists and Johnnie's there, a shadow with the fluorescent light behind him. Smoke funnels from his nostrils.

The light goes on. Before I can even see straight, Johnnie's got me in a headlock.

"Seymour, if I were you, I'd take off," Johnnie orders, and then Seymour's gone. Johnnie chokes harder, even harder, and I can't breathe. I drop the board, and the wheels go wild.

He chucks me into a chair. I lean over the tub and toss; beer flushes out my nose.

"Talk," he orders.

I wipe my arm across my face. "Fuck you."

His fist nicks my jaw and I fall against the table. "Just had to cause trouble, didn't you?"

Fuck off, I want to say. "You're just pissed."

"What was that?"

"P-I-S-S-E-D," I say. "Rich bitch doesn't want Chinatown homeboy in her pants, does she?"

I block a punch. The blow stings. I look him in the eye, like, Go ahead, Asshole. I'll take you on.

There's a knock at the door. Johnnie pushes me aside and I trip over the board.

The first person I see is Seymour. Then the fucking popos. Two of them, sandwiching him. One's got his hand on Seymour's shoulder. "This the home of Eric Tsui?"

The precinct stinks of fat cops and old papers. It's puke green and white. The plastic tiles are chipped at the corners and coming up in places; the windows are covered with a hundred years of dirt. Five puny stairs go down to the main door. Two squashed beer cans sit on the cop's desk. Evidence: one taken from my jacket pocket, the other labeled "Weapon," which they probably found beneath some parked car. Shit's separated into bags.

Johnnie says, "You really fucked up this time."

"Where's Ma?"

"She's not coming."

"You're an asshole, you know that?"

Johnnie comes at me, but all he gets is a weak jab at the shoulder before a cop pulls him away.

"Ungrateful little shit," Johnnie says. "She's at the hospital begging the bastard not to press charges." He takes off, jumping the stairs. "I hope they lock up your sorry ass!" He slams the door and leaves me alone at the precinct.

Popo pushes me into a chair. "Take it easy. A few questions, okay?"

Half an hour goes by before Ma shows. She comes up to me, and just as I think I'm getting a hug, she stops, stares, then smacks me across the face. Her eyes puff. She signs whatever papers the cops give her, and we leave. Outside, she walks a step ahead. She sighs. I know what she's thinking. Things would be different if Dad was still around.

"I'm sorry, Ma," I finally say. She sighs and shakes her head again.

At home, she shuts herself in her room, and I can hear her crying. Johnnie's already in bed, so he doesn't fuck with me. He gives me a look, like, Just you wait. I climb up to my bunk and pass out in my clothes.

It's still dark out when Ma shakes me awake. "Get up," she says.

There's the smell of fried eggs, which makes me want to toss. It isn't until I sit up that it all comes back. I climb off the bunk. Johnnie's still sleeping, his jaw open so that the world can see his gross white tongue. Ma's got a tray of food out. A mug of tea, an egg sandwich made with Wonder bread, rice congee with a quartered thousand-year-old egg, wood chopsticks she gets from the restaurant, and a folded napkin.

"What's that?" I ask.

She makes an impatient throat-clearing sound. "Bring to Lao Gong," she whispers.

"No way I'm going into that rat hole."

She sniffles and watches me through big-ass eyes.

"Smells like piss," I say. "You can smell it in the hallway."

"An old man." She sighs. "All my fault. Didn't raise you good. No, not a good mama."

"Ma, stop—"

"If only it had been me and not your father. He would have taught you right. He would have known what to do." The skin around her eyes looks like mashed paper. She balances the tray with one hand. "An old man. No one to help him. No one to buy food for him."

"Grocery drops stuff off every Friday."

"So smart. Know everything, hah? Store has new owner. No more deliveries. Old man didn't eat for two days." She shakes her head and moves toward the door, balancing the tray on one arm.

"Wait," I say.

She hands the tray to me, adding a pad and a pen. "Make a list of things to buy. What he wants to eat later."

"You're going to shop for him now, too?"

Ma's stare makes me nervous. "You are."

Ma stands at the top of the stairs. "Careful—don't trip," she says.

"If I knew this would be the deal, I would've stayed in jail," I grumble. The tray jiggles unsteadily. Tea spills, soaking the napkin.

"Not too late," she says.

The moldy old-people stink reaches me halfway down the stairs. My stomach flips.

"Not too late," I mimic.

Outside Lao Gong's door, I listen for some kind of sound. The guy could be sleeping; he could be sitting in an easy chair with the cane resting across his lap, waiting for the littlest bit of noise. Who knows? He could have his ear up against the other side of the door.

"What you waiting for?" Ma yaps from above.

The tray wobbles. "Ma, will you go inside already?"

In front of me, the door swings open, and the first thing I see is the gauze bandage wrapped around the old man's head. A raw patch of scraped skin, swollen and black-and-blue, stands out on his cheek. He's still got that coat on. There's a tear at the pocket.

"Hello," I say.

"Hello, Lao Gong," Ma corrects.

The old man stares at me blankly. He blinks slowly and scratches his head like he doesn't have a clue why the hell I'm here.

"E-lic?" he finally says.

"Yep."

"Ah?"

"Eric."

"E-lic," he says then, in Cantonese: "You're standing on my newspaper." I step back. He moves his hands like he's scrubbing them in a sink or something. His fingers look waterlogged; the nails are black and fucked up. Without another word, he places the paper on a stack by the door, then returns to the darkness.

One step and I bang into a wall of newspapers and nearly drop the tray. It takes a second for my eyes to adjust, and when they do,

I can make out the piles that line the hallway on both sides. I get this sticky warm feeling, the kind that happens when you never open a window. "Lao Gong?"

I find him in the main room. The layout's the same as ours: tub dead center in the kitchen. In one corner, a large cot stacked with more newspapers. There's only one clear path, which goes from hallway to desk and desk to bathtub. The rod above the tub has metal links but no curtain. A towel and one set of underwear—old and see-through—hang from the rim of the tub.

The old man's at his desk, poring over a paper with a magnifying glass. There's a small lamp, the kind with a pull-on, pull-off tassel, and a black-and-white picture of a woman with small, fuzzy eyes. He turns the page, and under the light, I see dust rising into the air. The newspapers are yellowed and frayed. "So much work," he says. "Must hurry, hurry."

I check out the stacks that cover the floor. "Guess you like newspapers, huh?"

He looks at the room like it's the first time he's really seeing what's in front of him. "Sitting all these years," he says. "No time."

What the hell's he been so busy doing all day? I wonder.

"So much to do now," he says. A headline in the paper catches his attention. "Ai-yah, those no-good Communists."

I place the tray on the desk. Half the tea has spilled. "Careful," he says. "Don't mess the newspaper." His teeth are so big and white, so perfect compared with the rest of his face. No way they're real.

"Ah? What do we have here?" he asks.

"Breakfast."

"What's that? Speak up." He notices me staring at the bandage and fidgets with it the way you do with your nose when someone stares at it too long. For a minute, I almost like the guy. He mixes the thousand-year-old egg into the congee, stirs it with the chopsticks, and slurps from the bowl. Black egg dribbles from his chin, and I can't watch anymore. The newspaper's turned to an article headlined "Ho Chi Minh Makes Deal with Mao." The thing's dated October 3, 1958.

When he's finished eating, Lao Gong makes a sucking noise through his teeth. "Not bad," he says, setting the empty bowl on the tray and drawing the mug of tea to his mouth. He takes a sip, and when he places the mug on the desk, congee shit is floating on the surface.

"Ma said you needed food?"

Lao Gong examines the next page. The heading reads "Nationalists Flee Tachen Islands." "Ai," he growls. "Those Communists. We have to fight. Fight, I say. Don't you agree?"

"Guess so."

He drops the magnifying glass to the table. "Guess so? Guess so?" Spit hits me in the eye and I back off. Whacked, I think.

His eyes go blank again. "Chow fun," he says, licking his lips. "Across the street. Old man Chu cheaper." He reaches beneath layers of clothes and pulls out a small change purse. Lao Gong hands me three dollars and seven cents.

"Beef?" I ask.

"Shrimp. Lots of chili sauce. And soy milk. Yes, ah. Soy milk." He digs into his clothes again and pulls out the door key.

I leave and get back with the carton of noodles in less than ten

minutes. When I walk in, I hear the guy yammering away to himself. "Soon, any day. We'll run those Communist scoundrels away
and we'll go home for a look-see." By the time I make it to the
main room, the old man is quiet again, the magnifying glass moving from top to bottom over the page.

Ma gets a kick out of the whole thing. "So?" she asks.

I circle a finger at my temple. "Cuckoo . . . Cuckoo. Goes on
and on about Communism. How we gotta fight."

"Poor man. At hospital, all confuse. Thought I'm dead cousin.
Si-mong, he call me. Thank God niece was there. Remember—that
girl who move him in? Gives him money every two weeks. Ai.
Good girl. Doctor, too. Check everything all right." Ma unravels her
apron and tries to press out a wrinkle.

"I'm telling you," I say. "The old man's loopy. It's a garbage
dump down there."

"Comes from Shanghai," Ma says. "Ran away before the Communists—kept talking about taking Si-mong home one day. So sad,
ai?" She sighs and settles in her chair, turning on the TV.

Johnnie comes out of the toilet. He's dressed in one of those
preppy plaid shirts with too much pink.

"Damn troublemaker," he says. "Ma should have let you rot."

"Johnnie," she warns.

"Like I give a shit what you think?" I say. Ma jumps between
us. She does one of her "So tired, so tired" sighs.

"You two. It's New Year's. Bad luck to fight."

Part of me wants to shake the hell out of her. The bigger part of me feels sorry to be alive; sorry to be one of the disappointments in her life. I grab my knapsack and board, and before Ma has the chance to say anything else, I'm out of there.

Weeks later, when I get back from the bakery with a tsoa su bao, the old man's going on about the island of Quemoy. "Those Communists," he says. "Can you believe this? Rascals, I tell you."

I nod, even though I don't have any idea where Quemoy is, or even who those Communists really are. Through the magnifying glass, the characters get as large as nickels. Ma took Lao Gong to the doctor's yesterday, and though he's still got the bandage, it isn't as large or thick as the one he had before. Soft baby hair pokes out from beneath the gauze.

For the first time, I notice the thump of footsteps upstairs. Johnnie's plastic slippers. He's headed down the hallway to the shit hole. I borrow the cane propped at the side of the desk and move slowly toward the bathroom. When I hear him fart, I bang the cane against the ceiling.

Johnnie curses. I hear him jump off the toilet. "What the heck?"

I don't want him to hear me laughing, so I make my way back to the main room. Lao Gong turns the page. Hasn't heard a thing, I think, shoving the cane back up against the desk. But then, he looks up and through the glass, his eye huge like that Cyclops dude we read about in school. I wait for him to say something, but he goes back to reading the paper, and it's like I'm not even there anymore.

A couple days later, the old man's reading about Nixon. "What a good man," he says. "Such a good president." The bandage came off yesterday, and because of the uneven patches of hair, Ma shaved his whole fucking head. It's like a salted duck egg.

I hand him the tray of tea and sa ping yiu tiao. Lao Gong bites into the fried dough, chews quickly, swallows. Grease sneaks down his chin.

"What do you want for lunch?" I ask.

"Buy? Oh, yes. Let me think."

I tap my foot. "Mei fen?"

"Not today."

"Chow fun?"

He makes that whistly sound through his teeth. "Didn't I have that yesterday?"

"No. Gai lan and fish."

"Ah? I did? No, can't be."

"How about spare ribs?"

"Spare ribs, spare ribs." He stops to consider it a moment, but his gaze fixes on the article again. He shakes his head. "Ai-yah. This Watergate. What's so big deal? Simple. Just chop fingers, then no more burgle." He flips through the paper.

Crazy old man. I give in and sit on the finished-reading pile. Lao Gong calls it the throwaway pile, and now it's me who gets to do the dumping. The room is the same, nothing more, nothing less, except every day there are fewer newspapers to read. The path to the tub gets wider; the dump stacks by the desk taller.

"How come you waited so long to read these?" I ask.

"Very busy," he says. "You don't know. After Si-mong died . . ."

The sound of that last word stuns him.

"Lao Gong?"

"Thinking," he says, smoothing a hand over the newspaper. "Thinking, thinking."

Shit. I know what he means. When Dad died, nothing else mattered. Dust rises from the desk. The specks drift under the lamplight.

"Don't you ever get lonely in this place?" I ask.

"Lonely?"

"I mean, don't you have friends or anything? Family? Ma said you have a niece or something?"

He blinks, then sweeps his arm over the room of papers. "This is my family."

"Newspapers?"

"Ah."

I shake my head. "I don't get it. I mean, where do you sleep?"

"You see, you see?" He ignores my question and points to another article. "Those Americans not so stupid, after all. Hospitals using acupuncture to anesthetize patients before surgery. See? Eastern medicine much better."

He rubs the back of his head where he got the stitches.

"Lao Gong?"

"Ah?"

"Where do you sleep?"

He looks about the room, then up at me. "Why, here, the desk, of course."

"On top? Just like that?"

"What kind of question is that? Floor so dusty. Not possible."

"But why don't you sleep in bed?"

He places the magnifying glass on the paper. "Then no place for newspapers. This here is enough. Bed so big. Too big for one person." He shakes his head at the woman in the photo. "Young people. Can't tell when they see a busy man. No worry. Soon I come, ah?" He touches the picture frame.

Come where? I wonder. What a spook.

After school, Seymour's like, What do you mean you got things to do? He wants to head to Astor, where a bunch of thrashers hang out. I don't tell him the Asshole came after me this morning 'cause I took my sweet time taking a dump. Said I was going to make him late for some job interview, but I knew it was 'cause of the girl. He called last night and couldn't get past her father.

My side throbs. "Got things to do," I say.

"Come on—it's not like I shouldn't be getting to the store. We'll hang for an hour. What's an hour?"

A green Volvo passes us, nearly swiping Seymour's leg. He punches the trunk. "Fucking idiot Jersey drivers," he says, and I wonder if his dad's having one of those fits again. It's whack the way the guy cries and paints—scrapes and stabs at the canvas.

"So? Coming or what?" Seymour asks.

"The old man," I say. "Gotta take him to the doctor's. Ma's got day shift today."

"Fuck him."

"Shut up, man."

"You getting soft on me?"

"I said shut up." A pain stabs me between the ribs and I wince.

Seymour backs off. I don't have to say anything else. He knows, and he's thinking, We should have pegged the Asshole when we had the chance. I try to smile.

"Well, catch you later," he finally says. "Watch your back, man."

"Yep, later." I drop the board to the ground, and even though each bump feels like a knife sticking me in the ribs, I skate all the way home.

I can hear the guy rambling as soon as I walk in the door. "Can you believe? The *president.* Ai, no respect, these Americans."

"Hello?" I whisper.

"Ah? What you say? Speak louder, Si-mong."

"Lao Gong?" I say, my sneakers thudding against the floor. "Ready to go?"

He places the photo back on the desk and looks at me. "Go, ah?"

"The doctor."

He nods, ignoring what I've said, then taps at Nixon's face in the paper. "Ah, E-lic. Sit here. Look how Americans want to impeach their own president. So shame. Don't you think?"

"Guess so."

"Guess so? Guess so?"

Shit, not again. "Yes, I mean yes."

"Ah. Shameless, these reporters. So what he lies, ah? Good

man, that Nixon. Smart. No one else goes to China. Now look. Open doors, ah?" He stares at me through the magnifying glass. "We have to do something," he says, a hand over his chest. "Chinese for Nixon, ah?"

It's going to take a million years for this guy to catch up. He goes back to finish the article.

The room looks different. Newspapers remain heaped on the cot and around the bathtub, but the paths seem wider. The dump piles by the desk get higher and higher. Lao Gong says, "Hurry. No time, ah? Have to finish." Every day now I dump them in the basement fryer.

When I try to lift a stack, a sharp pain gets me in the side, and I drop the stuff. I can't even breathe. Quickly, before he notices, I gather the newspaper back into a neat pile.

Lao Gong places the magnifying glass on the desk. "E-lic, ah?"

"What?"

"Doctor," he says, using the cane to push himself up.

"Doctor? I don't need no doctor."

He shakes his head. "Ai, didn't you say I'm going to be late?"

Air fills me up again. "Yep," I say. "That's right."

Johnnie starts up first thing in the morning. I know it's coming because he didn't get that summer job he applied for. I'm on the can, thinking about some whack dream I had. There are only bits and pieces, like, I'm in a bathtub, sleeping. The thing's filled with water. My side beats like a heart. It opens up and a rib cooked with spicy barbecue sauce comes out. But then what happened?

In the kitchen, Ma's stir-frying beef in oyster sauce for us to warm later. The smoky smell reaches me at the end of the hall. The popping sound, the burning oil, was in the dream, too. But how?

Johnnie starts pounding against the door. "Hey," he says. "Get the hell out already."

"I'm taking a shit. Too bad." I love it in here, I think. A closet with a sturdy lock. He kicks the door.

I hear Ma say, "Ai. You two. Why always fight? Fight, fight. Mama so tire." Johnnie shuts his face. I wipe, and pull on my jeans, but by the time I get out, the front door shuts and Ma's gone.

"See what you did?" Johnnie says.

"Shut up."

He grabs me by the cuff. "Say it again. Go ahead. Say it."

I look him in the face and what I see is the loser who always wants the girl he can't get or the job no Chinatown homeboy's going to ollie up, and when he stares back at me, his nose all swollen and pink with hate, I know he sees the part of him he hates most, the part he won't ever be able to get rid of. And somehow, I know the old man's standing in his hallway, right below our feet. He's listening. Waiting. His cane is pointing up in the air, ready to knock against the ceiling.

Before the Asshole lands his first swing, I say, "You fucking lose, man. You really do."

By the time I get to Lao Gong's, it's already too late to meet up with Seymour before school, anyway. I've got the board in one hand, the tray of tea and congee, beef and yellow radish in the other. A hamburger the size of a Big Mac covers my right eye. It's hard to blink, the thing waters so much, but it doesn't hurt. Nothing does.

If Lao Gong brings it up—if he says, I was knocking and knocking but the noise didn't stop—I'll say, I don't know what you're talking about; I'll say, Mind your own damn business, old man. This got nothing to do with you. The only *ba-la-lang* going on around here, I'll say, is in your big fat head.

The food Ma made smells sort of sweet. It goes up my nose and makes me sick.

Before I get to the bottom of the stairs, I notice the newspaper still on the mat outside the old man's door. Shit, I think. He up and died. Just like that. Up and died on me, the fucker.

I leave my board at the front door and let myself in. That's when I really freak. The piles of newspaper over the floor and cot are gone. What's left is in the dump piles around the desk and chair. The lamp is still on. The magnifying glass and cane sit on the desktop.

"Lao Gong?"

The bumpy linoleum is covered with dust. The tub sits empty in the middle of the room. Underwear hangs from the rim. Lao Gong lies on the cot in the corner. He holds the picture close to his face. I place the tray on the floor and step closer to him.

"Lao Gong?" I whisper. "Hello?"

"Ah?" He doesn't open his eyes. "Yes, soon," he says.

"What's soon?"

"So much to do."

I look at the empty room. One large tub, the cot, the desk. The floor is more uneven than ours. A tile is missing by one leg of the cot. "It's finished," I say.

He smiles and hugs tighter to the picture frame. "Soon I come home, ah? Yes, yes. Come now. We go home."

I start with the piles around the desk, move them to the basement. Downstairs there's a moistness that smells moldy. I open the furnace and feed each bundle to the fire. The flames singe the edges first. My hands get covered with soot and ink.

It takes three hours to dump the papers. When they're gone, I go back upstairs and watch the guy sleep. His hair has grown back silver and straight. Three months, and all of a sudden he seems too small in that gray coat.

The desk is clear except for the lamp, magnifying glass, and cane. I place the tray of food on the desk. The tea is cold. I brush my hand over the desk. What would it be like to sleep here? Here, alone, on this hard, smooth desk. I hug the board to my chest, spin a wheel, and decide on a bowl of Shanghai noodles and soup dumplings.

I shut the door and let the old man sleep.

GENTLEMAN

SHOELESS AND dressed in a double-breasted tuxedo, I pour myself a short glass of Macallan. On the desk facing me is a photograph of Her Royal Majesty Queen Elizabeth II, taken thirty, no, forty years ago. The young lad bowing at the foot of Our Royal Highness is, of course, me. Yes, me: Henry Wong II, owner of Royalty Decorating, Ltd—that's *the* Royalty—established in 1949 on D'Aguilar Street, Central, Hong Kong. The whiskey warms my gullet, leaves a welcoming bite at the back of my throat. Fernando, my butler and driver, appears with my shoes shined to perfection. He places them at my feet.

"You look very good in your tuxedo, sir," he says, with a singsong Filipino accent.

This amuses me. "Would you like a drink?"

"No thank you, sir," he says. "I am working this evening," he adds, reminding me of his place in the order of things.

"Why, of course." I finish my drink. Fernando pours another, but only one-third of the way. I give him the eye, and he shrugs, filling the glass.

The Queen smiles from the picture frame. Her crown shimmers with diamonds. Her white rhinestone-studded gown flows to the floor. A weighty feeling fills my lungs. Today is the thirtieth of June, the eve of the Hong Kong Handover.

"It's the end of an empire," I pronounce.

"I'm so sorry, sir," Fernando says. His voice catches in his throat, and I realize he's referring to Royalty Ltd. My sister, Esther, has gone so far as to "buy" the warehouse. A temporary loan, really, yet what was understood to be a favor of sorts has suddenly transformed into a claim of ownership. Imagine.

For without the warehouse, what would become of Royalty? My goods?

Dear, darling Esther. Go ahead. Sue if that would please you; sue to have my goods removed. I sip my drink, taste the sweetness over my teeth, and take up the picture frame. "Look closely," I say, pushing it at Fernando.

"It's you, sir, presenting the chair at Buckingham Palace."

"Throne."

"Of course. Throne, sir."

"Ah—look at the workmanship. Those carvings. Fine, uh? Took my best men a year to finish the frame. And the velvet. Isn't that a rich color? That red?"

"Rich, sir. Very rich."

"What standards. They don't make anything the way they used

to, Fernando. See the emblem there? The crown? Contains exactly eight hundred eighty-eight stitches."

"Lucky eights," Fernando says. He's been in Hong Kong long enough to know such things. "Just like the one at the warehouse."

"Its sister." I thump the glass onto the desk. My drink splashes. Fernando is quick to wipe the spill.

"A hand with your shoes, sir?"

"I can manage." I press my feet into the shoes. Unfortunately, my belly obstructs any view, and I'm forced to reach and fumble with the laces.

"I'm sure you haven't forgotten, sir, but your niece will be arriving momentarily."

"Ah, yes—the niece." I suspect my dear brother has sent the younger of his pigtailed daughters to help her uncle "see the light," so to speak. I've been known to be persuaded by the younger, more gentle kind. He called to say, "For the sake of the family, let it go. You talk about honor—but it doesn't mean much these days. Woolworth's went bankrupt here and no one so much as batted an eye."

Young Amy has been staying with Esther on the Peak, and doubtless, they all see this as the best opportunity to charm poor Uncle into conceding to their demands. Why else would Esther go to such lengths to deliver the girl prior to the dinner in which she, too, will be in attendance? Why not simply convene at the Club?

Fernando attends to the laces. The wax-tipped ends tap at the leather. The sound is vaguely familiar, gives me the sense of déjà vu. Fernando takes my glass. I get to my feet. "Missus ready?" I ask.

There's an awkward pause of the sort that reeks of trouble. "Her arthritis, sir."

A muscle at the side of my jaw contracts. "Good God," I stammer. Each seat cost ten thousand Hong Kong dollars. I rap at the door separating Judy's chamber from mine, then enter. The thick scent of perfume overwhelms me. The terrier leaps off the bed and begins its angry tirade. I back out of the room.

Judy shushes the dog, her tone thick with practiced innocence. "Oh, Henry," she says, craning her neck to look up at me. She lies diagonally across the queen-size bed. The masseur leans into her shoulder. She moans, her wretched fingers clutching at the sheets. Her knuckles are red and as swollen as marbles. "You're dressed," she says. "You look so gentlemanly, Henry."

Her robe opens, revealing two deflated breasts. She pinches the neck closed. Her fingers bend to the sides, resembling claws. She sees me looking at her crippled hands and quickly tucks them into the sleeves. She excuses the masseur. When he speaks, I can't help pitying the American accent. "I'll just get myself a cup a cawfee," he says. Imagine.

Our wedding photo hovers over the bed. Those large, wistful eyes, and those long lashes. This was the beauty who, once upon a time, turned heads. Judy focuses those dark, sad eyes on me. Her lashes droop. To think that look was what I'd once found so intriguing. It now inflames me. When did the good feelings stop and the bad ones begin? Does it matter who betrayed whom first? Love, it seems, is comparable to business. One day, you're thinking "future," "expansion." The next, "downsizing," "restructuring," "chapter 11."

The doorman calls up from the lobby. I hear Fernando say, "Send her up."

"Is that Amy? Oh, goodness. I can't go out such a mess." Judy runs her bent fingers through her hair.

I fix my bow tie and vest. "You look lovely as usual, my dear."

Judy forces a smile. "Send my regards to Mother," she says. "Say I'm not well. I'm ill."

Ah—Mother. I should have figured. "Of course. I'm certain Mother will *miss* your charming presence," I say.

Judy rubs her bloated knees. "These bones. Just awful, this weather. Rain tonight. I'm certain of it. I'll have to watch the fireworks on television." An elaborate laser and fireworks display will take place in the harbor. Just about everyone will be dining at the Club, enjoying its spectacular view.

The doorbell buzzes. The beast braces itself on the mattress and howls. "Shush!" Judy orders. She smacks Boo-boo on the backside, causing him to whimper. His ears draw back. I hear Fernando in the living room inviting the girl in, taking her wrap and offering her juice. I straighten my tie, vest, and jacket.

"You just stand right up to her, Henry," Judy says. She's referring to dear Esther. Judy doesn't know the papers have been served. She still thinks Esther is bluffing.

I nod farewell to my wife, then step back and shut the door.

In the living room, I find a buxom woman with long black hair, dressed in a loose-fitting black men's cheungsam, which trails to the floor. The manifestation catches me off guard. The outfit hides most of her body, but the gold-embroidered dragons provide a lovely pattern. Except for her lips, she has sharp features. Clear brown eyes; cheeks powdered and blushed with rouge. She tosses her hair, and the long string of pearls sways over her breast.

"My dear child," I say. "I was expecting pigtails."

"Hi, Uncle. Guess it's been a while, huh?"

"Why, of course. My mistake. Your father mentioned college."

She pouts. "Um, Harvard, I bet. Georgie went to Harvard. Georgie was summa cum laude. Georgie, Georgie. It's like, Get off my back already." Her perfume smells vaguely of strawberry. She puckers her lips, so red and full and perfectly defined, and I find myself at a loss for words. My hands tremble.

"Uncle?"

"If you would kindly excuse me a moment." I retreat to my room and shut the door. I dab at my brow with a handkerchief. On the shelf, I locate a worn leather-bound book, *Etiquette & Modern Manners*. I take the manual from the shelf, sit at the desk to peruse it, and pour myself another drink. I underlined whole sections, it seems, in pencil.

Meeting Royalty: *It is usual for men to bow and for women to curtsey on being introduced to and taking leave of Royalty. If the Royal hand is extended, take it lightly and briefly, at the same time executing a brief bob with the weight on the* front *foot, or a bow from the neck (not from the waist). If she wishes, a woman may bow instead of curtsey: it is the acknowledgement that counts, not the exact form it takes.*

Direct address: *The Queen and the Queen Mother should be addressed as "Your Majesty" for the first time and as "Ma'am" (pronounced like "am" not "arm") on subsequent occasions. . . . Other members of the*

Royal Family should also be addressed for the first time as "Your Royal Highness," and subsequently as "Sir" or "Ma'am."

I continue to search for marked paragraphs. "Courtship" is the only section missing. It is, perhaps, lost now. When I first arrived in Hong Kong, I carried those pages in my pocket, reading them religiously prior to each date. Paper dust rubs onto my hands. I swill the whiskey in my mouth, swallow, feel the sweet fist of liquor warming my chest.

We descend the Peak. The road snakes downward at long, wide angles, passing private mansions and apartment complexes discreetly hidden amid dense foliage. From where we are, there is a clear view of Central. Glass buildings and mirrored skyscrapers compete for attention. At the heart of it all reigns the Bank of China, a mirrored fixture with angles as sharp as swords, which cuts directly through the government district. That I. M. Pei—the scoundrel. He should have known better. A Western education doesn't make one a guai lo.

Outside it has started to drizzle. There is the damp smell of monsoon. I press the handkerchief to my brow, and without saying a word, Fernando increases the air. The engine rattles, threatening to stall.

"I'm quite all right," I say. "No need."

Amy takes the long strand of pearls from around her neck and winds it around her wrist. The result is a four-stringed bracelet. She rolls her window down as we circle past the new condos along Magazine Gap Road. Wisps of hair blow from her face. She snaps her chewing gum, making a restless clacking similar to that of mah-jongg tiles being shuffled on a table. "What an interesting sound," I finally say.

"Sorry." She spits the purple mass into a tissue, careful not to spoil her lipstick.

We pass the cemetery, then descend into the chaotically congested streets and walkways of Central. Chinese and Brits and other guai lo. A group of Americans parade about with champagne bottles. Kazoos whine. Fernando brakes, sounds the horn at a lad racing across the street fluttering a British flag. We pass the Landmark building, soon to be a hallmark of the postcolonial era. Amy stares out the window at a blond couple wearing coolie clothes and pointed farmer's hats. "Psych," she says, crossing a leg. A shoe dangles capriciously off the tips of her toes. A sickle-shaped scar runs over the knot of her pale, thin ankle. Imagine. To take the small foot in my hands, to kiss the pale white moon. I tooth the end of my cigar, feel it get soft and wet.

Fernando catches my eye in the rearview mirror. "Front entrance, sir?"

I tug at the lapels of my jacket. "Certainly."

"We're there already?" Amy asks, playing with her pearls. "I was hoping we could, you know, stop for a chat first."

My mouth feels thick and dry. If only I'd filled a flask. "Chat?" I say.

She bats those charming lashes. "You know, chat. Um, chitchat."

Did Paul advise her to approach me in such a manner? Does he think his daughter's charm will make me hand over what rightfully belongs to me? I remove the cigar from between my lips. "It would

be poor form to arrive late on such an occasion, don't you agree?"
I say. "Mother will be waiting."

"Oh, Uncle," she says, seemingly disappointed.

"Did you know that guests do not leave a function before a
member of the royal family?" I say. "Likewise, one does not make
her wait."

"What? Grandma?"

"That's correct. Such is her place in the family."

"Oh, boy. You and daddy are just alike. Auntie, too."

"Beg your pardon?"

"Come on, Uncle, loosen up. Can't we get a drink first? Auntie's so uptight all the time. It's, like, impossible to talk to her."

I taste the tobacco on my lips. It's true about Esther.

"And what's with that accent?" she says. "She gets this English
thing going when other people are around." Amy mocks Esther's
voice with incredible accuracy, exaggerating all her mannerisms. I
keep a straight face, though it's difficult to resist a hearty chuckle.
The pulpy end of the cigar flattens between my teeth.

"Fernando? Hyatt open?"

"Coffee shop?" he asks. "I believe so, sir."

"Coffee shop." Amy grunts and presses my arm. "Can't we grab
a Bud somewhere?"

"I'm sorry?"

"Beer, Uncle."

Beer? Why, yes, a beer, I think, salivating. I lick my upper lip,
tasting salty beads of perspiration. But I catch myself. No, no—I
mustn't. She is but a child. My brother's child. I clear my throat,
say, "Why, that wouldn't be a proper activity for a young lady."

"I hate to break it to you, Uncle, but I'm one of the best funnelers at school."

Horrified at the possibilities of the word "funnelers," I muster a smile. "Americans have such colorful expressions," I say.

"Please? Just one itsy-bitsy beer."

I ponder this: One drink. An "itsy-bitsy" one at that. I touch the handkerchief to my brow.

Amy bounces a leg in front of me. She winks. "How 'bout it, huh?"

Why not? I think. Why should I allow the petty constraints of society to keep me from enjoying a simple drink? Next year, she'll be off to university. That constitutes adulthood, does it not? Fernando brakes at the intersection. A group of guai lo step into the crosswalk. One is dressed in a coolie costume, the others in bright scholarly robes and cheungsam. They all have black braided pigtails. I pass the cigar to Fernando.

"Well, Miss Amy," I say. "What would Your Highness prefer?"

An hour and a half and four pints later (and four half-pints for the young lady), we stop for a "quick peek" at the warehouse. "God," she says, laughing, "Auntie's probably hitting the roof right now, waiting and all."

"Let her wait," I say, knowing Mother will be just as upset, perhaps more so. A few kind words, however, and all shall be forgiven. I step out of the car first, giving Amy my arm. Fernando hurries toward us with the large umbrella. During the course of the trip, I've been explaining the details of Esther's suit against me. The patter of the summer shower against the tin roof fills my chest with a dull, weighty apprehension. At home, my wife is lying in bed, her spoiled fingers perched at the edge of the sheets, watching a muted television and listening to the rain.

"So let me get this straight," she says. "Royalty *was* going bankrupt."

"It was having a few difficulties, yes, but nothing—"

"The government was about to confiscate the warehouse, so Auntie bought it from you and put it in her name."

"It was merely a temporary loan," I insist, avoiding the fact that "loan"—the word itself, that is—did not actually enter the discussion. It was merely suggested, understood.

"She set you up?"

I nod gravely. "That sweet aunt of yours is attempting to make off with my life," I say, patting the steel door. "My work. Isn't that right, Fernando?"

"Yes, sir." Fernando holds the umbrella over us. I search for the key in my waistcoat.

Amy waves a finger from side to side. "That's not what *they* say."

"Lies," I say.

She pouts. "Dad says you're just clinging on. You know, grasping at straws. Or maybe it's gasping at straws? Anyway, he thinks it's just a matter of time before you've got to close shop."

"As always, your father is terribly misinformed. He has a way of believing everything dear Esther tells him. He was prone to that since he was quite small."

Amy laughs. "Auntie's been going off about how Royalty went under. How she bailed you out and now you won't hand it over."

"Is that so?" I am tempted to enlighten her of Esther's past. The lecherous woman ran off on a husband and son. What now of the forgotten family? Simply erased. Imagine.

Amy mimics Esther's voice again—"He keeps the key on his body night and day"—thus I pluck the key from my pocket and laugh until I'm coughing.

"Sir," Fernando says. "You're expected at the Club."

"Why, the Club, the Club," I say, fumbling with the lock. "In a moment, Fernando. A moment."

"You wasted or what?" Amy takes the key from me. She jams it into the slot, and with a swift turn of her wrist, the door clicks open. Musty, cool air rushes out at us. We're about to enter a dark cave filled with ivory and cherry-wood antiques.

Fernando backs toward the door. "I'll wait in the car, sir."

"Yes," I tell him, "wait."

Amy takes my arm and we step into the dark. I locate the bulb on the wall and turn it clockwise. The harsh light forces me to blink.

"This," she says, circling and waving the key in the air, "is *it*?"

I survey the goods. Everything from dining tables to bedboards. Items such as sofa frames and desks awaiting reconditioning. Bureaus with missing handles. "It doesn't seem to be much." I notice a patch of leather peeling from an ottoman. Yellow stuffing peers from under the fabric. Garbage, Esther would say.

"Hey." Amy leads me to an oak dining table with a crack on the surface. "Mom and Dad have one of these."

"Yes," I say. "Same collection. The set was my wedding gift. This one needs a bit of reconditioning."

She nods and presses the key to the flesh of her cheek. "I like this place." Her voice is soft, tender, and I think: She understands; she sees the beauty.

"Is that so?" I make my way to the rear of the warehouse, where I store my prize. A large white canvas covers it.

"Let me guess," Amy says sarcastically. "It's a chair."

"Ah, not just any chair, my dear." I tear the canvas away. The throne stands with its back to us, square and stiff as a red knight. The mahogany frame is dark, sturdy; the velvet soft and cool to the touch. Gold tassels fringe each arm. I smooth a hand over the royal crown.

"Wow—awesome," she says. "Can I have it?"

"That, unfortunately, cannot be arranged."

"Why not?"

"Why—it belongs to Her Majesty."

"Her Majesty?"

Americans. Just imagine. "The Queen, of course," I say.

"But I want one." Perhaps it's my expression, because she adds, "Wait—you mean, Queen queen?"

"Her Royal Majesty." My fingers trace the gold double stitching. I explain that Royalty need be kept alive only until the Queen replaces its tired mate. Then everyone will see. Royalty will rise once again. "In another forty years' time," I say, "this will be sitting in Buckingham Palace."

"But Elizabeth'll be dead," she says. "*You'll* be dead." She seats herself on the throne, dust rising around her like a spell. "How's this for the Queen?" She crosses a leg and exposes the sickle-shaped scar at her ankle. The sight of Amy taking the throne—a Chinese girl in a man's cheungsam—stirs in me a hopeful sensation.

When referring to a member of the Royal Family in his or her presence or in the presence of other Royalty, the following descriptions . . .

I take Amy's hand, kiss it and say, "Your Highness."

She bobs her foot in the air. I want to drop to a knee, devour the ankle with kisses.

Fernando appears. "Sir?" he says. "The Club, sir."

"Ah yes, the Club."

"God," Amy says, her bulbous lips parting ever so slightly. "Auntie's going to flip, I tell you. Totally flip."

I look at her, dwarfed on the throne, and pat the dust from her hair. She rubs her hands over the red velvet, jangles the tassels. I extend my arm. "Shall we?"

On arriving at the Club, we discover Mother and Esther waiting at the front entrance. "Uh-oh," Amy whispers. Mother notices us immediately and waves. Esther shakes her head. Her jaw is set for battle; her torso seems slightly off balance. Beyond, dinner is being served buffet style. On one side of the hall is roast beef and ham; on the other is broiled lobster. Between them are tables topped with everything from smoked salmon to filet mignon to Peking duck. The hall is congested and difficult to navigate. People wait in line as if they were prison inmates. Waiters cut and serve. Busboys weave through the crowd carrying trays laden with dishes.

"Where have you *been*?" Esther yells. Chinese and British alike turn to stare. I tip my top hat; allow myself the pleasure of a pleasant grin. Esther stabs her watch with a finger. "It's been over two and a half hours. Mother has been waiting—"

The accent. Amy and I exchange glances.

"Is there a bar this evening?" I ask. Esther glowers. I must be smirking.

"Where's that no-good wife of yours?" Mother says, fingering her rosary. "It's her fault you're late, isn't it? Slothful woman."

"She's not well this evening," I say.

"What? Oh, I feel faint," Mother says. She knows the cost of each banquet seat. She presses a hand to her chest. "My heart. My heart."

I take her by the arm. "It's okay, Mother. Lean against me, why don't you?"

Esther waits for an explanation from Amy.

"We were chatting and lost track of time," Amy explains. "Sorry."

"Is that alcohol I smell on your breath?" Esther snips.

"Holy Mary, pray for me," Mother says.

"How could you?" Esther turns to me, and I expect she'd like to say something along the lines of, Go ahead and destroy your life, but leave hers alone. I'm tempted to comment on her slipped prosthesis.

"It was just a couple of beers," Amy says. Esther's mouth falls agape.

"Oh, merciful Mary . . ." Mother continues, "Hail, Mary, full of grace . . ."

I reach into my pocket for my handkerchief. "Perhaps Mother should be seated," I suggest. "Esther, would you mind terribly fixing Mother a plate?"

"Yes, yes," Mother says, relying on my arm, "a plate."

Crimson splotches materialize over her face and neck. Without a word, she turns and reenters the crowded serving hall. I can't help chuckling and winking at Amy. She smiles. She, Mother, and I enter the dining room, set up with cloth-covered tables and two television sets, one airing news, the other the laser performance in the harbor. The brass band bellows "High Hopes." Amy glances at the tuxedoed men gathered about in small circles. "Wow—some of these guys are actually pretty cute," she says. "I'm, um, not usually into the Asian thing."

I haven't a clue what she means by this. Nevertheless, I nod. Table 38, a small round one set for five at the far end of the room, is empty and waiting. I help Mother to her seat. She tugs at my arm. "Did you really take the child for a drink?" she asks.

Amy turns her back. Clearly, the redundancy of events bores her. "I'll go check out dessert."

"Go ahead. Anything you want. Just go ahead."

Mother sits. "How could you take the child to a bar?"

I check to make sure Esther is not present. "We went to the warehouse," I explain.

"The warehouse?"

I nod, pat my waistcoat, and only then remember that Amy still has possession of the key. "Esther told her my goods were nothing more than junk," I say. "She told her she *bought* the ware-house."

"She didn't."

I flag the waiter for a scotch on the rocks. "She did. I brought the girl to have a look. Evidently, your sweet daughter is broadcasting to the world that I refuse to get out. Everyone knows about the suit."

Shame drains the blood from her cheeks. "She wouldn't."

The waiter brings my drink. I smile, salute my mother with the glass, and add, "She did."

Esther arrives with two plates, one obscenely stacked with lobster, the other overflowing with sushi. She places the dishes in front of Mother. "Here," she says, thrilled to offer Mother something I cannot, "all your favorites."

Mother forces a smile. Her lips are pursed.

"Something wrong, Ma?" Esther asks.

I finish my drink, watch her distorted face through the bottom of the glass. *Conversation is an art, and like all arts, it is improved by experience and practice.*

"No, no," Mother says, pushing the dishes away. "I just don't have any appetite. Maybe later. You two go ahead."

Esther settles into her seat and stares angrily at me: What did you say to her?

I signal the waiter, order another drink, draw the lobsters toward me. Esther watches as I lift one to my plate.

"Those aren't for you," Esther says. "I didn't get them for you."

"Really?"

"Really."

I fork the meat out of the tail. "So sue me," I say, then place it in my mouth. The lobster is sweet, rich with butter.

A pinch of red appears at Esther's forehead. She is about to retaliate when Amy reappears with a cream puff the size of a coffee cup.

"Enough." Mother hisses and glares at Esther. "No face, you two."

A rash of color spreads over Esther's cheeks and neck. "It's not my fault," she defends. "He forced me to—"

Mother silences her with a look. Your big brother, her eyes say. Shame on you.

Esther's jaw clamps shut. She picks up two lobster halves and moves them onto Amy's plate. She takes the other two for herself. Amy scoops a bit of cream from the pastry with the tip of her finger, and before it topples, she shoves it into her mouth. She makes a smacking sound with her lips. "A dream puff," she says.

"To dream puffs," I say.

"I would have thought some things were perhaps a bit too young even for *your* tastes," Esther says.

"Esther," Mother scolds.

Just beyond Esther's smug face, I catch sight of a lad at the next table watching Amy. He's dressed in one of those sharp-looking Italian tuxedos, cut high and with the extra button. I stare him in the eye: Ready to prey on the innocent, are you? I'd like to hurl him across the room.

Esther notices the indignant flare of my nostrils and turns to look. "Jonathan, hello!" she says. "Goodness, your aunt didn't mention you would be in Hong Kong—"

"Auntie Ming doesn't know I'm here yet," he says. "I only just arrived yesterday afternoon. For work." He explains he was chosen for a position at one of the funds here.

"Is that so?" Esther nods but looks him over with a critical eye.

The boy maneuvers to our table. "Anyone sitting here?" he asks, withdrawing Judy's seat.

"Terribly sorry," I'm about to say.

"Not at all," Esther blurts, extending me a fake smile. "Henry, don't you wish you were still so slender?"

I turn my attention to the boy. "Might you be familiar at all with Chaucer?" I ask.

"Sure," he says.

"You've come across that saying, then—'Those who live in glass houses shan't throw stones'?"

The boy clears his throat to keep from laughing. He hides a smile behind a fist, careful to avoid Esther's eye. I search the room for a waiter. Mother clears her throat. She feeds her rosary through her fingers.

"Jonathan, you've met my mother, haven't you?" Esther says.

"Why, yes." He greets her in Mandarin and addresses her politely. He is a smooth small-talker, knows how to win her attention by admiring her dress. "It becomes you," he proclaims, which I didn't imagine young people knew to say anymore. Esther introduces Amy as her "niece from the States."

"How do you do?" the boy says.

"Just fine, thanks." Amy tilts her head coquettishly. His brow lifts; a flirtatious dimple presses at his cheek. Esther looks askance, and it becomes evident enough that the boy is of questionable background.

I step between them. "To the *Britannia*," I toast.

"I'll drink to that," the boy says, tasting his gin and tonic. Outside, jeweled with a single string of lights, the royal *Britannia* waits patiently in the harbor. Tonight the ship will begin its last journey home. There it will be laid to rest; disassembled and left for scrap metal.

Rain patters against the window. "Ai," Mother sighs. "No good, those Chinese."

"An unreliable bunch," the boy states. "Who knows what they'll do?"

"True," I add.

Amy laughs. "Um, hello? We're only, like, Chinese."

"Certainly not," Esther says, emphasizing her accent.

Amy and I exchange glances again, and this time I can't help chortling. Mother jabs me in the side with her elbow.

"What's so funny?" Esther asks.

"Nothing," I say. "Truly."

A frown creeps over Esther's face, but she's quick to compose herself. The waiter passes. I order another drink, despite the fact that I'm not quite finished with the first. Esther watches me with disgust. I relish a smile. Amy and the boy trade uneasy glances.

"Perhaps it's not such a bad thing that the Brits are leaving," Esther says. She knows the mass exodus has doomed Royalty, which caters solely to those of the highest social standing.

"Baked Alaska—that's what I want," Mother announces.

I look Esther in the eye. As straight-faced as I can manage, I say, "Out with the old and in with the new, is it? Well, well. Perhaps you shall be trading in that British accent? Or might I say 'aborting' yet another happy family?" Spittle hits her cheek. Her eyes bulge, the whites circling her dark irises. Her eyes skip from

Amy to the boy to Mother. Amy raises a curious brow. Esther wipes her face with the back of her hand.

"You . . . you're . . ." Esther starts to say.

"Baked Alaska," Mother repeats, and waves a hand for a waiter.

"You're . . . ?" I continue, laughing now.

Tears tremble at the rims of her eyes. "You're *drunk.*"

"Fireworks!" someone calls. "Yan huo, yan huo! They're starting." The word rushes like a collective force across the room. The crowd presses toward the windows. People hurry from their seats for a better view of the harbor. Mother retrieves a tissue from her purse and sneaks it into Esther's hand.

"Would you like to have a look?" the boy asks Amy. He fixes his bow tie.

"You bet." The couple excuse themselves. I notice the way the boy brushes his hand over the nape of her neck, the quick smile she flashes at him before they disappear. The room dims and the first set of fireworks go off. The explosions have the sound of cannon fire. The night air reverberates with the clack of firecrackers. Colors light the room. Red then white; red then white then green.

"You know," Esther says, getting up from the table. She pats the corners of her eyes with the tissue. "The one thing I respect most about the Brits is they know when not to overstay their welcome."

"Dear sister—they've *already* outstayed their welcome. The question is: Will everything go to pot now that they're gone?"

The waiter arrives with my drink. I take it from him, and when Mother asks again for the baked Alaska, he informs her that the regular menu isn't being offered this evening.

"No? Did you say no?" Mother cries, and I see that she's teary-eyed. Her voice goes hoarse: "Do you know who I *am*?"

The waiter turns to me for help.

"You heard Mother," I say. I finish my drink in three large gulps. "Tell shi fu that Wong Tai is here. He knows."

"Sir." The waiter shakes his head and disappears to the kitchen.

"Ma," Esther says, patting her arm. "Don't you want to see the fireworks first?" She moves toward the windows, where people oooh and ahhh. Mother pauses. Green, white, then red light fills the room. The colors tint her skin.

"Son?" Hope crackles in Mother's voice. I love you most, her eyes say. You are my number-one child. My number-one son. But I can tell she, too, is eager to see the fireworks.

"You go ahead," I offer.

"Come, Ma," Esther says.

Mother looks helplessly from Esther to me, reluctant to leave me alone at the table. I stand, take her hand and kiss it, nod for her to go. She smiles and follows Esther into the crowd. I sit back at the table clustered with half-finished dishes and enjoy the rest of my drink. The television airs the Handover ceremony. One at a time, the Queen's armies march steadily across the platform, halt, and when signaled, turn and march off the screen. First the Beefeaters, then the Scots with their hats and kilts. Steadily they come, tirelessly, row after row after row. Rain beats down.

I scan the crowd in the room. The gold-embroidered dragons on Amy's dress catch the light. The gown hides those sweet bare ankles. The boy places his hand at the small of her back. Fireworks patter through the sky. A pain resonates from the core of my bones. I shut my eyes, picture the *Britannia* blinking its lights. Fireworks sound; light filters through my eyelids. "Oooh," the crowd sighs.

I toast the crowd gathered at the windows, the Royal Navy marching across the television screen, my dear wife watching all this at home. Yes, Judy. The woman I once loved, the woman who'd once given me the world.

It is time, I think, to go home.

But back in the car, I say, "To the warehouse."

"Yes, sir," Fernando replies. As always, he hands me a fresh cigar and the lighter. Outside, people dance in the street. The crowds push and pull, forward and back, forcing people off the walkways into the streets. Fernando continues through Central. The neoclassical architecture gives the district its handsome character and clean, bold lines. There is something comfortable, familiar. Central does, in fact, remind me of home, of Shanghai and the area around the Bund. Boutique windows showcase the latest and smartest fashions. Scarves, jackets, shoes, luggage.

Colors and sounds swirl and mix. I light the Cohiba, fumble with the bow tie and attempt to prize it from around my neck. The headlights of the car behind us reflect off the rearview mirror, framing Fernando's eyes. All this time, I'd taken them for brown. "Goodness," I say. "Your eyes. They're hazel."

He chuckles. "One too many tonight, sir?"

The car fills with the sweet aroma of the cigar. We crawl up

D'Aguilar Street, the engine shifting into gear. For a moment I think I see Amy, but the girl turns out to be another woman. Disappointment settles in my mouth.

"You seem exceptionally tired this evening," Fernando says. "Perhaps it might be better to go home, sir?"

"Certainly not. Macallan's in the boot?" I ask, puffing on the cigar.

The glove compartment opens, and Fernando passes me a glass wrapped in plastic. A sniff and I can tell it's my favorite whiskey. "Happy Handover, sir," he says.

"Good man, Fernando." I reach over to pat him on the back. "Good man."

We pass an English pub where Frenchmen are singing bar songs. A group of Americans compete, chanting, "Fifty-six bottles of beer on the wall, fifty-six bottles of beer . . ."

By the time we arrive at the warehouse, the rain has let up, and I'm still preoccupied with that horrendous American pub jingle. Fernando pulls up to the brick building, parks, helps me out. He unlocks the boot, hands me a fresh bottle of whiskey, and waits as I make my way to the door. On the way, I break the seal of the bottle, pour myself a drink, take a sip. "Ninety-nine bottles of beer on the wall, ninety-nine bottles of beer . . ."

I place the bottle on the floor and reach into my waistcoat. The key. Where is it? Something stirs, catching my attention. The door, I realize, is ajar. I toss the cigar to the ground, push the door open, and once inside, arm myself with a desk leg. A creaking sound issues forth from the back of the room. The throne. I move closer, closer still, and then I see it. My prize—its back regal and sturdy, its arms draped with black silk patterned with gold dragons.

Creak, creak. Dust rises in clouds.

The ankle. Thin and naked and scarred. Pale and vulnerable. The arches bowed, the feet dip and rise, dip and rise. Skin smacks at skin. Sigh follows sigh. They rock, desperate and slippery, the odor of sex permeating the room.

Heat swells through me, and I want to kill; bludgeon the scoundrels. But I gaze about, and what I notice are sofa frames haphazardly strewn about like abandoned fossils. Along one wall, chairs stack to the ceiling. Heaps of remainders lie helter-skelter over the floor. Some of the desks lack drawers or handles; a dining chair remains split down the back; in the corner, bedboards and bureaus await reconditioning.

Amy's pearls snake to the floor, clattering against the concrete, and in the moment's passing, I see the flickering lights of the *Britannia* receding from harbor to sea. Dust rises from the wasteland.

Creak, creak; creak, creak; creak, creak.

Silently, before the desecration has been fully consummated, I retreat to the car. There I find myself shaking.

"You all right, sir?"

"Certainly," I say, clutching the useless leg of mahogany. I direct Fernando to take us home.

I shut myself in my bedroom, sit at the desk and hold my face in my hands. Fernando has retired, and the sun has started to rise. The beast yaps in the next room. Judy stirs and hushes the dog. She appears in the adjoining doorway. Lamplight filters into my room. Her hair has gone flat on one side. Her nightgown falls loosely from her body. "You're home," she says.

I suck at the cigar. It's not the time for idle chatter.

"How was dinner? Did you see the fireworks?"

A pillow of ash lands on the desk. Judy retrieves a tissue tucked up her sleeve and sweeps up the mess. I push the chair back. The leg squeaks against the tiled floor. "It's over," I say, reaching for my shoes and grappling with the laces.

She quiets. She knows what I mean by this.

I remove the cigar, balance it half on, half off the desk so that the tip points outward.

Finally she says, "Would you like a hand?"

"Not at all," I say, but she kneels at my feet. There's a soft tapping sound, a spell of déjà vu. The laces, I think, but when I look, it's her bent fingers. She clamps the lace between thumb and first knuckle. She pulls the knots free, the rest of her fingers trembling with exertion, the nails tapping against each polished shoe.

Breathless, she removes the shoes, looks at me with those dark, resigned eyes. Her scalp is damp with perspiration. "My bones," she says.

I take her hands, touch the twisted knots, turn them palms up. The skin is shriveled but soft, and smells of sleep. The oddest thing comes to me: *It is considerate of each party to make sure that the other knows how much commitment is intended.* I cradle my face in her hands. Just imagine. Right there in the cupped hollow of her soft, wretched hands.

STAR

THE BUZZER goes off like a bug zapper: *Tz-zz, tz-zz, tz-zz.* It's the first Friday of the month—Garbo night with Mom. When I open the door, I find a Chinese Greta attired in a flapper hat, her eyes heavily lined and her lashes coated thick with mascara. Her face is powdered and pale, her bobbed hair curled up at the ends, and for full effect she's knotted a silk scarf at her neck. She's laden with shopping bags filled with prepared dishes. Along the sidewalk, people converge from the direction of Grand Army Plaza, passing our stoop on their way toward Seventh Avenue.

Mom dumps a worn Loehmann's bag into my arms. "Ay—take this."

"You're early," I say, as we head inside.

"Really?" From her tone, the practiced surprise, I know something's up. "Careful—fish. Flounder—I make it just the way you like."

Uh-oh, I think, my intestines stiffening for the blow. The last time she troubled to prepare this dish, I ended up on a date with one of her friend's daughters.

Mom peeks over my shoulder. "Jack here?"

"Of course he's here," I say. "He lives here."

Jack appears from the bathroom, smelling of lavender. He hurries into the kitchen and takes the bag from Mom. "Hi, Mrs. Wong," he says, pecking her on the cheek. He tucks his hair, brown and cropped at the shoulder, behind his ear. He's wearing a pair of my jeans, which are a few sizes too large, and which he has to curl over at the top to keep them from falling down. At the knee there's a nickel-size hole, which drives Mom crazy whenever she sees me wearing them. "I'll buy you a new pair," she always insists, and when I say no, she nags, "What will people think?"

Mom, of course, picks up on the jeans and looks away. "What's that?" she says, pointing to a fishbowl on the kitchen counter. The goldfish noses the glass, searching for the way out.

"Georgianna's," I say. "One of her patients gave it to her."

"He's fish-sitting while she's on vacation," Jack explains.

"Why'd you lug all this food?" I ask. "Didn't we agree we'd do takeout from now on?"

"Yeah, you shouldn't have," Jack says, pulling a container out of the bag. "Oh, my—is this what I think it is?"

"Sesame noodles," she replies, and I think, Big trouble.

"Oh, goody," Jack says, his green eyes round like a child's.

"Grandma Wong in town?" I guess.

"Ay," she says, shushing me. "Ma's food much better than order-out."

"Yeah." Jack gives me the eye. "Much better."

Mom smiles that safe, diplomatic smile, and I can feel the lunch in my system lurching to a halt. As soon as she goes to use the bathroom, Jack ribs me one. "What's your problem?"

I rub my gut. "Something's up."

"What?" He dishes noodles into bowls.

"I don't know—something."

He looks at me, sighs and shakes his head like he's totally exasperated. He divvies the gai lan and string beans onto plates.

There's a pause before the toilet sounds. It's the kind of silence that makes me wonder if Mom's checking the contents of the medicine cabinet. The faucet squeaks on.

"Just be nice," Jack says, cutting the fish and separating the meat from the bone. He severs the head and places it on Mom's bowl. He does this matter-of-factly, as if the skull were nothing more than a piece of broccoli. The fact that he doesn't get grossed out anymore makes me want to hug him. "Be a good boy," he tells me, "and maybe—just maybe—I'll stop off at the pharmacy later, and you know, pick up some more goodies." It's such a sweet gesture I want to kiss him. The condoms are really my deal. I'm the one still not ready to take any major leaps.

Mom returns from the bathroom. "Goodies?" she asks.

"Just look at all these goodies," I say.

"Right." Jack smiles and hands Mom a bowl of noodles and a plate with the fish head, and we move to the den. He returns to the kitchen for drinks.

"Give me a viskey and ginger ale and don't be stingy," I say in my best Garbo accent.

"Diet coming up," Jack replies.

Mom giggles and sits in the easy chair. With her chopsticks, she draws the fish head to her lips and sucks out the eye. "Tasty, quite good," she assesses. She uses her chopsticks to pick a thin piece of cartilage from her tongue.

The phone rings and Jack answers. "Hey, Fred. I didn't know you were going to be in town. . . ."

Mom slips into Chinese: "Oh, yes. Auntie Esther is arriving next week."

Bingo. Esther, of course. Haven't seen Dad's sister since the funeral four years ago. I settle into the couch and fast-forward through all the previews. Voiceless people jerk here and there, disappearing from the screen and then reappearing.

Mom sucks at the other eye. "Rai-cho's at college. Some place in Boston, I think."

"Little Rachel?" I ask.

Mom sighs. "Ay—all getting old now."

"Did she really have an abortion?" I ask.

The skull pops off the chopsticks and smacks against the floor. "Who told you that?"

"You."

"Ay," she says, picking up the head and placing it on a napkin. "Poor Esther. She would chi si—so heartbreak—if she found out about that daughter of hers."

"She probably knows."

"Don't say anything-ah? We know nothing. Nothing to do with us."

"Like I'm going to go up to her and say, 'Hey, Auntie, heard your daughter got an abortion. Can you confirm that for me?'"

She points the tips of her chopsticks at me. "Always have to be smart-pants-ah? Anyway, ay—she wants you to have dinner with her."

Dinner—is that it? True, Esther can be an overbearing, nosy bitch. And Uncle Philip—now, there's a prick of a guy. He used to bully me around, never relinquishing control over the television, forcing me to watch mad-shark movies or cowboy-and-Indian flicks. But hey, it could be worse—it could be Grandma. Last time I phoned, she invited herself to stay at my place on her next visit. She'd be giving me face, she explained. Choosing me over everyone else in the family.

"Well," I say, pausing the video machine. I pick up my bowl of noodles, relax back into the couch, push food into my mouth. "When?"

"Friday." She tastes the noodles and, after a critical pause, decides that she didn't use enough sauce. "And oh, yes," she adds in Chinese, "maybe it's better not to bring your friend."

I swallow, feeling the clump stick in my chest. My muscles tense.

Jack hangs up and enters the room with a tray and three tall glasses of soda. "Here we come," he sings, "Miss America . . ."

"Hurry, Jack," Mom says, switching to English. "Ay—everything getting cold."

Jack places the glasses on the coffee table and settles next to me on the couch. He takes up his bowl, and with chopsticks sweeps a tangle of noodles into his mouth.

I pick a piece of fish from the bone. "He's coming," I tell Mom in Chinese. As if interpreting, I turn to Jack and say, "Fish is good."

He tries a piece. "Oh, great."

Mom crunches on a piece of gai lan and replies to me, "I think better not," and I know she's concerned about Esther. What would Esther say? And Tai-tai. Her only grandson. Ay!—she would have another stroke, I tell you.

"What do you expect me to tell *him*?" I demand.

Jack glances from me to Mom to me. "Hey, no fair," he says, laughing. "How do I know you're not talking about me?"

Mom and I both smile at him, like, Aren't you silly? I click off the lights and start the movie, then sit again. I draw the food to my lips and eat.

At the end of the movie, Garbo looks out from the stern of a ship. She sails away from her country, her home, her people. It is her moment of freedom, her chance at love irretrievably lost. She watches Sweden shrink, disappear. A steady good-bye, her face betrays neither smile nor frown nor tears.

I'm thinking about Dad. If only I had told him. But there was Mom: "He's in so much pain already. You want to kill him?" All those months while cancer devoured his body, I thought, Wait— he'll be better tomorrow. So I waited, and when tomorrow came and he was worse off, there was still tomorrow. All of a sudden he was dead.

I flick on the light and rewind the video. "Oh, Greta," Jack whimpers. "Poor Greta." He has his feet folded beneath him on the couch.

Mom remains silent. Her face is clear and smooth, stripped of weariness and grief. Her tattooed eyebrows have begun to fade. Lonely clusters of hair struggle to exist within each ashen line. "Ay." She sniffles, fingering the fabric along the armrest, and despite myself, I can't stay pissed. She tries, I know she tries.

"It's getting late," I say. I start clearing the table and moving the dishes to the kitchen sink. Mom hangs her purse from her shoulder. The weight forces her to lean to one side. "Why don't I walk you out?" I say.

Outside, the crisp air reminds me that fall is creeping into the nights. Gingko trees remain full of leaves, but beneath them is the stink of overripe nuts. Mom and I walk toward Grand Army Plaza. The drone of traffic reaches us from Atlantic Avenue; otherwise, the brownstone-lined street is quiet, overtaken with shadows. Ahead, an older couple survey their house. The woman has a hunched back. They hold hands, discuss the state of their roof. Or perhaps they are pointing at the curve of the moon. The woman has to strain her neck in order to do this. Mom watches and follows their gaze.

She sniffles. "Work is okay?"

"Fine—the same." I'm the production manager for a series of business magazines. With my managerial skills, I'm well suited for the job. The pay is decent.

At the end of the block, we stop and wait for the light to change. A cab slows, I wave it away, and it takes off. The light turns and we cross to the subway station. Mom retrieves a tissue from her purse. "Must you say anything?" she asks, picking up where we left off earlier.

"What—say nothing? Come home a couple hours late smelling of Chinese food and act like I had a tough day at work?"

"Ay—I ask you to do one thing."

"Wait a minute, there. Didn't I go on that date? The one with your friend's kid?"

"That was Auntie's friend, not mine."

"Yeah, but I did it because *you* asked me to." The ground trembles as the subway pulls into the station. Mom pats the tissue to her nose, stuffs it back into her purse, then starts down the stairs. "Never mind."

"I am what I am," I say.

She pauses, glances back. Her age reverts to the skin around her eyes and mouth. She shakes her head, turns and steps into the station.

Jack's in the kitchen washing dishes when I get home. He's changed into a nightshirt that comes down to his knees. The backs of his thin legs seem pathetically pale, almost greenish from too much vein. He has the kind of body, small and fragile, that elicits in me a paternal protectiveness. I hug him from behind and nip him on the neck.

"You okay?" he asks, soaping a bowl.

"Yeah. Why? Do I look like something's wrong?"

He shrugs. "You didn't finish dinner. Stomach acting up again?"

"A little," I say, noticing a paper bag on the counter. "Couple of deadlines coming up at work, that's all. What's this?"

"Goodies." Jack smiles devilishly. In the time it took me to walk Mom to the station and drop off the movie, he went to the pharmacy and back. In the bag I find a thirty-six-pack of condoms, a supertube of K-Y jelly, four boxes of enemas, and a bag of Circus Peanuts.

"What the hell?" I ask.

Jack simpers, and I can tell he's been up to no good. He places the bowls and chopsticks in the dish rack, then wipes the counter-top with a wet sponge. He scrubs with a circular motion. "So I'm standing in line with these condoms, right? You know, minding my own business. Doo-dee-doo. And out of the corner of my eye, I see this guy doing one of these conspicuously inconspicuous elbow things to his girlfriend. You know, 'Check out the faggot with the rubbers.'"

He tosses the sponge into the sink, and I hand him a towel to dry his hands. "So I look back at them, right? And they turn away. The girl, she's got so much foundation on, you can see this line across her neck, and she looks at me like *I've* got the problem. Me. So I step out of line, make my way back through the aisles, and— ta-da—all this."

"Enemas," I say. "Should I take this as a hint or something?"

"Shush, I'm not finished." Jack's nightshirt hangs from his body. I run my hand at the dip of his waist. "So I get back in line, and the couple does another one of those elbow things, only this time . . ." He digs out two boxes of enemas and, to demonstrate, holds one in each hand. "This time, I lean over to the girl and say, 'You think the latex-free kind works better than the latex kind?' God, if only you could have seen their faces."

"You're too much," I say, laughing.

"I have my moments. It's my flair."

"You mean like that time you appeared at work in your pajamas?"

"Oh, you." He dumps the boxes back into the bag. Bloomingdale's nearly fired him for that stunt. "Besides, you love it, I know you do."

I hug him real tight. "I do."

Jack pulls out the condoms and looks at me like, Yes? Still want to use these, right? I nod. The phone rings. I go over and mute the sound and let the machine take it. He opens the box of condoms, pushes one into the elastic of my pants, and leads me by the drawstrings to our room.

It's morning when I wake. I've been dreaming about schedules, and I can still hear the echo of myself insisting, "We have to ship copy today, not tomorrow—today. We have to ship. We have to ship." And Dad. He was there, too. But why? How? Jack is sitting at the end of the bed, watching the sun peer through the blinds. He circles his palm over the stump of bedpost. Outside, a gingko tree shivers in the breeze. Its fan-shaped leaves wave hello, good-bye. The shadows dance across his face.

"Hey," I say, sitting up.

"It's beautiful, isn't it?" He's quiet for a moment, then says, "It just kills me, you know?"

"What?" I ask, and he reaches back for my hand. I give it to him.

"Do you ever wake up, and it's sunny and pretty out, and people are strolling along the sidewalk with their coffee, and you think: What a perfect day to kill myself?"

"Jesus, don't talk like that."

He glances at me and turns back to the window. I wonder if he's thinking about his parents out in Greenwich: Wasps as open to gays as the Chinese. Could it be the condom thing? No—he's onto me about dinner. That's it. He knows something's up.

I stare at the desktop, where there are photos of us taken in Miami around the time we first met, in Australia sometime after that (God, Jack looks so pale and thin next to me), and in Montreal last February (never go that far north in winter). "My aunt's coming into town," I say. "She wants to get dinner Friday. . . ."

Jack pushes to his feet and shuffles to the closet. His heels pad against the wood floors. The blinds tap against the windowpane. He withdraws his robe from the closet and puts it on.

"It's going to be such a drag. Esther's going to go on and on about how I look exactly like Dad—which I totally do not—and how many girlfriends he had when he was young. I can hear it already: 'Steven, it's time to settle down, find a nice Chinese girl.' Wish there were some way I could get out of it."

Jack ties the robe and nods. "She the one who set you up with some girl?"

"That's her."

"Couldn't shit for a week, right?"

"Went through a box of prunes." I chuckle. "So I heard you on the phone—friend in town? I guess you've made plans for Friday?"

Jack hooks a strand of hair behind his ear. "No, actually I haven't."

"Oh. Well, you can if you want."

He blinks tiredly.

"Or not," I say.

He shakes his head. "Whatever." He meanders down the hallway to the kitchen.

I trail behind. "You angry?"

"Who, me?" He listens to last night's phone message. From the voice, I can tell it's Nell, one of his closest friends. "Call me when you get this," she utters, her voice hoarse and whiny. Jack picks up the phone and starts dialing. "Can we finish this later?" he asks, and then into the phone says, "Hey, good-looking . . . Oh darling, what's wrong?"

Fine, I think, heading back to the bedroom. Talk to Nell. Good old suburban Nell. I fix the pillows, lay against them, and flip through a recent issue of *Condé Nast Traveler.* The magazine opens to an article about Brussels: "Manneken Pis: Maybe the best emblem of Brussels's irreverent spirit is a bronze statue of a whizzing boy. . . ." I fold the page at the corner—Jack would get a total kick out of this.

"Gone?" I hear him say. "With her?"

"The figure has acquired more outfits than Barbie—all 600 housed in the Museum of the City of Brussels." It occurs to me that we could make a trip to Paris this summer, and stop in Brussels on the way.

"Of course, darling," Jack says into the phone. "I'll be there as soon as I can, okay? You'll be okay? You sure?" He hangs up. There's the creak of the floorboards, and I hear him scurry into the bathroom. The shower goes on.

I follow him into the bathroom. He's already in the shower. "Hey," I say, meaning to tell him my idea about Europe. Jack scrubs his armpit. "I don't have time for this right now," he snips. "I've got to get to Nell's."

I put down the toilet seat and sit. "What's going on? She all right?"

"Breakup or something. The girl's talking crazy. Says that no-good boyfriend's sleeping with her best friend."

"When you going to be back?" I ask.

"Depends." He tilts his head, and the water rinses the suds away. He pours a creamy-blue conditioner onto his palm and massages it through his hair.

"Listen," I say. "It's not like you can't come if you want."

He leans into the water and rinses out the conditioner. "Spare me, okay?" He shuts the water and pushes the curtain aside.

I pass him a towel. "What?"

He rubs his narrow chest, legs, and back. "You want me to go see my friend on Friday, right? That what you're saying? Fine—I'll meet up with Fred on Friday."

"No, really—come if you like."

He looks at me like, You mind? I realize that I'm in the way, so I move into the hall. Jack foams mousse into his palm, rubs his hands together, and styles his hair. "Who's Fred?" I ask.

"Someone from my former life. Trust me—you don't know him."

To shut me up good, he switches on the hair dryer. I return to the bedroom, chuck the magazine onto the floor, and fall back in bed. In the pillow, there's the smell of lavender soap.

Mom orders the courses for the evening's dinner. She pauses for the waiter to leave before she says, "Why did you have to mention it to him? Didn't I tell you? Of course you hurt his feelings. Ay—so stupid." She twirls a finger in her long gold chain.

Jack has spent nearly every night this week with Nell, and after work, either he comes home only to get more things he needs or he goes out to meet that guy Fred. When I asked if I could meet Fred, Jack told me, "It's probably not a great idea—Fred's real shy."

With her chopsticks, Mom clips a string of chilled jellyfish and drops it on her plate. Before she eats it, she rearranges the strands so nothing seems missing. "Went and told him," she reproves in Chinese. She sniffles.

"He knew something was up," I say. "He could tell I was keeping something from him."

"You and your father—always like that."

"Don't go warming up for Esther. You know as well as I do that we weren't anything alike." I have to restrain myself from using the word "bastard." Father wasn't the type to hug or kiss or say kind words. I didn't feel anything for him until the day Mom told me he was dying.

"That's not true, Steven," she says. She crunches a piece of jellyfish.

I rub my sore eyes—where's Esther?—and wish we could get this damn dinner over with already.

"Fine—don't listen to your ma. But don't wonder why you're getting silent treatment. Ay—hurting his feelings."

I'm about to say something I'll probably regret, when Esther steps through the door. "Quiet," Mom warns, plastering on a false smile. Esther seems stockier than I remember, with more folds about the neck. Her chest looks the same. I can't tell which breast is real and which is fake. Besides that, she bears a remarkable resemblance to Dad and her brothers. Esther's coat drapes off her shoulders. Rachel appears directly behind. Unlike her mother, she's all bones and sharp angles. She's wearing a tight-fitting silver dress with lavender swirls, which accentuates a look of cultivated starvation. Her head seems too large and heavy for her body, as though it might snap off if she's not careful. Though it's still early, and the dinner crowd has yet to arrive, mother and daughter make a show of searching for our table at the back of the room.

Mom waves. The hostess notices and leads them to the table.

"Esther," Mom welcomes. "Wah—you look wonderful. How you feel?" No one ever mentions the word "cancer."

"Fine, just fine," Esther states, mid-embrace, forcing an English accent. "Oh, Virginia. More and more Steven looks just like Peter. Did you know that, Steven? You look just like your father."

I force myself to smile. "Hi, Auntie."

"Don't you think?" Esther asks Rachel.

"Just like Peter," Rachel echoes. I notice a scar over her left brow.

"Philip ne?" Mom asks, since the guy doesn't seem to be around.

"Last minute, he had to go to Beijing for work," Esther says, touching the area just above her left breast. The guy lost his shirt in last year's market and has nothing better to do now than employ himself.

"Too bad," I say. Rachel stifles a smile. She knows I'm full of shit. The waiter pulls out their chairs and the two of them take their seats. "Where are your cousins?" Esther asks. She's referring to Georgianna, once the golden child and now the black sheep of the family, and Amy, once the black sheep of the family and now still no golden child. Georgie's big "mistake" was to marry a black guy, a lawyer who I made the mistake of thinking must be pretty cool simply because of the mix. As it turns out, he's one of the most homophobic pricks I've ever met. Amy, on the other hand, has a reputation for scandalous, sensational acts, which, when it comes to the family, seem always to spell "Fuck you." She was in Hong Kong over the summer, and word has it she won't be invited back.

"Amy has a work engagement," I say, though her exact words went something like, Sorry, but I've, um, got a date. "And Georgianna's away." I pour tea.

"Hawaii," Mom adds, serving Rachel a segment of jellyfish.

Esther tsks. "Shame, ah? Georgie had so much going for her."

Mom brushes the tip of her nose with her napkin. "Tragedy, really a tragedy."

Rachel breaks a piece of jellyfish in half with chopsticks.

"Anyway," Esther says, holding her cup like we're at high tea, "your ma mentioned you have a new girlfriend?"

My hand wavers. Tea spills from my cup and dots the tablecloth. Mom's eyes dart at me. I go for the plunge. "Actually—"

"Very sweet girl," Mom says. "Carries herself well."

I bite the inside of my lip. Rachel looks casually down at her watch.

"From a good family?" Esther asks.

"To be honest—"

"Old money," Mom blurts. "Father's a judge. High federal court."

So she's been listening, anyway.

"Not Chinese?" Rachel peeps, and I sense some kind of melancholy, some kind of connection between us.

I swallow, muster a quick "Nope."

"Your ma mentioned this." Esther shakes her head. "Lucky your father's not here. If he knew his son might marry a na gua ning, he'd roll in his grave."

"There isn't so much he wouldn't roll in his grave about," I say, and wink at Rachel. She smiles. The waiter delivers bean curd with shrimp, sautéed string beans, sesame chicken, pepper steak, steamed yellowfish, and fried rice.

"Grandma told me you bought her a new dress," Mom says to Rachel. "Such a good girl. So thoughtful."

"Thank you, Auntie." Rachel attempts a smile. Her teeth have that overly straight retainer look. I can tell she misses the old bat. Out of all my cousins, she's the only one who could take all those bullshit stories: "When I was little, my father had two tigers. Can you imagine? And trunks of gold this big."

Mom spoons tofu and pepper steak onto Rachel's plate. "She's so skinny, Esther," Mom says. "All skin and bones."

"Really, Auntie," Rachel blocks her plate with a hand—"I can help myself."

"No, no," Mom says. "Eat, eat. Quite tasty."

"She's quite discerning when it comes to *food*," Esther says. Rachel looks down at her lap.

Mom stops mid-chew. "How grown-up Rachel is," Mom intervenes. "College. I remember when she was just a baby."

"Pretty soon they'll be having children of their own," Esther adds.

Immediately I can feel the activity in my intestines lurch to a halt. Rachel turns quiet, grayish, especially around the eyes. She excuses herself to the bathroom. Esther starts yammering about the obscure family poem from which those in the patrilineal line get their Chinese names. Since I'm the only one to carry the family name, the burden falls on me.

"Enough with this bachelor life, Steven," Esther says. "Find a nice girl. Settle down."

Mom sips at her tea. "One has one's duties," she says.

"I have to make a quick call." I hasten my way to the phone sandwiched between the men's and women's bathrooms. I call home, knowing Jack isn't there—he's out with Fred for dinner tonight—but I try anyway. Please be there, please be there, I think, and when the machine picks up, I get an excruciating pang of loneliness.

There is no way Esther can leave tonight without my telling them, I decide. No way.

I hang up just at the beep, and Rachel steps out of the bathroom. She smooths her dress. "Oh, hi," she says, suddenly noticing me. We head back to the table.

"So," I say. "Mom says you're here for school?"

"Wellesley."

I pull her seat out for her. "Good school."

"It's okay, I guess," Rachel replies. She gives her attention to a piece of chicken. Esther digs through her purse.

"Harvard's up there, isn't it?" I say. Georgie went there.

Esther flushes, the color distributing unevenly over her neck. Rachel coughs the chicken onto her plate.

"Jesus," I say.

"Rachel—" Esther reprimands, her eyes bulging. She plucks a business card from the side pocket of her purse.

"Sorry," Rachel whimpers, pointing at her throat. "Wrong tube."

Mom calls the waiter for a glass of water and pats Rachel on the back. The hostess seats a couple next to our table, and I'm forced to pull in my chair so they can get to their seats.

Esther places the card near my plate. Chrissy Tung. Freelance writer. "She lives a few blocks from here, I think. Very pretty—like Gong Li."

"Auntie—" I try to avoid Mom's stare. "I'm actually very happy with my friend."

"Friend?" Rachel looks at me.

"Have more chicken," Mom says, putting a piece onto Rachel's plate. The waiter arrives with a platter containing a fish, the last course of the meal, its scales thick with crust, dressed with scallions and red sauce. Mom cuts the thing up and serves it. "You must try," she insists, "it's delicious!"

"Call her, Steven-ah?" Esther says.

That's it, I think. "Listen—"

The woman at the table next to us leans over. "Yes, yes. Whatever is that?" she asks with a low, sultry voice. My gut tenses.

I turn around stiffly. It's Jack. He's wearing a white dress embroidered with pink flowers. It's a simple, almost dainty floral dress, no doubt something out of Nell's closet. On him, though, it seems awkward: too suburban. Foundation cakes his skin. His lashes are as dense as Garbo's, his hair is pinned back into a tight bun. He blinks, waits for an answer.

"Yellowfish," I say, trying not to spit the word through my teeth.

He points at the dish closest to Esther. "Whatever is that?"

"Bean curd," I reply coolly. "With shrimp."

"That's exactly what I want, hon," he tells the guy in a tux next to him. Fred.

"That's what you shall have, my dear," Fred smirks, and my fist tightens, ready to knock his teeth out.

"Oh, goody," Jack says.

Mom glances over and practically jumps out of her seat.

"Rai-cho—what a beautiful dress. Where did you get it? Did you buy it here?"

"DKNY," she replies. "It was on sale."

"Beautiful on you," Mom says. "Oh, yes. Such a lovely figure."

The waiter comes to take Jack's order. "We'd like whatever they've got there," he says. "Yes, yes. I want it like I'm seated at that very same table."

"Steven?" Esther scolds. "Will you please answer me? You'll call Chrissy, won't you?"

"Sorry," I say. "Of course."

"Good," she says, winking at Mom. "You'll like her. Chrissy's *very* pretty."

"Very pretty," Jack repeats under his breath.

"Sale at Bloomingdale's," Mom exclaims.

But Esther turns to the next table, her eyes narrowed and her lips tense and angling down at the corners. Her eyes open wide. She leans toward me. "That woman," she whispers. "She's . . . he's . . . a man."

"He is?" Rachel turns to stare.

Mom interjects, "We can go shopping tomorrow if you have time."

"No he's not," Rachel decides.

"Stop staring," Esther hisses.

"I'm not staring. You're the one who's staring."

Esther glares and Rachel zips her mouth.

Mom cracks off the fish head and spoons it onto her plate. The eye is crusty.

Rachel excuses herself to the bathroom a second time. I feel the urge to use the can, too, but to judge from the pull of my bowels, a movement isn't about to take place anytime soon. Jack notices when our bill arrives. He gets up, and I have to inch my chair to let him by. He disappears to the bathroom just as Rachel returns. He looks back at me, expecting me to follow, but I pretend to be focused on the bill. We leave while he's still in the restroom.

Outside the restaurant we say our good-byes. Rachel whispers to me, "Think he really was a man?" There's something naive but sad about her, layered, and more compassionate than someone her age ought to be.

We look back at our mothers gossiping now about Grandmother, who is going deaf, though the doctors can't find anything ("Those Western doctors—what do they know?" Esther says), and how Esther overheard Grandmother in her room talking out loud to her dead sister.

"A man," I say, nodding.

"Thought so," Rachel says, and after a beat the two of us burst out laughing.

In the bedroom, a box of prunes is the first thing I see. Jack left it on the new issue of *Traveler*. "Cruise Guide: How to Find the Best in the Americas," the cover reads. He's also moved the fishbowl into the room. The fish swims in circles, still searching for a way out.

I open the box of prunes and am caught off guard by the scent of dry Chinese plums, the kind Dad kept all over the house, which came wrapped in blue-and-white paper. Lemon-essence pitted prunes. Jesus. He used to keep a bag of plums in the magazine rack by the toilet. I squeeze a prune between thumb and forefinger. The dried fruit squashes open, revealing its soft center. I put it in my mouth. At first there's a tangy mixture of sweet and sour. But soon my tongue goes numb and the sticky mass loses its taste. I try another prune and the same thing happens. Sweet with a hint of sour, then a dull nothingness. I pour the bag onto the desk, separate the prunes, and try another, another.

By the time Jack returns, all that's left are gummy brown pockmarks on the desk and an empty box. I'm still at the desk, rubbing my sticky brown palms together. He comes down the hallway toward the bedroom. His heels click against the wood floor. He stands in the doorway, removes the pumps and comes toward me.

"You never mentioned you do drag," I say.

"I don't."

I flick the empty box into the trash.

"You finished the whole thing?" he asks, his voice squeaky and tender. "All twelve ounces?"

I rub my hands, and prune junk crumbles to the desk.

"Oh, darling—it was all in fun," he says, peeling off a thick eyelash. "I always thought you lacked a sense of humor."

"Jesus—what the hell were you trying to prove, huh?"

He blinks—one eye naked, the other fully dressed—and says, "Let's not go there, all right, Mr. Constipated-up-the-ass."

"And what do you mean by that?"

Jack peels away the other lash and clutches the two caterpillars in his fist.

"You smeared your lipstick," I say.

His jaw clenches. He moves to the bed, raises the dress to his knees, and steps onto the mattress. He settles into the comforter, allowing the dress to fall around him. He plucks bobby pins from his hair and releases the bun.

I say, "I was about to tell them, you know."

"So? You didn't, did you?"

The prunes flush through my system. "Well, what was I supposed to say? I have a boyfriend—here she is?"

Jack folds his hands in his lap. His body seems to deflate. "Yes?"

I go to him, crossing the bed on my knees to unzip the dress. The thing opens to the waist, revealing light freckled skin. I run my hand down his back.

"Don't," he says, wincing. "I'm tired."

Maybe it's my expression, because Jack pats the space next to him, and I sit. The down comforter squishes under my weight. "He's left her," he says.

"Who—Nell?"

He nods. "Just up and moved in with that backstabbing whore."

We shut the light, hold hands in the dark, and watch the gingko tree, alone and shivering in the cold. "You going over to her place?" I ask.

"She needs me," he says.

I need you. Just as quickly as it enters my mind, I sense Jack waiting for me to say it. That easy. Say it, you bastard: I need you. But I hold back. I don't say anything, just as Dad hadn't, and in the end, maybe Mom was right—Dad and I are the same that way.

Outside, the moon is nowhere, and I think, Maybe it's behind us now.

Mom comes over on Garbo night, and this time she brings dumplings. I don't say anything. We watch *Ninotchka*. Jack and I hold hands. We've been through a two-week separation, during which Jack moved into Nell's place, and afterward, a weeklong get-back-together period, during which Jack returned his belongings bit by bit home. Everything feels fragile, tender.

Throughout the movie, Mom squirms in her seat. She laughs a beat too early or too late. When she notices us watching her, she says, "American humor . . . Ay—what's so funny?"

Because of that stunt in the restaurant, Mom can barely look at Jack without going red in the face. She practically froze when he greeted her at the door, and she sniffled nervously when he pecked her on the cheek. After the movie, Jack cleans up and I walk Mom to the station. It's cool out. We can see our breath.

"Thanks for the dumplings," I say.

"Don't thank," she replies, pulling on her gloves. "I'm your ma."

At the end of the street, we wait for the light to change. Without the brownstones blocking it, the wind hits us straight on, cutting through our clothes. Mom clips her fingers at the collar of her coat. She waits until the light changes and we're crossing the street. "So?" she asks. "Did you call?"

A train rumbles into the station. My stomach buckles. "No."

Mom sighs, and I can tell Esther must be at her about it. Despite my frustration, I feel sorry for Mom. It is her duty, as a mother, that is, and she has failed. She retrieves a tissue from her purse. "You'll call?"

Weariness overcomes me. I kiss her cheek. "Probably not."

"Ay, good night." She returns the kiss, then rubs the lipstick from my cheek, and soon she disappears into the station. The dimly lit brownstones of Park Slope call me home.

TRADER

AFTER THE global meetings in Australia, the bunch of us met up at the Billabong, a pub out in the Rocks area of Sydney. Precious Metals kicked ass—we announced a total profit of forty million dollars. The guys crowded around the bar, challenging one another to shots. Thomas, my boss, and I discussed UTG's hostile takeover of Cross Bank. I suggested he hire one of the marketers for the London office.

"Guy's good," I said. "Just moved to Cross a month ago."

Thomas sucked on an unfiltered cigarette. "Mate of yours?"

I nodded. "We played rugby at school—"

"Congratulations," Thomas said, which seemed from out of nowhere. I turned, and only then did I notice Justine. She was there next to me.

Justine kissed Thomas on both cheeks. The rock on her slender finger seemed larger than it was. She was small, compact, and sometimes reminded me a little too much of home. A "Chinatown homegirl," as my brother Eric liked to call them, but really, because of a scholarship to Andover, Justine was as refined as any Wasp. She was maybe a little too thin—the slightest bit of anxiety would upset her stomach—but she had these expressions that could fill an ocean. Really. We were twenty or so meters down at the Great Barrier Reef when I gave her the ring—picture white coral, a school of black-white-and-yellow-striped butterfly fish, twelve-foot manta rays—and what I remember most was Justine's "It certainly took you long enough" grin.

Thomas threw an arm over her shoulder. "Good man you got here," he said, nodding at me. "A real mate. Take care of him, eh?"

"Don't you worry." She cracked a smile. "As long as I don't have to cook, Jonathan'll be just fine."

Thomas drew his glass to his lips. "Bra-burner, eh, mate?"

"She means it literally," I explained. For a "homegirl," she couldn't cook for shit.

Justine burst out laughing. "The last time I made dinner? Oh, boy. You should have seen him."

"What's that you Aussies always say?" I asked. "Chunder, right?"

Thomas laughed and ordered another round of drinks. Justine asked for a diet Coke. She never got buzzed—it made her feel out of control. It'd been a couple of hours, and I was hungry and tired enough to pass on the pint, too. We'd be taking off for dinner soon, anyway.

"Don't be a wowser," Thomas said, thrusting a glass into my hand. "It's early yet."

"Helen coming?" I asked.

He checked his watch. "In a bit."

"Why don't you two join us for dinner?" Justine offered. She knew I was waiting to discuss my long-term goals with the company. "We found this cute place up the street. Right on the water."

"Dodie's," Thomas said, lighting another cigarette. "Helen and I used to go for barbie. Haven't been there in years. Imagine it must still be pretty good, though. Try the bugs. They're really good."

"Bugs?" Justine had that grossed-out look on her face. "Icky."

Thomas was charmed. "Beaut you got here," he said, winking.

"He knows," Justine replied confidently.

"Balmain bugs," I told her, "are a type of crawfish, I think."

"You'll like them," he said. "No worries—you two come out on the *Lookout* tomorrow, and I'll have Helen make up a batch."

"Boat," I explained to Justine. "Thomas rented it for the day."

"Oh, cool," Justine said. "How fun."

"We'll bring wine," I told Thomas.

For a moment he seemed preoccupied, the way he got when calculating figures.

"Problem?" I asked.

"Not at all," he insisted. "Meet us at the marina at noon. It's a must, mate. You haven't been to Australia until you've been to Australia."

Justine gulped her diet Coke as if she might get a buzz off it.

"So this tennis mate of yours," Thomas said to me. "Only a

month at Cross Bank, eh? What sour luck—in his last life, poor bloke must've killed a Chinaman."

Justine looked as if she'd been struck dumb. She never did "get" subtlety.

"No offense," Thomas said.

"None taken," I answered. He exhaled, smoke rushing from his nostrils, and gulped his beer; he licked the foam from his upper lip. One of the Tokyo guys checked his Quotron, asking Thomas about a position.

"What's up with that 'Chinaman' stuff?" Justine asked, the second he moved out of earshot.

I shrugged. "Aussies have some strange colloquialisms."

"Yeah, but what the hell's it supposed to mean?"

"Come on—aren't you the one who's always saying we need to understand cultural differences better?"

"Differences, not—"

"James," I interrupted, noticing a trader from the London office. Justine put on her happy smile. I introduced Justine, and successfully passed her off while he explained the rules of cricket to her. The Zimbabwe–Aussie game was on TV. The Hong Kong guys had a hundred bucks each on Zimbabwe; the Londoners watched smugly, arms crossed and feet firm on the ground. The guys next to me were talking about the NBA.

The bar got packed, people standing as far back as the door. Waitresses pushed their way through the crowd. The guys didn't mind getting rubbed up against—the girls wore gold-colored bikinis and heels, and went around offering tequila shots for five bucks apiece. A cell phone rang. Thomas reached into his jacket—we all did—but it turned out to be mine.

"Jonathan Tsui," I answered.

"Yo—what up?" It was Eric, my twenty-three-year-old fuck-up of a brother who'd been MIA the past two weeks. A few years ago, just to add more grief to Ma's life, he dropped out of school. Always was a damn troublemaker.

"Where you been?" I asked. "Mom's worried sick. Said you're going around now with some band." On his end of the line, there was the twang of an electric guitar, and he mumbled something I couldn't make out.

"What? What was that?" I asked. "Listen—I'm right in the middle of something. Call me later, all right? I've got a few things to say to you."

He responded again, but the only thing I could make out was "Justine." I looked around, but she'd been swallowed up in the swarm of people. "Can't find her," I said. "Later, okay?" I hung up and tucked the phone back into my jacket. Thomas took my empty glass and stuck a fresh pint in my hand. "One more, eh, mate?"

When Helen called to say she couldn't make dinner, I went to find Justine. The guys stood in an arc around her. She ate up the attention. "There you are, Jonathan," she said. "We were just talking about you."

"They're lying," I said, playing along.

"Don't worry, man," one of them said. "We didn't mention that affair you were having or anything."

Justine laughed it up.

"Let's take off," I told her. "I'm starving."

"Helen here?" She leaned on my shoulder, then shifted onto the ball of her foot, trying to get a peek over the crowd.

"Nah. She's still out in the 'burbs with her folks or something."

She checked her watch. "It's nine."

I shrugged. Who knows?

"Give me a sec," she said, handing me her diet Coke and disappearing to the bathroom.

The guys had heard about our engagement. "Don't do it, Johnnie boy," one said.

"Get out while you can, man."

"Death do you part," a buddy added, gesturing as if he were strangling someone. The other guys laughed, put in their two bits, and started a round of tequila shots.

Thomas made his way over and patted me on the back. He was drunk. I could tell by the glob collecting at the corner of his eye. Other than that, he seemed fine. He wasn't the slurring type. "Dags—all of you," he said, waving a hand. "What do any of you know between a sheila and a *sheila*, eh?"

We were cracking up hearing Thomas go on like that, when Justine walked into the middle of it. "What's a sheila?" she asked.

Thomas took Justine under his arm. "A sheila—" he started to explain.

"A pretty dog—" one of the guys blurted.

"In heat—"

"No, no—it's a *pussy*cat."

Justine looked suspicious. "It's something crude, isn't it?"

The guys went nuts. A waitress came by with another round. She had an all-around golden tan that seemed almost fake, tits like you read about, and was wearing a bikini with one of those strings that went up her ass. "Body shots," she announced.

The guys pushed and shoved over who would go first. Justine bit her lip. I could tell she wanted to intervene, say something sensible, maybe even prudish or earnest. For a moment, I despised her for those damn diet Cokes.

Thomas laughed at the first guy up. The waitress poured a shot and shifted her weight to her back leg. Her skin was smooth, and I couldn't help noticing the sharp curve of her hipbone. The guys made a racket.

"Get tit, man."

"No, arse. Definitely arse," someone said.

Justine flashed me this "Oh my goodness" look, but I laughed along with everyone. Her attitude made me think of this bitch I once went with—what was her name again?—Jenny Chow, that's it. We met at one of those Asian parties. That Scarsdale CAP fucked anything, except, of course, stupid shitheads from Chinatown.

The guy doing the shot leaned over the waitress and licked the area just below the bikini strap. He sprinkled salt, threw back the shot, and went in for the kill. The sucking sounds created a frenzy.

"That's not how to do it, mate."

"You're slobbering, man."

"Time's up, eh."

The waitress yawned. The guy was still going at it, making wet, slippery sounds with his mouth. "That was not a body shot," Thomas yelled. The other guys paid no attention. They were too busy one-upping each other for the sake of the waitress.

Thomas dragged Justine to the bar. She caught my eye. She had that raised-brow bewildered look. "Don't you worry, love," Thomas was saying. "I'll show you. Old Thomas knows."

"Um," she stammered, "well, I—"

Thomas ordered a shot of tequila. Old Thomas with his face in Justine's neck. It was a funny sight; *I* was laughing, anyway. Without much ado, he sprinkled salt over the area. "Now, this is how you do a body shot," he said, closing in on her throat.

Justine stood very still. She craned her neck stiffly and looked at me as if to say, Do something.

What? I thought. What exactly do you expect me to do?

Something, her eyes said.

"Hey, Thomas," I called, moving toward the bar. "Thomas."

But he went for the dive, and when I got there, he was still going at her neck. Justine stood motionless, her arms stiff at her sides and her eyes squeezed shut. A bald spot at the top of Thomas's head peered at me like an octopus eye. I just stood there. I mean, what the hell was I supposed to do—tell my boss, the one man who has backed me up from the very beginning, to fuck off? Plant my fist in his face? Besides, it was all in fun.

Finally he came up for air. "Now, that's a body shot."

There was a red patch the size and shape of a two-headed strawberry on Justine's neck. She forced a stiff smile. The three of us looked at one another, then away. "That's how it's done," Thomas said, punching me in the arm. "Eh, mate? See that?"

"Yeah, man," I chuckled. "Saw that, all right."

Justine pushed her way to the door.

Thomas said to go ahead to dinner without him. Since Helen wasn't around, he wanted to hang with the guys. Outside, neither Justine nor I said anything. I listened to her shoes smacking steadily against the planks of the walkway. We passed a couple of opal shops, a souvenir store with stuffed koalas hanging in the window, an apothecary's, and a leather-goods place showcasing water-proofed canvas raincoats. The harbor seemed a dark wall covered with lightning bugs, and though it was still warm, Justine clasped a shawl to her neck.

After ten minutes, she suddenly stopped, and I nearly walked right into her.

"What was *that*?" she demanded.

"He was drunk."

"Oh, please." She shook her head and turned to the rocks displayed in a store window. At the center was a blue opal the size of a large walnut. A beam of light shifted right, then left. The stone turned from sea blue, to something close to black, to cobalt; from certain angles there were hints of magenta, even lime.

"Amazing, huh?" I said. "Thing's gotta cost a good buck or two."

Justine snapped out of whatever bullshit was spinning around in that head of hers. "What?"

I nodded at the opal.

"Oh," she said. "Yeah, uh-huh, beautiful."

"Listen—it was all in fun. You know, like ha-ha?"

She looked me straight in the face and responded, "Ha, ha. Happy now?"

As soon as we got to Dodie's, Justine bolted for the restroom. I ordered a diet Coke for her and a glass of Merlot for myself, and perused the menu: *Balmain bugs, broiled with a blend of the chef's secret seasonings and chilled on bed of ice.* Shit. I remembered tomorrow's boating plans.

I didn't say anything when Justine got back, but I hoped she'd let it slide. She had obviously been rubbing the area on her neck, and now the strawberry had grown to the size of a plum, which she kept covered with a hand. "He gave me a hickey!" She hissed.

"Looks fine," I said. "Nobody'll notice."

She whipped open the menu and spotted the bugs. "Do we have to go tomorrow?" she asked, not looking up.

Why was she blowing this out of proportion? Why did she always have to do that?

"We'll tell them we have an earlier flight," I said. "We won't have to stay long."

"Do I absolutely, positively have to be there?"

An angry rush shot through me, but I tried to stay cool. "Come on—Helen'll be there. Thomas'll be doing time in his best-behavior cell." I reached across and took her hand. "We'll be out of here tomorrow, okay? It'll all be over. That'll be that, and we'll take off for Hong Kong."

"But I really don't want to go," she complained.

Does she think she's some kind of princess or something? Before I could stop myself, I banged my fist against the table. The glasses spilled water onto the tablecloth. Justine startled and drew away.

"I'm sorry, I'm sorry," I whispered, reaching for her hand again.

People turned to stare. The waiter backed off from taking our orders.

Justine had one of those disappointed "Oh, Jonathan" looks on her face. Shame pricked my skin. I wanted to kick myself. Why did I lose control? Why did she have to keep on me like that?

Justine's lips tensed with disapproval. That pissed me off. Who was she to judge me? Who the hell did she think she was, anyway?

"What?" I challenged, careful to keep my voice down.

"Nothing." She looked away.

Fine. I let it go at that, and signaled for the waiter.

All through dinner, Justine twirled and retwirled her pasta without eating. What does she want from me? It wasn't like I told old Thomas to fuck around like that. Besides, he's a good guy. Just having fun. How to get that through her thick head?

She circled a string of pasta onto her fork. Her eyes glazed over, carrying her to some distant place. I wanted to say "Fuck this" and walk away. At the same time, I wanted to kiss her, bring her back. It just killed me to see her looking so sad. I wanted to fix things, make everything all right.

When it came time for dessert, I said, "They have *crème brûlée.*" I knew it was her favorite.

"Okay." Her voice wavered.

She was still quiet as hell when we got back to the hotel, and in the suite, the first thing she did was jump in the shower. I got out of my suit and dumped my tired ass in bed. The bathroom was open, steam poured out in clouds, and I listened to the water, the way it sounded when Justine moved in and out of the shower. She came to bed smelling of soap, and she wore the hotel robe, many sizes too large. The mark on her neck was pink down to the clavicle. Her eyes were swollen.

"You crying?" I asked.

She sniffed. "No."

I pulled her down onto the bed. We kissed. I fingered her skin just at the robe's collar, felt heat rising from her body, a wetness between her legs. My prick went hard, and my underarms went damp, and I wanted to put it in, put it right in there, and fuck her slowly and softly until she gave into the pleasure.

"Don't," she said, drawing away.

What?

She clutched the robe closed with a hand. "I'm tired."

I throbbed, and it hurt I wanted it so bad. Bitch wasn't kidding, though. She rolled over, her back to me, and it was as if I'd swallowed an enormous stone. Who was she to hold out? I wondered. She too good for me all of a sudden? I wanted to remind her of who she was, where she'd come from. She knew it; I knew it.

But I heard her sniffling, and this sick feeling came over me. I could've punched myself. It reminded me of Ma—all those times I listened to her crying—and it made me so fucking helpless. I was beat. I turned away, punched at the pillow to make it right. Sleep fenced me in. I drifted. Then, just as I slipped into sleep, an idea leaped from out of the darkness: the opal. I'd get her the fucking opal. Yes, first thing tomorrow morning. My body went slack. The opal, yes, the opal. In my mind, I could see bright cobalt and aqua, with a hint of magenta.

The next morning, Justine and I packed and showered. It would be cold out on the water, and so we threw on the new sweaters we had bought on our first day in Sydney. She didn't say much. Just got ready, putting on makeup that was supposed to give her the appearance of having been born that way. Every once in a while, I'd catch her rubbing her neck, and I'd feel like *the man* to have come up with the opal idea, especially when I pictured Justine's killer grin. We had breakfast in the Rocks, then passed the shops on our way to the marina, and when we got to the one with the blue opal in the window, I stopped to browse.

A saleswoman noticed us as soon as we came through the door. *"Arigato,"* she said.

Justine laughed. *"Arigato* to you, too."

The woman went red in the cheeks. "May I help you?"

I asked about the opal, and then understood why she took us for Japanese. The stone was beyond tourist expensive. It was Tokyo expensive. "Shit," I mumbled.

"Wow," Justine said, "for that little thing?"

"It's quite unique, love," the woman said, handing it to her. "Quite exquisite."

Justine shifted the opal to and fro. The stone went from copper blue to light seaweed, then cobalt. "Honey, look how it does the color thing." Her eyes went big with excitement. She smiled. "Wow. See? See that?"

That's more like it, I thought, placing my gold card on the counter.

"You didn't have to, you know," Justine said. She clenched the little package against her chest. "I almost wish you hadn't."

"What're you talking about? You're my girl."

Her smile fell away. She gave me this long-faced look.

"It's as beautiful as you are," I said, feeling my patience edge.

"I guess."

You guess? Here I go out of my way to get you something you want—get totally ripped off doing so—and all you can say is, "I guess"? Fuck this. Fuck you. Who do you think you're kidding? Think you're Jenny Chow with your mommy's gold charge card and your daddy's brand-new Beemer? You come from the bottom, bitch, don't you forget that. All the prep school in the world can't erase that.

I made straight for the dock, moving at a pace that I knew would be too brisk for her. We followed the boardwalk all the way around to the marina. The boat was down at the far end. There was a sharp breeze. The glare hurt my eyes. Boats rocked in their slips. Somewhere, a loose clip knocked against a boom. It made a hollow, metallic sound.

Thomas was on board, in white tennis sweaters and khakis. He was prepping the sail, his back to us. There was no sign of Helen. Boats were out on the water, their white masts struggling to catch the breeze. Beyond, at the mouth of the harbor, cliffs jutted out on both sides. A wave rushed up the rocks, spraying and foaming.

"Jonathan," Justine said. "You mad?"

Me, mad? "No," I replied. "Why?"

"Well, for one, you're walking like a mile a minute."

I slowed. "No I'm not."

"Yes you are," she said. "You were."

Thomas was too busy adjusting the ropes to see us approaching. When we got up to the boat, I heard Helen from below deck. "Our plan was to talk, Thomas," she said.

He checked that the sail would rise without a hitch. "Later."

"No, now, Thomas."

"You didn't think it was so urgent last night," he snarled.

Helen banged around down below. "You know as well as I do that there was no way we could have talked about anything. You were drinking with the boys. I would have been lucky if you hadn't invited them to dinner with us."

Justine and I looked at each other.

"Uh, hello?" I said, knocking against the side of the boat.

There was a moment of silence, and down in the cabin, a door slammed shut.

"Eh, mate," Thomas said, hurrying us on board. He and Justine did the two-cheek kiss greeting. She stiffened. He poured Justine a Shiraz-Cabernet, and today she took it. "Why not?" she said, placing the opal in its box on the seat under her.

"That's my love," he said.

Thomas served me a Foster's. "Helen'll be up in a moment. She's made those bugs for you."

"Oh, she shouldn't have," Justine said. She took a large gulp of wine.

"Eh, she loves it, really."

I sat across from Justine, trying to do the footsie thing, but she shifted her foot whenever I came near.

Helen came up with a dish of cheese and pâté and crackers. She wore a white outfit and the kind of sneakers old ladies wear. The bulb of her nose was pink.

"Oh, how wonderful," she said, fully composed now. She congratulated us on our engagement and asked about our trip to Lady Elliot Island. She explained she and Thomas had gone there for their honeymoon twenty years earlier, before Thomas got transferred to New York.

"Wasn't it lovely?" Helen asked.

"Like paradise," Justine said. She sipped at her wine.

"You two dive?" Thomas asked.

Justine nodded and looked down at her ring. "Jonathan proposed down there."

"Oh, love." Helen spread cheese over a cracker and passed it to Justine. "Isn't that romantic? Down there with all those fish?"

"Thousands of them," Justine said.

"We saw a couple of stingrays, too," I said.

"Interesting creatures, those rays," Thomas added, drinking his beer.

"Terribly prehistoric, don't you think?" Helen spread pâté over another cracker and handed it to me. Thomas backed the boat out of the slip and steered us swiftly into the harbor. He cut the motor and brought the sail up. Justine watched. Hair fluttered across her face. A strand caught in her mouth. The wind picked up, but the conversation flat-out died.

"So," I said, and from the corner of my eye, I watched Justine take another sip of wine. Thomas's kid popped into my head. He had Helen's small nose and tight pursed lips. "Griffin's in college, now, isn't he?"

"Freshman," Helen said, clearing her throat. "Williams."

"You must be proud of him," Justine said. "That's a great school."

Helen sighed. "I miss him mostly."

"You going to visit?" Justine suggested. "Parents' weekend is probably coming up."

Helen mustered a smile. "Actually, I'll be spending some time here with my parents."

Thomas lost grip of the rope, and the sail fluttered in the air. He took his beer and downed it in three gulps. Helen quickly excused herself and went below deck. From where I sat, I could see her quartering a lime.

My phone sounded from my pants pocket.

"Aren't you going to get that?" Justine asked, sounding miffed.

Thomas caught the tone, his eyes darting from Justine to me. His brows lifted questioningly.

"It's just Eric," I said, swigging my beer. "He called looking for you yesterday."

The whites of Justine's eyes had turned pink. The wine was

getting to her. "When?" she asked. "You mean he called and you didn't tell me?"

"I'm telling you, now, aren't I?"

The phone went off again. She slouched into her seat, crossing her arms in front of her.

Fine, I thought, answering the damn thing. It was Eric all right. "Boulder," he said.

"What?" I asked.

Thomas threw back another beer. A glob formed at the corner of his eye.

"Colorado," Eric said. "That's where we are, yo."

"Twenty years," Thomas toasted the ocean. A northerly breeze carried us swiftly over the water. We headed out to sea. The Cliffs grew larger. The water turned from sapphire to olive to black ink.

"Listen, Eric," I said. "This isn't a good time—"

"I gotta, man. It's, like, important."

Justine reached for the phone, but I pulled away.

She folded her arms over her chest and glared at me. "He listens to me, you know," she murmured.

And what the hell's that supposed to mean? I wanted to say. She actually believed she was responsible for getting us on talking terms. Did she think the idiot wouldn't call whenever he needed more cash?

"Uh, actually," Eric said, "I'm getting married."

It took a second for this to sink in. The water was murky, impenetrable. Did Mom tell him I'd asked Justine? Was he doing it because I was?

In the background, I heard a girl giggling. Was it her? Was she hot? No, I knew the kind of girl Eric hung around with these days, and that couldn't be it. In my mind, I saw one of those tangly-haired, Birkenstock-wearing tree-huggers. At least he didn't go for those big-haired Chinatown types anymore.

Thomas said something, but I ignored it. "Stay away from the Cliffs," Helen yelled from below. She was preparing the bugs. I could hear Eric's girlfriend humming a tune. She must have backed him into this. The boat rocked, and Helen's tray slammed against the rim of the table. My stomach lurched.

"You knock her up?" I whispered.

"Fuck you," Eric said.

Fuck me? "No, fuck you. Are you stupid or something? Got any brain left in that fucking head of yours?"

Justine flashed me that look again, that "Oh, Jonathan." She stood, braced herself against the side of the boat, and held out her hand.

Fine, I thought, giving her the phone. Go ahead, Miss Know-it-all-he-listens-to-me. "You talk to the idiot," I said. Fucking un-grateful little shit.

Justine brought the phone to the bow of the boat. She sat with her back to us, her legs dangling over the side.

Thomas steered us in the direction of the Cliffs. He popped the cap off another beer. A collection of empty bottles began to fill up the cooler.

"Hey," I said, nodding at the icebox. "Go easy, man."

"You don't," he was saying.

What the fuck is he going off about?

"Biggest mistake you'll ever make," he said. "You work your

arse off to get her that house, that car, those ten million pairs of shoes she'll never wear. What for, mate, eh?"

Helen dropped what she was doing and shut herself into the bathroom. The bugs sat over a bed of lettuce. They were arranged in a circle, their heads facing one another.

"Truth is—you're on a bad streak, just like this bloke here," he said, pointing a thumb at his chest. "You just don't know it yet." He beat his chest with a fist. I could hear the meaty thuds. He was getting drunk, all right. Stupid drunk.

Why was he telling me this shit, anyway? I finished my beer and chucked the empty bottle back into the cooler.

"No," Thomas insisted, "not yet. You don't know."

The Cliffs towered into the sky. The closer we got, the more immense they seemed. Exposed parts had eroded, and what remained jutted sharply from the sea.

The wind shifted. Waves gushed against the rock, folded back onto themselves, belly-flopped onto the water. Cool spray came over us, and just as quickly evaporated. Another wave went up, rocking the boat. I moved toward the bow, straining to hear what Justine was saying.

She had plugged a finger in her ear. "You love her? You certain about this, Eric?"

The boat tipped. The cooler slipped from one side to the other, glass bottles knocking against one another. Thomas worked the sail, and we buoyed upright.

"Well, you haven't known her for very long," Justine said. "Yeah, uh-huh, I know. . . . Wish I could be there, too, sweetheart."

After all these years playing Dad to that fucking pothead, I thought. That ungrateful little shit. All those years and all he can do is fuck everything up. Just wait until I get my hands on him: I'm going to beat some sense into that stupid bastard. Damn trouble-maker. Water splashed and soaked my khakis.

"It's never enough, mate," Thomas told me. We closed in on the mouth of the harbor. He steered us closer to the bend.

"Uh-huh. I will. I'll tell him. . . ." Justine went on. "He does, you know. Very much. Yeah, as soon as it starts, okay?" Justine clutched the rail and snapped the phone shut.

"That's it?" I said. "You mean to tell me you just let him go?"

"What did you want me to do?"

"Oh, I don't know—maybe talk him out of it? Jesus, Justine. You got your head screwed on right? He's going to fuck up his god-damn life."

She sighed. "He says he's in love."

"He says? Who gives a shit what he says. The kid's fucking high. He can't even get through college. You think he knows what the fuck love is?"

"And you do?" she yelled. "You're the expert here?"

I could feel Thomas's and Helen's eyes at my back. "In this case, yes, I do," I answered.

The color drained from Justine's face, and she looked at me with a pity that pissed me off. "You just don't get it, do you?" she said, as if talking out loud to herself. "You're never going to get it."

Then, in the middle of all this shit, it seemed like we were go-ing to smash into the rocks. Water splashed on deck, jerking the boat sideways. Helen scrambled up the stairs. "Thomas," she called. "The Cliffs, Thomas."

He stared at her blankly. The ocean roared. Waves crashed, deafening every sound. The Cliffs pulled us into the shade. A wave went up and turned a fist at us. Justine screamed, and I caught hold of her.

It was Helen who let loose the sail. Almost instantly, the boat changed direction. She gunned the engine and we sped toward the open ocean. The sail flapped, surrendering to the wind.

Once docked, Justine and I tried to walk it off. We left Thomas and Helen on the *Lookout,* and after an hour the two of us wound up in Darling Harbour. Justine was wet and trembling. The opal rattled in its box. Her eyes started to tear. "Oh, shoot," she said, brushing her face with the back of her hand. "God—I'm crying."

"It's okay," I said. People stared. They shook their heads at me as if I were the culprit. You've got it all wrong, I wanted to say.

"Oh God," she said. "Everyone's staring."

"No one's staring." I ducked into the aquarium and took her with me. I paid for two tickets and we stepped into the darkness. Inside, a tank took up an entire wall. Light shimmered, filling the room with bluish gray. There was a sacred, hushed silence. We were back at the bottom of the ocean. The water seemed textured and grainy. Seaweed stretched its green arms. A school of neon-colored angelfish dashed across the glass. Sharks cut through the water. A manta flapped its wings.

The phone rang, the sound reverberating off the glass walls. "It's Eric," Justine said. "Talk to him, Jonathan. Don't take this away from him."

I felt so damn tired, so fucking tired. "Hello?" I answered. The line was full of static.

"Yo, Asshole," Eric said. "It's the big moment. Her name's Melissa. You'd like her, I know you would."

Justine went up to the glass wall. She seemed small, distant; she was beautiful that way.

"She kind of reminds me of Justine. Not Chinese or anything like that. It's just—she's got all these faces, you know? And her eyes. Like marbles, man . . ."

The manta came forward, fluttering its black cape wings, and swooped up the glass. Its whitish belly couched a rectangular mouth and gills. The tail trailed as sharp as a fencing foil.

"Hello?" Eric said. "You there, dude?"

I couldn't speak. Justine took the phone. "Sweetheart? Are you ready?" she asked, her voice soft, maternal. A greenish-blue light rippled over her face. "You are? You mean right now?"

The ray doubled back. When it got closer, I realized it wasn't the same one. This was much larger. Its eyes were solid black.

"Wish I could be there, too," Justine added. "Uh-huh, he does, sweetie. You know that."

A shadow passed over us. The ray had sharp, crisp movements; grace I couldn't understand.

"We're right there with you, sweetheart." Justine took my hand. "We are. Go ahead. Tell us, then. We're listening. Uh-hum. Parking lot outside the stadium. Bunch of guys. The band. Uh-hum. Yeah, go on."

I watched the ray circle up and around, and disappear into the distance. It transformed into a massive flying mushroom. On the other side of the world, in some abandoned parking lot, my brother was about to take the plunge. Justine leaned close, and I felt the warmth of her breath. Music blared in our ears: the rhythmic beat of drums, the resonance of a bass, the angry edge of an electric guitar, the deep lull of the cello.

A cello. How fucking lovely.

"Here she is," Eric said. I could hear that giggle again. "Say hi."

"Hi," she squeaked. A school of bright yellow fish darted toward the glass.

"That's her," Eric said. "Isn't she great?"

A sudden ruckus of voices and laughter came from his end of the line. Some idiot was blabbering, "So you know what the master says? He says, 'A crystal vessel filled with ice has no shadow. A monkey reaches for the moon in the water.'"

"Yo, back off, dude," Eric responded. "It's my brother and his girl."

Justine and I looked at each other. I got that sick feeling again, as if I'd been kicked in the stomach.

"Listen, I gotta put you guys down for a minute," Eric said.

"Go ahead." Justine slipped the phone back into my hand.

The receiver thumped. I realized Eric's phone must be swinging against the booth. The music went silent. Voices hushed.

"Dearly beloved," someone said. "We are gathered here . . ."

Justine leaned her head against my shoulder. I got that feeling again like I'd swallowed a stone, a fist. I shut my eyes. A wall of numbness circled around; it saved me. Through my eyelids, I could see the changing light.

"Eric, do you promise to love, cherish . . . till death do you part?"

"Yo, I do."

"Melissa, do you promise . . ."

The world held its breath. There was applause, cheering. Music commenced. I remembered once way back when Eric had pissed me off, and just as I was about to beat the crap out of him, he'd looked straight at me and said, "You fucking lose, man."

The words rang in my ears. They felt familiar and, oddly, right. I opened my eyes.

Justine forced a smile and handed me the opal box. "Give this to Eric for me," she said. She turned and, without looking back, went toward the exit. Fine, fuck you, too, I thought. Go ahead—take off—see if I care. See you on the goddamn plane.

A ray fluttered through the water.

I opened the fucking box. The rock sparkled. She'd taken out the opal, replaced it with the ring. The diamond shimmered rainbows under the light. I looked up in time to catch her disappearing into the darkness.

B E A U T Y

HIS PERSONAL says: "Well-traveled, good-looking, thirties."

This boils down to ripe-honeydew eyes, thick rusty-brown triangular brows, a freckled complexion. He's a lanky five-eight, maybe nine, balding. Poor thing combs a lock of hair from one side of his scalp all the way to the other. Guy must be terrified of wind. Other than that, he's okay-looking. Pushing it about his age—let's just say I wouldn't be surprised if he turned forty tomorrow—but not bad, really not bad.

"So Thomas—" I pluck his eight-liner from my purse. "Says here, you're looking for an Asian beauty?"

His grins as big and wide as a Cheshire cat. In that sexy Australian accent of his, he says, "Looks like I've found her."

The waiter arrives with the bottle of Château Haut-Brion. I cover the personal with my hand. Thomas goes through the ritual of squeezing the cork, swirling the wine, sipping. "Good," he says, and nods. The waiter pours. I order the Valentine Weekend Special: bouillabaisse for starters, lobster in vanilla cream sauce for the entrée. Thomas decides on the carrot soup and rack of lamb.

"Where were we?" He clears his throat. Lines fan from the corners of his eyes, "Oh, yes—Asian beauty, was it?"

I flash him that vulnerable look I've practiced so many times in the bathroom mirror—slight tip of the head, lift of a brow, large upturned eyes, pouting lips—and watch his eyes trace the full shape of my mouth.

He clears his throat again. "Now, let's see. You're Asian, that's apparent. You look it, anyway." He takes me in at different angles. "You *are* Asian, aren't you?"

I can't help laughing. "I don't tape back my eyes, if that's what you're asking."

I can tell he's thinking, That's certainly an odd thing to say. "Okay, then—that's taken care of," he says, rubbing his palms together. "Now, as far as beauty goes—well, there are sheilas and there are sheilas. What more is there to say?"

"Plenty." I examine my fingernails, each one manicured to perfection.

"Mh—you're right. You're simply exquisite," he says. From the slight tweak of his eyes, I suspect he's got a hard-on under the table. "Cheers."

"Cheers to you, too, Mr. Well-traveled, Good-looking, and um, Thirties."

He smiles sheepishly. Busted. Our glasses touch with an awkwardly loud clink. He looks at me, then away. Candlelight reflects off our glasses. The Bordeaux leaves a dry, fruity taste, a hint of licorice.

"So tell me," I ask, "how many responses you get?"

He chokes on his wine.

"Come on, Thomas. We talking more than ten, less than ten? What?"

He sets his glass on the table. "Curious thing, now, aren't you?"

"I would think you'd appreciate the direct approach."

He offers me bread from the basket. I pass but he takes an herb roll, squeezes it between his fingers, rips off a piece. He butters it, places it in his mouth. "Six," he finally says. "Maybe seven."

"And the last date before this?"

He rests his elbows on the table, folds his hands in front of him. "Let's talk about you. Shall we?"

"Last Wednesday," I say, knowing it will stun him. "One tonight—that's you. Another tomorrow for the big Valentine's Day."

He forces a weak smile. "You have the loveliest hands. An artist's hands."

I pucker my lips, wiggle my fingers at him. My nails are painted a color called teaberry, a mauve-red with hints of brown. "There's not an ounce of creativity in this entire body, unless you count painting these nails or plucking my eyebrows, which I wouldn't honestly think you would."

"Likely not."

"I didn't think so." I uncross my legs and recross them the other way. I sit back, relax into the seat, allow a thin ankle and a black Versace pump to protrude from beneath the tablecloth. He watches my bobbing foot. There's a light scar the size and shape of a fingernail over my ankle.

"Of course other things compensate," I say.

"Of course," he says.

"Like warmth," I say, pointing at the personal, "and humor."

The soup arrives, steam rising from it. "Hot," the waiter says. Thomas moves back from the table. I spoon a shrimp from the bouillabaisse—careful to get it into my mouth without ruining my lipstick—and chew it slowly. He watches me over a spoon of his pureed carrot soup.

Go ahead—want me, baby, I know you want me.

"Mh—you're absolutely exquisite," he says.

"You've, um, said that already."

"I couldn't emphasize it enough." His hand snakes across the tablecloth.

"Careful," I say, sticking him with my spoon. "Hot."

After dinner, Thomas drives me home in his silver Mercedes. He takes Third Avenue downtown, blathering on about his separation. I gather his wife is Helen, who decided to split after their son went to college. Yeah—and I care? I'm thinking, Let's get to my place and fuck already. His hand rests over my thigh, squeezing it as if it were one of those warm rolls. I want you, those fingers say, God, I want you. We pass clothing stores, boutiques, a supermarket; I imagine Thomas's face between my legs—the carpet of hair at the peak of his head flapping the wrong direction—and I can't help laughing.

"Something funny?" he asks.

I lean close, smooth the hairs stretching over his scalp. His body goes rigid. "How about letting me give you a haircut some-time?" I ask.

"Why?" He checks the mirror to make certain all is in order. "What's wrong with it?"

"Nothing," I say. "It's just that naked's in."

He glances at me, turning onto my block, Tenth Street. "I don't know about that," he says. "Hey, look—Ben and Jerry's. When Griffin was little, I used to take him to get a banana split every week. Back then, it was Baskin-Robbins on every corner."

"Nothing like trying to buy love."

"It wasn't like that." The hurt shakes in his voice. This moves me.

"Smooth spots are sexy, you know." I stroke his baldness, then sniff the tips of my fingers; his scalp smells of braised lamb and Head & Shoulders.

"You think so?" he says, squeezing my thigh.

"If you sit still the whole time and be a very good boy, I promise to take you afterward for an ice cream."

We get near the end of the block. I point out a gray four-story building. Cars line both sides of the street. Thomas pulls over near a rusted white Cadillac. He cuts the engine.

"So," he says, "are you my Asian beauty?"

I make my pouty face again. "You tell me."

"Mh." His eyes droop with lust. "You are a beaut." He runs a finger along the side of my jaw, leans to kiss me. The leather seat squeaks under our weight. He pushes his tongue into my mouth.

He's so hungry he's got one hand squeezing my breast, the other trying to find the hem of my dress. The back of my head presses up against the window. "You want me, don't you?" I whisper.

"God, yes." He shudders.

"You want to fuck me?" I say.

His hand locates the bottom of my dress. He reaches under, slides his hand up the inside of my leg to my knees and thighs. He feels the outside of my panties. "You're wet," he whispers. "So wet."

The flap of hair falls to the other side of his head and hangs over his ear like a limb. For a moment, I can see him as the boy he was—carefree and full of himself—chasing the pretty girls for a quick kiss. I stood aside. Want me, I yearned, want me. One day he did come after me, only it wasn't for a kiss. He slammed me to the ground, screwed my ankle into a shard of glass with the heel of his sneaker, chanting, *Chinese, Japanese, dirty knees . . .*

"So wet." He makes his way into my undies.

I catch him by the wrist. "You never did tell me about your last date," I say.

"What date?" He tries to shut me up with kisses.

"Last week?" My tongue tangles with his. "Last night?"

He draws away, sits back into the seat, the leather pushing and pulling under his weight. He fixes his hair.

"Did you fuck her?" I ask. "Was she good? A good fuck?"

"Look—I don't know what you're trying to get at."

"Was she?"

"You have a problem or something? Masochistic tendencies?"

"Thomas." I demand an answer.

"Yes," he finally replies. "All right, then? She was great. It was great. We 'fucked' on the kitchen floor. Happy now?"

"As a matter of fact"—I open the door, step outside, wrap my coat close around my body—"I am."

The door slams shut in his face, trapping his voice inside.

My place stinks of ripe apple. The first thing I do is call Angel, my best friend from college, who still lives with and supports her parents in Chinatown. My hands are unsteady. I sit with my coat on, engulfed with that peculiar sensation that something just happened, something bigger than I can understand. I get this weird feeling that it's me—something's terribly, terribly wrong with me. After three tries, I finally get the number right.

Angel's mom answers. "Weh?"

"Yang, Auntie," I say, failing to dig up any Chinese. "How are you?"

"Amy-ah? How you? Angel not home."

"Zi?" Mole? I ask. Meaning, of course, Jim, the pig who got drunk at a high school party and called me "Chink." He has this black dot just above his right nostril.

"Hai . . ." From her tone, I sense she isn't altogether happy about the situation, either. That's the thing about Mrs. Yang—she's got good instincts. "Two weeks. Three times they go outside to eat."

Damn it, I think. That fucking Mole. I could kick myself for bringing Angel to that stupid high school reunion. Left her for five minutes to get drinks. When I got back, Jim had secured a space for himself at her side.

On the end table sits Georgie's fishbowl. She gave it to me when she and Mark split up. The goldfish's dark shape rises to the surface of the water, searching for food.

"You must come for dinner soon," Mrs. Yang says.

"I'd love to," I reply. Mrs. Yang cooks the best Cantonese around. She knows my parents took off for Hong Kong way back when sweet darling Georgianna broke their hearts, so every time I go over, she cooks as if Mom had died. The only thing is space. The bathtub is in the middle of the Yangs' main room, which happens to also be the kitchen and a bedroom for the kids. Whenever I eat there, Angel's younger sister and brother have to eat outside in the hallway. "I've been so busy lately," I say.

"Next week-la? I'll make gai lan—all your favorites."

"Please. Don't go to any trouble. I love everything."

Mrs. Yang's still going on about dinner when the elevator in the hallway dings. Through the peephole, I watch Angel step off. She's wearing a knock-off Armani coat with square silver buttons. She grows larger with each step, coming closer, closer. She reaches into her pocket, pops a black watermelon seed into her mouth, cracks it with her teeth. She spits the pieces of empty shell into her hand. Up close, I can see the mascara layered onto her curled lashes. She rings. The bell thumps. It sounds as if a spoon had knocked the bottom of a glass.

I cover the mouthpiece and swing the door open. "Where's Mole?"

"Downstairs—and stop calling him that," she says, peering over my shoulder, squinting into the dark. She picks another watermelon seed out of her pocket, puts it in her mouth, cracks it.

"You alone? What happened to your date?" Poor Angel. She gets so jing zang about this Personals stuff. She must think one of these nights I'll get hacked to smithereens.

"Did you see a silver Mercedes double-parked outside?"

She spits out the shell. "No."

"Went home." I point to the receiver: "your mom."

Angel takes the phone. She switches into Cantonese, speaking at such a speed that I can't decipher it. She runs through seeds as only an expert could, cracking each directly down the middle. She's getting her fix. Americans, she says, can't appreciate this kind of thing, which must translate, I suppose, to Jim's thinking it's a gross habit.

I drop onto the couch, kick off my heels. Angel feeds the goldfish a pinch of food. Finally, after a few minutes, she hangs up. "I told Ma I'm sleeping over tonight," she says, in case I need to cover for her. Her parents don't bend when it comes to old-world ways.

"You staying at Jim's?" I try not to sound snotty.

She nods, and fidgets with the button on her coat. I've told her my history with the pig. "You don't really know him." She cracks another seed. "People change."

"Right," I say.

"They do," she insists. I don't argue. After all, as Angel has pointed out, I may be convinced he's just using her, but the fact remains she's still a virgin—plans on remaining one until she's married—so if he is in fact using her, it isn't for *that*.

I'm about to ask why Jim didn't come upstairs with her, when it occurs to me that, despite promises, she's probably blabbed to him about the Personals thing.

"You told him, didn't you?" I say.

"No, of course not." A guilty look skips over her face. She spits out another shell.

"Oh, Angel," I say. Do I really want that pig to know about this?

"I didn't tell him," she swears. "He thinks I came up to borrow a dress."

"A dress?"

She nods, but too urgently.

I sigh. "Whatever—take your pick." I point to the closet. She goes straight for the black dress I'm planning to wear tomorrow. "Just not that one," I say.

She returns it to the rack and flips through the rest of my things. "You okay?" she asks. "You seem funny."

"I don't know. . . . I feel kind of funny. This date was like, one minute everything's going fine—I'm really turning this guy on— then bang, just like that, for no reason, everything feels totally wrong, I hate his guts and it's like I'm egging him on for a fight."

She draws a short black skirt up to her body. It comes way above the knee, so she puts it back. "That always happens. You say that every time."

"I do?"

She shakes her head. "Why you do those things, I don't know."

"It's fun."

"Fun?"

"Sort of. Sometimes."

She shoots me a look.

"Oh, I don't know. Tomorrow will be fun. I can feel it in my bones. His personal said, 'Be Asian, be sweet,' and honey, boy, can I do sweet."

She shakes her head, picks a red lace dress. "This is pretty."

"Isn't it a bit formal?" I ask. "Where's he taking you, anyway?"

"I don't know." She shoves another seed into her mouth, cracks it, then starts on another. "He says we need to talk."

"Talk?" I try not to sound too skeptical.

"No, no," Angel breaks into a smile. "He bought me something. I saw it in his drawer." She holds the dress up to her body again.

"How big?"

"Jewelry-box big," she whispers, as if saying it too loud might make the thing disappear.

"No!"

"Yes," she says.

I look at her: You certain?

Her eyes light up. "You'll be my maid of honor?"

We hug, rocking from side to side. "Of course," I say, though part of me hates her more than that pig she's choosing to spend the rest of her life with. Why is she choosing that fucker over me? Hasn't she heard a thing I said? Maybe she'll che ku, eat bitterness, and come to see the bastard for what he really is. Yeah, that's right. Che ku.

But I catch myself. What's wrong with me? My friend tells me she's getting engaged, and all I can do is hope she gets burned? Am I that fucking small? I mean, maybe Angel's right—people can change. The fish swims a circle in her bowl.

"You better get your buns out of here," I tell her, and push her to the door. "Your soon-to-be-fiancé's probably freezing his ass off and wondering if I'm holding you hostage." She laughs, covering her mouth to do so, and hurries to the elevator. A final crack of a watermelon seed, and Angel disappears inside.

The wind rattles the storm window. I'm nearly asleep, with the TV on, when that rhyme starts going off in my head again: *Chinese, Japanese, dirty knees* . . . What is that last line? *Chinese, Japanese, dirty knees, wash them please. Chinese, Japanese, dirty knees, watch me beat. Chinese, Japanese, dirty knees, make her plead. Chinese, Japanese, dirty knees* . . .

An angry gust knocks at the window. In the apartment across the way, my neighbor ices a chocolate cake. On TV, a commercial for fruit juice comes on. My eyes droop shut. A child laughs. *Ha-ha-ha, ha-ha-ha.* Somewhere a metal lunchbox rattles. I feel myself falling. Dust rushes up my nose. I open my mouth to scream, but instead I hear myself say, "Nobody does it like JuicyQ. . . ." *Chinese, Japanese, dirty knees, touch me please.* A boy laughs. "You're wet," he says. "You got a problem or something?" He has Thomas's worn face and a child's small, underdeveloped body. He swims up between my legs, sinks his teeth into the apple, crunches its crisp meat. "So wet," he says. *Chinese, Japanese, dirty knees, fuck me please.* Somewhere a bell rings. He eats faster, crawling, pushing for more, more; just when his little feet get lost inside, I feel the pulsing thump, thump, thump of me chewing him alive.

The doorbell sounds, startling me awake. There's the smell of overripe apples in the kitchen. It's just a dream, I tell myself, it doesn't mean anything. I stumble to the door. It's Angel. Almost immediately, I can tell something's wrong. Her face seems too large compared with the rest of her body, distorted as though her face had been stretched outward by the ears. Her eyes are swollen, squinty. Mascara stains her cheeks. She clutches the red dress by the waist, the sleeves dragging on the floor.

"Oh, Angel," I say.

Her head drops to my shoulder. "Mei la"—It's over—she tells me.

"What?" I look into her face. But the ring, I want to say. What about that ring?

"Ta bu ai wo," she replies. He doesn't love me.

I pull off her coat, lead her to the bedroom. Watermelon seeds scatter over the floor. She moves stiffly to the bed, sits there in a daze. I brush my thumb across her cheek. Mascara runs onto my palm. "Talk to me," I say.

She gazes at me; I've become a stranger. "Maybe you were right," she says, her lips trembling. She clenches her fists, beats them against her head. "Stupid, stupid, stupid!" she screams.

I grab her forearms. "Stop it, hear me? Stop. Please, Angel. Don't."

"Ni bu dong," You don't understand, she says. In that moment, I know she despises me. I want to say, Yes, I do, I do. But I don't understand. I don't know anything. I am not Chinese. Not Chinese Chinese like her, anyway.

She lies down, her head on the pillow, her body shivering, cold. I fold the comforter over her so she's sandwiched inside and lie next to her.

Be Asian, be sweet. I'm huddled at a phone booth outside the movie theater. With the windchill factor, it's gotta be minus something. Too cold to snow. My fucking date is late. The movie, a special Valentine's Day showing of *Titanic,* starts in ten minutes. A man wearing a black baseball cap, a sailor's coat, and dark corduroys walks toward me. He's six feet, maybe an inch over that, and struts around like a cowboy. His eyes are the kind of hazel that goes green some days and brown others, depending on the color shirt he's wearing. He notices me, smiles.

Please, God, let it be him. Please. I return the smile, swear I'll go to church every Sunday from now until I die.

But he passes. In fact, he goes over and kisses the plain-looking brunette behind me at the other phone. She ends her call—pronto. She's got that artsy look: thick-framed glasses, all-black attire. She notices me eyeballing the cowboy, glares.

Honey, please, I want to say. You and I—we aren't in the same league.

But it's me who ends up outside waiting, freezing my ass off, asking myself why the hell I'm wearing a dress when it's so damn cold out. And these shoes. So fucking high they're killing my feet. What was I thinking?

Where the hell is *my* cowboy?

I call Angel. She answers with a drugged-out voice. "How are you feeling?" I ask.

"Not so good."

"Me, either," I say. "Get this—looks like I've got a no-show. Can you believe? It's fucking Valentine's Day and my date decides —*ha, ha*—joke's on her, why not let her stand outside in the fucking cold until she catches pneumonia." For Angel's sake, I laugh.

There's a pause, followed by a raspy, choking sound.

"Don't cry," I say.

"Chi si," she says. Heartbroken.

The wind tears through my clothes. "Would you like me to come over?" I ask.

"No."

"It wouldn't be a problem. I could just hop into a cab—be there in a snap—we could just talk and drink a cup of your ma's steamy hot Ovaltine."

"I hate her," she says.

"Oh, Angel."

"I do. You know, she's happy about this. She is. You should see her. She's scared one of these days I'll leave and they'll be stuck taking care of themselves. She'd like to keep me in this prison forever."

The front of the movie theater is walled in glass. People disappear into the theater. What would it take to smash the front of the building? A rock the size of a coffee cup? A Volvo going seventy miles per hour? I think about Mom and Dad—how they took off for Hong Kong: now, to assuage their guilt (I wasn't the troublemaker this time), they send a monthly check that pays my rent. Angel, on the other hand, has parents she supports. As a result, she can't afford to move out.

"Sorry," Angel says.

"Don't be." I check my watch. "I have a better idea. Why don't you come meet me here, and we'll get dinner and see a late movie? My treat, okay?"

"What about your date?"

"He's late—his tough luck."

"But it's Valentine's Day."

"Yeah," I say, my teeth chattering. "Happy fucking Valentine's Day."

She chuckles. I feel better. She says she's too tired to go out, so I tell her to get some rest, I'll call in the morning. An Asian guy pauses under the theater lights. He's a good height—taller than I am—and broad in the shoulders. Button-down leather jacket, jeans, brown bucks. He looks at me but I turn away. Sorry, dude—not into the Asian thing. There's been only one exception: this guy in Hong Kong a bunch of years ago, during the Handover. Jonathan Something-or-other. But *that* was just a result of an afternoon of beer-guzzling with pathetic Uncle Henry.

Get that—stood up on Valentine's Day. I purchase a ticket, ascend the escalator to the third floor. My fingers and ears still sting from the cold. The place smells of popcorn. I'd buy myself a bag if it didn't mean missing the beginning of the movie.

The theater is packed solid, except for the front row. Sitting in those seats means craning my neck for more than three hours. But what choice do I have? I sit as the last preview ends. The movie starts. I glance behind at the crowd of tinted faces. It spooks me to think the stupid guy might be here; for all I know, he may be watching.

Buttery popcorn wakes my hunger. I reach into my coat pocket, find a mentholated cough drop and a bottle of nail polish. On the big screen, a love story unfolds. The *Titanic* sails into the ocean. Though it is tragic that the ship will sink, I feel strangely comforted by the fact that it will vanish to the bottom of the ocean.

Someone sits in the seat next to mine, bringing with him the buttery smell of popcorn.

It's the mole I notice first.

Fuck. What the hell is *he* doing here?

"Popcorn?" he asks.

"What?" My voice falters. "How . . . ?"

"Extra butter," he says.

A guy in the row behind shushes us. On the screen, the ship drifts into a fog. Is this really happening? I dig my nails into my thighs until I am sure about the pain. Jim stuffs his mouth with popcorn. Angel's at home crying her eyes out, and he's fucking here, enjoying a movie?

Then, it hits me. "Be Asian?" I whisper.

"Be sweet," he responds.

I shut my eyes. Oh, Angel. My poor, sweet Angel. Jim moves his sweaty hand over mine. I push him away, knock the bucket of popcorn to the floor, jump to my feet.

"Wait," he whispers, snagging me by the coat.

I jerk free, race toward the exit sign.

"Amy," he calls. "Amy."

"Shhh!" the audience cries.

Outside, my heels stab at the pavement. Garbage whirls over the sidewalk. A napkin blows onto my shin. "Fuck," I say, trying to shake it off. My breath rushes from my mouth. The wind shifts; the napkin finally tears free. It drifts a moment, then is sucked into the street, a cab taking it in its wheels.

Jim catches up with me the next block over. "Just listen," he says.

"You didn't fool me for a second," I say. "I knew you were a fucking pig."

"Oh, that's nice."

"Pig."

"People change," he says. The dark mole stares me in the face. "I was a different person back then."

Cold air rushes up my dress. A scratchy sound forces its way out from my gut, and I realize I've waited for this. I've wanted to say: Who's the beauty now, huh? Want me. Go ahead and want me.

He leans in for a kiss. A voice inside me squeals, See? He wants me, he wants me. I want him.

But no. I draw back, find myself cracking up.

"Go ahead, laugh," he says.

Clueless. Totally clueless.

When I finally get a hold of myself, I say, "You need help. I'm talking professional help."

"Me?" he says.

I look at him. That's right.

"Wait—who's the one here who dates strangers from the Personals? Losers hot for Asian chicks?"

"Fuck you." I turn, storm away. Didn't I say he was a pig? Why did I even bother talking to him? I'm two blocks from home when Jim catches up again. "Just let me buy you a drink and explain—"

I confront him head-on. "You speak English or what? Which part of 'Fuck you' don't you understand?"

A bunch of guys start cheering. I realize we're standing outside a bar quarreling as if we were lovers. A guy wearing a Mets cap toasts me through the window. "Fuck him," he mouths.

"One drink," Jim says, holding the door for me. "Come on—be sweet." Reggae tumbles out the door. The place looks like the set of *Gilligan's Island*. Plastic flowers and palm trees, shiny bamboo furniture, floorboards covered with white sand. My dream flashes into my head. An apple. The wet sound of its meat crunching between someone's teeth. I look at the pig, all smug and full of himself. A part of me goes, You want sweet? I'll give you sweet. I know, now, exactly what I'm going to do.

You want to fuck? I'll give you a good fuck.

"One drink," I say.

Five drinks later, plus a trip to the bathroom, where I force myself to puke, the reggae has stopped and the theme song to *Gilligan's Island* comes on. A redhead climbs on the bar and starts dancing.

Guys hoot and clap. She sips her drink, sways her hips. I feel satisfyingly numb. Ready.

I dance my way to the door, stumble out to the sidewalk.

"No kidding around," Jim says. "Angel and me were just casual."

I laugh, take his hand, twirl under his arm. "No kidding around. Jim sings and he doesn't kid around. Quick stings. Wet dreams. Hey, that rhymed!"

Jim takes my hand, leads me to my apartment. He starts telling me he wants to see me again, next weekend, he says, since he's got to see his mother midweek. It's her birthday, which, I assume, explains the mixup with the ring. "Happy birthday to you," I sing. "You live in a zoo. You look like a monkey. And you smell like one, too!" I laugh, digging out my keys.

As always, the front door is ajar. We enter the building, and I make as if I'm oblivious about his coming up with me. The damn elevator's so slow I take the stairs. He follows behind. Halfway up the second flight of stairs, I turn, and catch him staring at my ass. "May I help you?" I step around to face him. My coat slips from my shoulders, thumps onto the stairs.

"God," he says. "You're so . . ."

I pout, look up at him with big eyes. "Exquisite?"

His nostrils flare. The mole seems larger, as if the edges had started to bleed into his skin. He holds me at the hips. I lean toward him. He reaches behind to squeeze my ass. We kiss. He tastes of sour beer.

I pet him until he moans.

In my apartment, we undress. Light from the streetlamp pours in
through the blinds. Ripe apples stink up the room. A faint scent of
nail polish remover calms me. I pull my dress over my head, drop
my bra and undies. My heels go back under the end table. I lie on
the couch and part my legs. My hands slide up and down the in-
sides of my thighs. "You want some?" I whisper.

"Oh God, yes." Cum hangs from the tip of his penis. He pulls
me by the ankles. He's trembling he wants it so bad. His erection
taps against my thigh. "You're wet," he says. "So wet." He pushes
the tip of his penis inside me. In my head, I hear the crunch of an
apple.

"You want to fuck?" I tease.

He forces himself all the way inside me, groaning, clenching
his teeth, shutting his eyes. He leans over, screws slowly; then
faster, faster. "Oh God," he croaks, "oh God." Just as he starts to
lose himself, I start singing, "Chinese, Japanese, dirty knees . . ."

He stops. His skin looks jaundiced in the light from the street.

"How does that rhyme go again?" I ask.

His dick softens, loses its angle. "I don't know what you're talking about."

I repeat myself. "It's driving me crazy that I can't remember."

He takes his penis into his hand, tries to massage it back to life.
"My apology not good enough or something?"

"Oh, that? You call that an apology?" I say, mocking him.
"'People change—I was a different person back then.'"

"They do."

"Right. And I'm Angel."

"You're a bitch, you know that?" He grabs his boxers from the floor.

"Is that official? Have I graduated from Chink to bitch?"

The shaft of his penis rears its ugly, swollen head. Before I know it, he's struggling to pin me to the floor. I thrash and kick. The end table goes down. The fishbowl crashes to the floor.

"Stop," I say. Like Divine Providence, the elevator sounds. Footsteps clap toward my apartment. "It's Angel," I say.

He leaps back. His penis falls limp again. It hits me that he actually cares about her.

An evil chuckle escapes me. "Just casual," I say. "No kidding around."

I imagine her standing in the doorway. The shock of witnessing him with someone else, seeing him for the pig he truly is. A pool of water expands and trickles toward the door. The goldfish lies flat on her side. She inches over the tiles, drifting with the flow.

Angel knocks. "Amy?"

I clutch my rumpled dress and scurry to the door. I'm here, I want to scream. Look at him. Look what he's done. But I picture her in the doorway again, the way her eyes would fix on me beneath those thick, dark lashes.

Oh, Angel. What have I done? A jagged pain stabs me in the gut.

Jim registers my reluctance. A scornful smile creeps over his face. He moves toward me, touches my left breast, rubs the nipple between thumb and forefinger. It rises under command.

"You there?" Angel calls, knocking again. Water trickles under my feet. I drop the dress to the floor.

"Go ahead, open it," Jim challenges, barely sounding the words. He crosses his arms over his chest.

"Amy? You there?"

The phone rings. Jim and I both turn to stare at it. The machine finally goes on.

"G'day. It's Thomas. I just wanted to apologize for last night. I'm not really clear what happened there at the end, but if I did anything to offend you . . ."

Jim's hand runs down my back, over my ass. Goose bumps race over my skin, and the soft hairs on my arms stand on end.

"Well, that'll be all," Thomas says. He leaves his number.

Angel waits on other side of the door. Through the peephole, I spy her enlarged face. Her eyes look swollen, slitty. Her long naked lashes capture my loneliness. *Chinese, Japanese, dirty knees.* Then I remember: *Look at these.*

COPYCAT

"I'M GOING to the A&P," I said. "Want anything?" Todd, our other kid, the live one, would be arriving soon. He'd spent the fall and winter traveling cross-country with friends. He wasn't planning to stick around long. Two nights and he'd be off again.

Gary mowed up and down, then diagonally. The lines staggered and ran over each other. He razored around the realtor's "Sold" sign, leaving a small island of unkempt grass.

He was doing it intentionally, the bastard. Trying to goad me into a fight so he could say: What's it to you? True, I'd put the house on the market. But hasty? It'd been ten years. Ten unforgiving years.

I was the one who'd been at home that day. Where were you? I wanted to ask, because I wanted to remind him: That's right—at the office. While *you* were at the office, *I* was in the study directly below Sarah's room—yelling, "Sarah Sheng-Stevenson, if you don't turn that music down this instant!"—when the gun went off.

All these years, and it was the little things I hadn't forgotten. Little things that should have meant nothing: the string pulley attached to the lightbulb over my desk, and how its metal tip had jangled against my scalp; the headline in the local paper, which had read "Cobain Copycat"; the dandelion spores, fluffy and round, ready to spread their seed.

"Well?" I asked now.

Gary shut off the mower and scratched his chin. "Let me see. Do I want anything?" He always had a way with sarcasm.

"It's not a trick question," I said.

He brushed past me into the house and slammed the screen door. In a few minutes, he'd be in her room. He'd play those Nirvana CDs; maybe he'd "talk" with her. The more time that passed, the more alive Gary seemed to make her. It had become a habit, an obsession.

Just as I got in the minivan, Todd arrived. I heard the high-pitched whine of the compact car as it descended Walbrook Lane. We were at the bottom of it. Before we bought the place, Mom had warned, "Bad feng shui, that house." But Gary and I had been above that kind of hocus-pocus superstition.

In the rearview I saw a cream-colored Volkswagen, one of those mini-Rabbits, pull into the drive. I smiled like any mother should, and stepped out of the van. The smell of grass gave me a headache. Todd swung his large pack onto his back. He waved. The driver threw her car into reverse. She had a round face and light complexion. She wasn't the least bit pretty, what with the knotted mass of unkempt hair and the knobby nose. She tooted her horn and disappeared as quickly as she'd come.

Todd seemed thinner about the face, more filled out in the shoulders and upper body. He had his father's large forehead and aquiline nose, my Asian eyes and high cheekbones. His shins were as thin as chicken legs, but covered with dark hair. He adjusted his cap. There was a certain rhythm to his step, a relaxed gait that seemed forced. He nodded. Here I am.

Here you are.

"How's the book?" he asked.

He was referring to my second novel, a story about a man who lost his son to the Vietnam War. "Longer," I replied. I'd been working on it the past twelve years, and the manuscript was closing in on two thousand pages. Only recently, ever since the house went on the market, had I stopped writing.

Todd looked up at the house. When I told him we were selling it, he said he wanted to "have a look around" before I packed everything. He meant *her* room; it was to be his first time in it since the "accident."

"Who's the girl?" I asked, trying to be casual.

Todd hooked an arm over my shoulder as if to share a long-kept secret. His odor was stronger, muskier than his father's. "What's with the lawn?" he whispered.

Gary came out onto the porch. "What's this?" He wanted to be in on things.

"Your son wants to know what went wrong with the lawn," I said.

"Neither here nor there, as your mother so often likes to say," he said, and winked.

"You could've invited her in for a drink," I told my son.

Gary hummed that Nirvana tune. He believed the answer existed somewhere in the lyrics. For me, the truth lay in research. Articles about Cobain's life, Nirvana, and Courtney Love. Whatever I could find in books and magazines or on the Net.

"Where are your things?" Gary asked.

Todd patted the backpack. "You're looking at it."

Gary didn't appear the least bit amused. I knew he must be wondering about the computer Todd had begged for and made us buy him the year before.

"What's her name?" I asked.

Todd removed his pack. "Have I ever told you the thing about the poet?"

"Poet?" Gary said.

"Yeah, there's this poet, you know? One day he asks his master, 'Master? If an ancient mirror isn't polished, how can it reflect light off a candle?' You know what the guy says? He says, 'A crystal vessel filled with ice has no shadow. A monkey reaches for the moon in the water.'"

Gary rubbed his chin.

"So this poet—he's clueless, you see?—he goes: 'Such things do not reflect light. Will you go on with your talk?' The master looks at the guy and says, 'If these aren't of any help, what do you want me to say?'" Todd looked at us expectantly: Get it?

Gary nodded. I, on the other hand, blurted, "What?"

Todd beamed, proud of himself the way he'd been as a child when he mastered another multiplication problem. "It's a koan."

"Well, does this 'koan' translate somehow into 'girlfriend'?"

Todd chuckled. "She's a friend."

"Friend like 'just friends,' or friend like—"

"Aggie," Gary interrupted, and from his tone, he may as well have said, Don't you ever learn?

My chest felt as if a brick threatened to smother it. Don't you dare drag Sarah into this, I wanted to warn. I have every right to know these kinds of things. Every God-given right.

"Hey." Todd patted his father's shoulder and drew me closer. I felt small next to him. He was the missing link between us, the human go-between. He gave my shoulder a tight squeeze. "Just a friend, okay, Ma?"

"Fine," I said. "See, that's all I asked."

Todd stared into the house. The front door was open, revealing the bottom of the stairwell. "Well," he sighed. "Guess it's that time."

At the A&P, I crossed off each item on my list: milk, cheese, eggs. Before I left, I'd told Todd everything in her room was the same; everything was the way she'd left it. What I hadn't said was that she'd put everything away. Photos and charms on her bureau were placed in the desk; clothes that had been on the floor were neatly folded into drawers. All for my sake. The only thing left out had been the CD player.

I made my way down the cereal aisle. What was Todd thinking now, standing there in his sister's room? Was Gary sitting at the end of the bed, playing that music for him?

There were no more than ten items on the shopping list, but when I got to the counter, the cart was nearly full. I placed my things on the belt, watching everything go by, and only then did it occur to me that for every one of Todd's favorites, I'd picked out one for Sarah. Doritos and Bugles; Mini-Wheats and Cocoa Puffs; apple juice and grape; ravioli with meat and with cheese; ice cream sandwiches and Heath Bar Crunch.

A soft voice behind me said, "Any day now."

I realized I'd been gazing at the woman next to me in line. At her belly, that is, which protruded like a piglet's bottom. "Oh," I managed. "Lucky day."

"A girl," she said, smiling openly, untouched by doom. She was young, maybe mid-twenties, petite. The pregnancy bloated her cheeks, neck, and arms. Her legs reminded me of overstuffed sausages.

"Congratulations," I said, though I was thinking, Just you wait. You'll make certain she eats right, takes her vitamins, cleans behind her ears each night. You'll make certain she looks both ways before crossing the street; that she doesn't speak to strangers. Later, you'll fret about boys and sex and grades. You'll do things you don't want to do: ground her for coming home past nine on a weeknight, yell when she's on the phone too long, and finally, forbid her to see the rich kid with the fancy Corvette. People will tell you, Relax—she's just a teenager. You try to relax, you focus more on the project you've been working on for two years and are about to finish. Then, on a perfect May afternoon, she'll put her things away—she knows how much you hate it when she leaves a mess—then lie between white cotton sheets to blow her brains out.

But that wasn't true now, either, was it? It had been me, only me. My little girl, not hers, not my brother Philip's—his precious little Rachel—not the neighbors'. No one else's but mine.

The woman rubbed her belly. "We're calling her Zoe—after my mother."

"How nice."

I paid the cashier and stacked the bags into the cart. My nose itched and I sneezed.

"God bless," the pregnant woman said.

What does God have to do with anything? After Sarah, that stupid neighbor of ours, Tung, had said, "It's God's will." I'd wanted to say, Fuck God and his damn fucking will. And secretly, when I'd heard their daughter was anorexic, I'd hoped the girl would starve herself to death. Try God's will then, I'd thought.

In the parking lot, the shopping cart banged into the van. The glare hurt my eyes. I slid open the back door and hauled the bags onto the seat and floor. The van was parked under a cherry tree. A film of pollen covered the windshield and gathered in pools along the edge of each wiper. Blossoms filled the air with their scent. Bees hummed.

I got into the van and started the engine, and just as I was pulling out of the lot, I noticed the pregnant woman out the window. She had one hand over her eyes, the other bracing the small of her back. Her belly protruded in front of her. My blinker clicked on, off; on, off. Part of me would have liked to back up over her, savor the thump of her under the tires. The other reprimanded: Only a monster would think such a thing. I turned onto Central Avenue, sped through a yellow light. Pollen rose over the windshield, giving with the wind.

———

The house was quiet. Gary, I knew, would be watching golf on TV. The light was on in Todd's room. I noticed a dandelion spore. Within moments, I was kneeling, spraying Weed-A-Cide. Go ahead. Try it; just try it. I dug my fingers around the naked stem and leaves, listened for the tearing sound, and delivered the culprit to the garbage. My fingers stunk of poison. Beneath my nails were bits of soil and grassy dandelion juice.

Just then, I heard the train in the distance. I used the trains to gauge time. The eight-thirty train signaled it was time to go into the study; the one at noon allowed me to break for lunch. This one, now, was the six p.m.—time I'd have called it a day. I went inside to start dinner.

At ten, I stopped at Todd's room to say good night. He hadn't mentioned Sarah since I returned from the store, and secretly, I wanted to keep it that way. But did he know that Cobain came from a broken home? That his father beat him with a belt? That he was diagnosed with scoliosis in the eighth grade, a condition that grew more severe because of the weight of his guitar? Did he know that the initial title of Cobain's last album was *I Hate Myself and I Want to Die*?

Did Todd know that his sister had nothing in common with any of these things? That Sarah felt certain she and Cobain were soul mates, based on the facts that—as Sarah so articulately stated—they both thought S. E. Hinton's *The Outsiders* was the "best

book ever written" and were both "hard-core" Pisces. Did he know
that Cobain left a letter written to an imaginary friend, who, inci-
dentally, had a name that sounded like "Buddha"—the name of
Sarah's childhood pal?

Todd's room had been pretty much untouched—a testament to
the fact that I wasn't the neatnik control freak Gary made me out
to be—though, admittedly, I put away some of the clutter. Even before the "accident," Todd had been actively involved in school
sports, usually arriving home no earlier than dinnertime at seven.
Trophies from Little League, felt letters from varsity soccer, and an
MVP plaque from his senior year crowded the top of the bookcase.
There was a baseball mitt signed by the Yankees. The shelves were
filled with books. Over the bed hung a poster of a red Ferrari.
Above the desk, a poster of a naked model wrapped in a boa con-
strictor.

A cone-shaped piece of incense burned on the sill. Smoke circled to the ceiling. It made me think of temples and foreign places.
The backpack was open on the floor. Old clothes overflowed from
a black garbage bag. I sat on his bed. Todd removed snake woman
from the wall.

"I always hated that poster," I said.

Todd held it at arm's length. He smiled. "Nastassja."

"I mean, how are you supposed to study with a naked lady
hanging over you like that?"

He shifted the poster this way and that. "You don't."

"See? That's what I told your father. Did he listen? Does he
ever listen?"

"It *was* my room."

"It *is.*"

He laid the poster on his desk and started on the Ferrari. "Didn't you say you're selling this place?" he asked.

"The house is on the market, yes."

He rolled the posters together, clapped a rubber band around them, and set them in the hallway. He started packing trophies into a box. The little gold men lined up in rows; they were soldiers. They dribbled balls between their feet. They stood at bat. They leaped to shoot.

"You going to save those?" I asked.

"Nah—Salvation Army, here they come."

"You can't do that," I said, taking the box onto my lap. "You can't just give these away."

"I'm not going to be needing them anytime soon," he said.

I hugged the box to my body. Todd started on the books, clearing them off the shelves and dumping them to the floor. "Look at all this garbage," he said. "You want any of these?"

I felt miserable, what with the mess he was making, and the fact that I'd given him most of those books. "Yes," I answered. Then, "No." I already had so many of my own books to move.

"No," I repeated. "You're right. Give them away."

One of the books, I saw, belonged to the school. It was *Nine Stories* by J. D. Salinger. Inside the front cover, the stamp read: "Property of Edgewood High." There was a list of names. At the bottom of the list, "Todd Sheng-Stevenson." Scratched in pencil; a gangly script. I picked it out and rearranged the rest of the books into piles, being careful not to bend the covers. I jammed the school's book between two trophies and got up to leave.

Todd emptied his desk onto the bed. Pens and notebooks, baseball cards, newspaper clippings, rocks. He fished out two quarters and a Canadian penny, then handed them to me. He looked ready to share something. Instead he smiled sadly and said, "Sweet dreams."

"You, too," I said.

The trophies jiggled, clacked against each other, making a hollow, tinny sound. I carried the box downstairs to my study. Inside the converted kitchen closet, the space was small, windowless. What I used to refer to as "cozy." But now, there were times when the space seemed too tight. It was like an aged relative whom you are eager to see yet, when you finally do, yearn to get away from. I pulled the string and the light clicked on. The metal tip swayed back and forth. It was bell-shaped, the size of a stud earring. I stopped it with my fingers.

The desk took up half the room. Shelves stuffed with books lined two walls. Between them stood a pile of books waiting to be read. On the desk, a computer, a lamp, a printer, and a tall pile of paper.

My hands spasmed. The box slipped from my hands and crashed to the floor. Little gold men spilled and fell over one another. A miniature foot splintered to the other side of the room. A bat split down the middle. I thought of the pregnant woman at the market. Sarah, had she still been alive, would have gone out into the world to start her own life, her own family. She'd be married, possibly have a child.

My heartbeat stuttered. Why did I continue to torture myself thinking such things?

Damn it, Sarah. What did I do that was so terrible, huh?

One by one, I packed the trophies back into the box. I laid the gold foot and bat on top of the manuscript. My eyes ached. A gasping sound escaped my throat, and then it was too late. I was crying. This time, maybe I wouldn't stop.

The lights were out in our room. Gary was already on his side of the bed. I slipped between the sheets and drew them to my neck. Outside, an owl hooted. The woods were dark nothingness. Exhaustion weighed at my limbs. Gary shifted, trying to get comfortable. I could see his eyelids blink as he stared up at the ceiling.

"So what'd he say?" I asked.

"Suppose he seemed a bit surprised," he said. "About the room."

"Surprised? Did he think we'd just pack up and give away her things?"

"It wasn't that. It was as if he expected to see something. "I don't know. Evidence, maybe. Something."

The smell of blood filled my nostrils. I went numb. My heart throbbed erratically, but it was distant, as if I were standing outside myself.

"What does a crystal vessel have to do with the reflection of a mirror?" Gary asked. "It doesn't make the least bit of sense."

"It's not supposed to."

Gary started up with the tune again.

"Do you have to hum that?"

He quieted. "He's turning into one of those New Age freaks," Gary said.

Now who's being the control freak? I wanted to say. "It's not any stranger than 'talking' with a dead daughter."

Gary froze. I loathed myself for having been so cruel.

"You're jealous," he said, stinging me back.

True, I was. After all, Sarah had never "talked" with me.

"I can't leave her," Gary said. "I'm not leaving her."

In the hall, I could hear Todd hauling bags of used clothes down the stairs to the front door. Gary stared at the ceiling. His lips moved silently, religiously. I watched him mouthing the lyrics, and wondered if sanity and loneliness were my just punishments.

For breakfast, Todd had his Mini-Wheats. Gary read the *Times*, shielding himself with the paper. I'd woken to the sound of the passing train, and by that time, he'd taken down the realtor's sign and called the agent. I sat across from Gary, completing the day's "To Do" list. At the bottom of it I wrote, "Return book to high school." My eyes felt tight. The night had been a river of unyielding, exhausting dreams. Only vague images remained: a snake twisting around my body, a forest of dandelions, the gold foot and baseball bat.

With his mouth full, Todd said: "There was this scholar, you know? One day, he goes to his master and asks, 'If it is doubtless that Mount Shumi can contain a poppy seed, then isn't it false that a poppy seed contains Mount Shumi?' So the master looks at him and asks, 'People say that you have read thousands of volumes of books, is that true?' The scholar guy says yes, you know? So the master goes: 'The body is as big as a coconut. Where can your thousands of volumes of books go?'"

Gary peeked over the top of his paper. The house reeked of incense, a smell that reminded me of cloves and cheap cologne.

"You're pretty serious with this Buddhism," Gary said.

"I've always been Buddhist. Just didn't know it." Todd shrugged. "Can I borrow the van?"

"Keys are in my purse," I said.

"Cool. Wanna drop stuff at the Salvation Army. Get some boxes."

"Oh," Gary said. "We aren't moving after all."

"Since when?" Todd stopped crunching his cereal.

I felt too tired to argue. The most I could do was smile the way you do when, hey, you win some, you lose some.

"Your mother and I discussed it, and it's final." Gary folded the paper and set it aside. He picked a banana from the counter behind him, peeled it, took a bite. He made a sucking noise as he chewed, started humming, and pretended to read the paper again.

Under the table, Todd reached across with his foot and tapped mine. It hit me how much I'd missed him. He looked up at the clock on the wall. "Shouldn't you be working?" he asked, referring to my writing routine: Eight-thirty to noon; one to six. No interruptions, the kids knew that. If one of them knocked, it meant a broken bone or an illness that involved bleeding, purging, or chills and fever.

Or death.

"Yes," Gary said, his tongue fishing food from the back molars, "shouldn't you be writing?"

I took my coffee to the study and shut the door. The mug was empty, yet still warm. I held it with two hands and watched the bell swing.

Todd drove off in the van. Gary went upstairs to pace in Sarah's room. He turned on the music, kept it low, not realizing I could hear it. I sat perfectly erect so that the small bell settled at the top of my head. The string twitched each time Gary stepped over the light fixture in the ceiling, and the metal doohickey tapped against my head. Gary talked. His muffled voice came through the ceiling.

A draft came in from under the door and circled my ankles. The manuscript stared at me. Every day I expected the story to end, and yet every day it continued to grow. I got up from the desk, left the room, and found Todd sitting at the top of the stairs. He had a bunch of brown boxes, folded and bunched, under his arm. In Sarah's room, his father was saying, "Who's Daddy's girl?"

Todd held his face in his hands, his feet turning inward.

Gary hummed the song.

I opened my arms to Todd. Come, come to Mommy. Todd descended the stairs one step at a time. I hugged him, tiptoed to kiss his forehead, and led him to the front porch. Outside, we sat together on the wicker loveseat.

"I'm losing it," he said, shaking. "I'm fucking losing it."

"I'm here. Mommy's got you."

He cried until he'd worn himself out. He hiccuped.

"Take some of that food with you when you go," I told him. "Those snacks in the kitchen."

"I hate Cocoa Puffs."

"I bought that for Sarah," I said. "Unfortunately, she's dead."

We looked at each other. It wasn't funny, we both knew it wasn't funny, but we laughed.

After dinner, Gary and I inspected the dead grass on the front lawn. It reminded me of a patch of bad eczema. Todd came outside with one large box on top of another. He walked over to us.

"Neighbor's dog," I lied.

"Neighbor's dog?" Gary said.

"Now that's some powerful piss," Todd said.

"Damn dog," Gary growled. "I'll shoot the thing if I ever see it—"

An invisible shock struck the three of us. We stared at the bald patch of lawn. How many times had I said, "If not this way, she would have found some other way," when really, underneath it all, an insipid voice raged: Why does he insist on keeping that gun?

"What's that?" I asked Todd.

Gary turned his attention to the boxes.

"Stuff." Todd continued walking toward the van. He'd be leaving in the morning.

Gary nodded absently, then went into the house. I had that fine-on-the-outside, sick-on-the-inside feeling I got the first time the kids left for summer camp. Only, this wouldn't be a fleeting moment of nausea that I could get over. Even now, after all these years, it was, would always be ongoing; perpetual.

I threw Todd a kiss as he drove away in the van, then went to my study, turned on the computer. I understood, finally, that the story was over; not done or finished, simply over. For no reason, except that sometimes the life of a novel evolved into nothing longer than a short story.

My fingers rested on the Delete button of the keyboard. Whole sentences, paragraphs, pages disappeared. I cut away at the manuscript as if I'd been storing energy for this moment. One line saved; two . . .

Only the rain let up. White petals fell to the ground, each plucked, as if by hand, and stamped into the red mud. Wind drummed against the barn. The walls were built of sturdy oak, but there were spaces, which allowed for the coming and going of voices, soft whistling voices, which were lost and trying to make their way home. John listened for the voice he knew. He understood he had to wait because of the great distance between continents, because of the great expanse of sea between the jungle trees and the dogwoods at home.

How long this went on, I couldn't say. But a soft, tentative rap at my door broke my concentration.

"What?" I thrust the door open.

Gary was in his rumpled pajamas. The collar was turned inward. A mark the size and shape of a red ant sat centered between his eyes. I hadn't noticed it before. Who are you? I wanted to ask. Maybe he was thinking along similar lines, because we stared at each other, quizzically at first, and then with that unforgiving knowledge that we'd lost her, we'd lost our baby girl. Between us stood our past. Between us stood our daughter's death, a cavern neither of us had dared leap to catch hold of the other.

"Todd's going to be leaving soon," Gary said.

It was morning. Through the window over the kitchen sink, I saw the sun was already up. I smelled a faint scent of incense. "Where is he?" I asked.

Gary nodded, Upstairs.

I pushed past him and climbed the stairs. The backpack was in the hallway. It was zipped, ready to go. Todd was in his room. He sat by the window with his eyes closed, his legs crossed beneath him, his hands palm-up in his lap. The expression on his face made him seem high. He was beautiful. A man, a stranger. The incense burned. His bed was stripped, the desk cleared, the bookshelves empty.

Todd opened his eyes.

"Hungry?" I asked.

"Lotus position, food for the soul."

"Sure you don't want me to whip up something?"

"My friend'll be here any second."

"That girl?"

Todd smiled as knowingly as if he were the Buddha himself. "Her name's Melissa—"

I cut him off. "I know, I know—'A crystal vessel filled with ice has no shadow,'" I mocked. "'A monkey reaches for the moon in the water.'"

He smiled and shut his eyes.

———

A frantic feeling came over me. It twisted around my body, ready
to choke the breath out of me. I went to the kitchen, poured myself a cup of coffee, and checked my "To Do" list. Except for return-
ing the book to the high school, every task had been taken care of
and crossed off. I washed the dishes, wiped the counters, put
everything in its right place. I cut a large piece of cantaloupe for
Todd, placed it on the table with a spoon.

Gary toasted himself a bagel and spread it with cream cheese.
He watched me darting about the kitchen and said, "He'll be home
before you know it."

I shut myself in the office. The metal doohickey swayed to and
fro. *John heard the horse braying. It was old and tired, alone within those
thick walls. John unlatched the doors, appeared with the rifle at his side,
and the horse fell silent. Its hoof was dried and splintered, as worn as the
barn under the summer sun. John cocked the rifle.*

Outside, a car tooted. Todd came to my study, opened the door
and stepped inside. His lips were shiny with purple lip gloss; he'd
been in Sarah's room again. The light gadget tapped at the crown of
my head. He kissed me. The lips. Right on the lips. One quick peck.
"Love you," he said, the bell jiggling at my scalp. The smell of grape
candy nearly swallowed me whole. I tasted the sweetness. It was
Todd who stood before me, and yet it was she; it was Sarah. She
flickered, went out. A moment; a century. The universe in a grain
of sand. A mountain in a poppy.

The car honked again, and it was over. From inside the house
I could hear the car radio blaring. Todd swung his pack onto his
back. He tightened the shoulder straps and stepped to the front
door. He turned and nodded. Here I go.

There you go.

He crossed the lawn to say good-bye to his father. They half hugged, half patted each other on the back. They were stoic and stiff, awkward the way men get when faced with too much emotion. Todd swung his pack into the trunk of the car. This time, in the front passenger seat was an Asian boy with long dreadlocked hair. He seemed younger than Todd. He got out of the car for Todd to get in the back. Melissa shut off the radio, and I could hear her giggling. Her voice squeaked when she spoke.

"Yo, dude," the boy said. "What up?"

He and Todd exchanged some kind of complicated high-five ritual. Todd climbed into the backseat. The Rabbit backed out of the drive. Todd waved and I waved. The patch of dead grass looked torched. When they were gone, Gary looked at me. What now? I shook my head, went upstairs to Todd's room, and sat on the floor by the window. The cone of incense was still burning. I shut my eyes.

John placed the rifle at the soft space equidistant between the horse's eyes and pulled the trigger. The blast exploded the skull. Bits of bone and blood covered his hands. The faint smell of burnt skin and the ripe, sweet smell of dung filled the air. John listened. Voices whistled through the walls. Not one was the one he waited for.

Later, in my study, I arranged the trophies on the desk. The gold foot and baseball bat reminded me of dice. I shook them in my fist, rolled them. The foot landed on its side. The bat rocked to a stop. I printed the story, left the two pages on the desk. With the school's book clutched under my arm, I went out to the van. The noon train sounded in the woods. From Sarah's window, Cobain sang: ". . . on the bright side is suicide . . ." I traveled down Central Avenue, passing shopping centers, apartment complexes, the supermarket. I wondered about the woman with the belly.

Today's her lucky day, I decided. Her lucky, lucky day.

I drove toward the red-brick buildings of the high school, and when I got there, continued past and turned onto the highway. I drove and drove.

Maybe this would be the day I wouldn't stop.

T H I E F

Y O U   S E E , I knew everything by heart: every detail about the house and who was in it. For ten thousand Hong Kong, the information "leaked" from the former cook. It was Sunday; hired help was off. I got in through the servants' quarters—the window was propped open with a warped wooden chopstick—and crept to the first-floor landing. The moonlight from the window made the marble steps look slicked with water. The hallway was cool but my hands were sweating in my gloves. Man, the rush made me feel like a kid again. This is the shit, as I used to say.

One flight up was the master bedroom. It was warm with sleep. The walls were upholstered with a slippery material. It was like being in a silk-lined casket. The floor was carpeted, the pile thick and silent beneath my feet. The safe was behind a series of cabinets on the west wall. It faced the foot of the bed.

I could make out the outlines of Sheng and his wife in the

king-size bed. She was the larger of the two—the bulk of her body practically dwarfed the guy—and she snored like gems were rattling at the back of her throat. To the right of the bed was an end table with a phone. There was also a desk lined with picture frames. Across from the door was a wall of windows.

I held the pistol close and cut the phone cord. The next thing, of course, was the safe. I opened a cabinet. The steel box was as cool as an ex-lover. I pictured the jade necklace inside the box. The missus had been featured in *The Hong Kong Daily* wearing it to a society ball. She had a round face and small eyes. Her cheeks seemed bloated, her neck lost in a ring of fat. The necklace bunched around her throat. The pieces of jade connected in a chain, each carved into an ornate lotus flower. Two million, the article said. Carved one flower at a time from a single stone.

I thought about Laurel back at the hotel. She had come to Hong Kong with me as a sort of vacation. This job would get her the ring she deserved. She could junk that job at Bloomingdale's and finally appreciate things from the other side of the counter. I went to the desk, pulled out the chair, and turned it to the bed. Then I sat back, parted my feet, and switched on the lamp. The room lit up.

The wife was closer to me. Her jet-black hair came to just above her shoulders. The roots were silverish, and at first, her scalp seemed to be perspiring. She gulped, then forced her eyes open. The lids fluttered. They were puffy and thick. Her skin was slick with oily lotion. There was a strange smell, something that gave me a bad feeling.

That moment—that *Oh, shit*—registered in her eyes. She went for the phone, kicking off the blanket at the foot of the bed, and took up the receiver. When she realized the phone was dead, she frowned, one cheek going red as if I'd smacked her across the face. I smiled, and she must have seen it through the hose, because she lay back, frozen against the pillow.

I turned the gun on her husband then, and she nudged him awake. "Phil-ip, ah," she whispered. "Phil-ip."

Sheng grumbled, turned to us, and blinked. He seemed confused, like he thought he should have known me. Then his eyes rounded out, and the stink of fear gave me another rush. That's right. I'm the one in charge here.

Sheng reminded me of a live turkey: a pocket of skin dangled below his chin, and tiny bumps circled his eyes. He had a large, flat nose, which dominated his face. His hair stuck to his scalp. His eyes veered toward the opened cabinet—the safe sitting inside—then back at me. "Take it," he said in Cantonese.

I gestured at the safe with the gun.

"Anything," he said. He clutched the sheets. "Whatever you want."

In a strained voice the wife said, "I think he wants you to open it."

"Yes, yes. Of course." He got out of bed, tried to jam his feet into slippers.

I jumped up and sighed impatiently. His hands flew into the air as though I'd said "Stick 'em up."

He sidestepped barefoot to the safe. He was shaking. In the privacy of their own homes, most of these Hong Kong types seemed either uglier or older. This guy seemed smaller. Smaller than he appeared in the papers, anyway, decked out in a bow tie and tux. How could this puny guy have a reputation for being such a brute? The cuffs of his pajamas were ratty, and you could practically see through the fabric at his ass. These rich guys who ran from the Commies. Never did get over starting over. Old man could've bought new silks every day, yet here he was, decked out like he was fresh off the boat.

Sheng touched the dial of the safe, turned it to the right, then stopped. "I can't remember," he finally said.

"Oi—didn't I tell you not to change it every week," the missus complained.

"I don't change it every week."

"There you go again," she said. "Fine, don't listen."

Shit, I thought. One in five jobs was going to turn nutty in some way. I accepted this. But to show I meant business, I swept my arm over the desk. Framed photos crashed to the floor.

"Five, twenty-nine, fifteen, three, forty-five," the wife said. She tried to be quick about it so I wouldn't catch the numbers.

"What was that?" Sheng asked, turning the dial.

She repeated herself.

"What?" he said. "Five, twenty-nine . . . ?"

"Fifteen," I shouted in Chinese. "Five, twenty-nine, fifteen, three, forty-five." My tones fell in all the wrong places.

The couple stared. "Get that—he's banana," the woman said.

That is: yellow on the outside, white on the inside. "Little banana," Ma used to say. It's the one thing I remember. Most things about her are gone now. Gone. Like her, a "missing person" since I was four. Went out for a quart of milk and never came back. "A bad man took her away," Dad explained. Abducted, locked up; possibly, and after a few years probably, dead.

Sheng kept fumbling with the dial. *Tick-tick-tick; tick-tick-tick; tick-tick-tick.*

"There's nothing in there," the missus said, in stilted English. "All le se," garbage.

I turned the gun on her; aimed at her head. Her eyes bulged. They weren't so much small as lost in webs of ruined skin.

"Want Rolex watches?" Sheng said. "We have. And pearls. Freshwater pearls from Japan. The best."

"The necklace," I said.

"We keep that in the bank," the missus stated.

"Oh, really?" I said.

She was sitting now, and I could tell something wasn't right. The top of her nightgown hung lopsided; there was the rise and fall of a breast, then a strange sinking. She was missing a breast.

Tick-tick-tick; tick-tick-tick; tick-tick-tick. Sheng tried the combination, but the safe refused to open. Frustrated, he shook the handle. "Si le"—dead—he wheezed.

"That's right, old man. Si le—get my meaning?" I dragged his wife out of bed, forced her to her feet, and held her by the throat. I tapped the gun at her temple, and wondered if it would be easier to try opening the safe myself.

"Take the necklace. Take everything. Just don't hurt her." Sheng turned back to the safe. *Tick-tick-tick; tick-tick-tick.* The woman was fleshy and soft. That strange smell came off her nightgown, and I felt a rage swoop through me. What was it? Incense? Perfume? I yanked a cord from my pocket and tied her wrists behind her back.

"You've got one minute," I told Sheng.

"Please," he begged. Sweat trickled from his hairline.

"Sixty, fifty-nine, fifty-eight . . ." My groin pressed against his wife's flabby ass. That's right—who's the boss now, huh?

All of sudden I was hard.

Shit, I thought. Be cool, man. Don't go losing your head right now.

But the woman shifted her weight, rubbed against me, making my dick throb. Bitch, I thought. She stiffened. A rush of heat—of shame, maybe—came off her, and she whimpered.

"I'll buy you another," he said to her. Right—just go on down and pick it up with the rest of the groceries. Man, what's another two mill? No fucking big deal.

"Ain't that the shit," I said.

Sheng's wife began to laugh. She didn't stop—she only got louder and more shrill—and it became clear from the look on Sheng's face that even he missed the point of her private joke.

I slipped my arm from around her throat to her waist and could feel the empty space where the breast should have been. Her body shook with laughter. She tried to speak. "It's—"

"Wife," Sheng warned.

"Get to work," I yelled, and he returned to his task.

The woman tried to catch her breath. "Bao ying," she said, and laughed. She was wishing whatever ill I was causing them now to come back to me later. What comes around goes around, as the saying goes. I threw her facedown on the bed.

Just then, the lock clicked and the vault opened. *Cl-tk*—like that.

I pushed the woman's face into the mattress, and took a paper lunch bag from the back of my pants. I threw it at Sheng. "Show me the necklace."

The man reached into the box, fidgeted with its contents, and brought out the necklace. The chain of lotus flowers hung from his hands, each petal and leaf precisely and delicately carved. There was a hint of blue I'd never seen in jade before. "It was handed down from my mother's mother's mother . . . her mother," Sheng said.

The missus cackled into the mattress. "Ha—garbage."

I lifted the woman by the arms. Her breast hung like a rotting melon. "What was that you said?"

"Fake. You'll be lucky if you can fetch more than a couple hundred."

Sheng stood with the offering in his hands. His face turned white. "She doesn't know what she's saying." A drop of sweat appeared at his temple.

"Phil-ip, ah? Nothing to hide. He's a thief, for God's sake. Who's going to know?"

"It's real," he insisted, short of breath. "From my mother's side."

She shook her face into the mattress.

"It is," he said, his voice nearly gone. He covered his face with his shaking hands. The jade pieces tapped against each other, pattering dully against his skin.

"Put it in the bag," I said.

His breath grew wheezy and short. He moved his hands. His face was blank, sweating.

"Hear me, old man?" I warned. "The bag."

He did what I said, and clutched a hand to his chest.

"On the floor," I said. "Drop it."

The woman continued to chuckle, her fingers wiggling behind her back. Yoo-hoo, they taunted, betcha can't get me.

My dick throbbed again. I thought about Laurel. How beautiful she was, how fucking lucky I was to have her. Yet here I was with a chubby. A fucking chubby. I wanted to kick the fat cow's legs apart, teach her a good lesson. She quieted and tried to look over her shoulder. I pressed her head into the mattress and lifted her nightgown. Her legs were tiered with fat. Half-moons of ass stuck out from her underwear.

"Son," Sheng whispered.

Son? It was like he'd planted a fist to my chest. He dropped to his knees and crawled toward me. "You don't want to do that."

I pointed the gun. "Don't be telling *me* what I want or don't want."

His eyes pleaded, Take me, blow my head off if you want, but leave her be. The look he gave me made my stomach turn. He didn't resemble my old man, and yet he was everything like him. One woman was enough to ruin a guy. My old man waited for Ma's return, on the same ratty couch, in the same room, in the same apartment. Before she disappeared, my old man ran a store and on the side painted still lifes—mainly fruit bowls and potted plants. Afterward, everything turned abstract. During his last twenty-five years, he worked on a series titled *She'll Be Back.*

Sheng coughed. "Take anything."

"Anything?" I barked. "Well, how fucking generous of you."

I dragged him to the bed, tied his hands and feet, then dumped him next to his wife. She was screaming now, flailing around on the bed, her nightgown tangled at her waist. Her scent overwhelmed me.

"Phil-ip," she cawed. "Phil-ip."

The house was secluded safely at the end of the road, and yet the sound of her voice got to me.

"Shut up," I yelled, and started to remove the pillowcases. I gagged her first, then him. The air conditioner blasted on, buzzing and rattling the window. All at once, the room went from being too hot and stuffy to being too cool.

On the bed, the couple were like a pair of fish at the market, alive and breathing at the gills, but otherwise laid out and still. Sheng was soaked with perspiration. They shivered. I did, too. It hit me how close I'd come to losing it—I could have fucked the bitch.

I knew then this would be the last job.

I took the blanket from the floor, waved it open and covered them. I picked up the bag and went to the safe. It was filled with jewelry, all of which I quickly scooped into the bag. There were a bunch of photos. On top was one of a woman in a white lab coat, maybe a doctor. She sat at her desk, which was covered with files and a glass bowl with a fat goldfish. I left the photos and made my way to the marble staircase, enjoyed a moment of moonlit silence, then exited through the front door.

———————

The exchange with Da Jie, an old high school acquaintance, was as always. We met at the back of the candy shop. In front, the store was stocked with everything from chocolate-covered peanuts to candied mango slices to dried squid. A salesman going gray at the temples helped a girl with an order of gummy bears. "That one," she insisted, pointing at a red shape at the bottom of a jar. The guy smiled. He tipped and shook the jar with grandfatherly patience, and fished out the candy with tongs.

I pretended to be interested in the cuttlefish. The strands were sinewy and dry, like overbleached hair. I knew there had to be a .22-caliber semiautomatic concealed beneath the man's smock.

When the salesman got around to me, I told him I was delivering a salmon sandwich. He glanced at the bag and then at me. He'd figured as much. Without another word, he took me to the storage room, which led to a secret room at the back. He knocked on a door, opened it to an office dressed up like a living room: TV and CD player, coffee table, couch. The salesman left me in the room with Da Jie. She was on the couch, in the middle of checking the books. She put up a finger to indicate she needed another moment of silence; I saw her circle several figures in red. I could hear the candy bumping against her teeth. She looked young, her skin smooth and clear, her features sharp and refined, but she handled business in an almost matronly manner. Her hair was rolled like a roast-pork bun at the back of her head. She wore a purple suit with gold buttons and shoes with buckles. This always got me. Way back at P.S. 445, she had big, mile-high hair, and wore tight jeans and

too much makeup. Back then, before she got recruited by Da Ge—
Big Brother—and the rest of them, she was still Sandra.

Next to her on the coffee table was an ashtray filled with the
night's cigarette butts. The TV was turned to the news. There were
also sandwiches out on the table, a vase filled with white tulips, a
pot of coffee, and a jar of individually wrapped candies. Though I
knew this was just an illusion of safety, I still felt comforted by it. I
helped myself to an aqua Gobstopper. It was sweet yet tart.

Da Jie tapped her pen against the page. She felt for a cigarette
on the table, lit one, glanced at the burning tip, then X'ed something from the books. I knew what this meant: Some idiot would
wind up at the bottom of Kowloon harbor. Either he'd scammed
her or he was in bad with the police—the kind of trouble you
couldn't buy your way out of. This could lead the police not only to
Da Jie's door, but to Da Ge and then the larger network, revealing
to you powerful people in all kinds of high places.

Da Jie cracked a smile. It was a natural part of her character—
the way her lips curled upward at the left side of her face but down
at the right—and this peculiarity, too, calmed me. Smoke streamed
from her nostrils.

"Doesn't the cat look as though he ate a fat mouse," she said.
"What'd you do—rob a bank or something?" She patted the seat,
and I sat next to her on the couch. She juggled the candy in her
mouth. "Haven't seen you in a while. Since Macau, uh? Now, *that*
was a gold mine of a job. Haven't seen a diamond like that in
years."

"Set me up pretty good," I said. "Just wanted a little more to
get my girl a little something, put down some roots—"

She flicked the tip of her cigarette into the ashtray, picked up the remote, and muted the TV. "Guai lo girlfriend want you to retire? She know all about this?"

"Course not," I said, smiling. "But hey—am I lying if I say I'm in the jewelry business?"

Her mouth went crooked again.

Out of the blue, I picked up that scent of incense again. Where the hell was it coming from? "Smell that?" I said.

Da Jie sniffed the air, then the inside of her wrist. "Chanel No. 5."

"No," I said. But then the smell was gone. "Nothing. Never mind."

She watched me for a second, inhaled her cigarette. "So how's your father?" She'd been around to see how the old man painted: the frenzied scrapes and stabs, the desperate strokes that arched across the canvas, the sudden fits of crying.

"He passed on," I said. "Few months back."

"Sorry to hear that, Seymour." She sighed, tamped out the cigarette, and offered me a sandwich. When I refused, she set the plate aside, uncovering a rubbery black placemat.

I laid the paper bag on the table. She poured everything onto a blotter. She separated the necklace from the rest of the jewels, then examined it through a magnifying glass she had pulled from her pocket.

It's fake, I thought. She thinks it's fake. The bitch had been telling the truth, after all. Get that. She's probably laughing her ass off right now, and you're ten thousand down. Bitch.

"Beauty you got here," Da Jie finally said.

I relaxed. The panic spinning in my head gave way to a quick rush. "Yes! I mean, I know."

Da Jie nodded absently. She peered through the glass. "I'll have to get my guy to take a better look tomorrow—"

"Can't get a thing like that anywhere. Worth two mill. Saw it in the papers."

"Really?" She seemed mesmerized by the necklace. "What an interesting shade of blue. You know, this piece'll be hot for at least ten years."

"Hot or not hot, it's worth two million."

She placed the necklace and magnifying glass back on the blotter, then folded her hands, interlacing her fingers. "One seventy-five," she offered.

"One seventy-five? Oh, Sandra, Sandra. What you trying to do to me?"

"That's my offer."

"Two twenty-five," I said. "I'll throw in the other stuff."

She studied the pile of jewelry as though it mattered. A piece of plastic caught my attention. "What's that?" she asked.

It was a ring. A plastic ring, the kind you get from a gumball machine. It was purplish blue, like a giant sapphire. My throat squeezed shut. That smell. It was sandalwood soap. Ma used to keep a bar in her top drawer. I'd reach into the bras and panties, feel the silk catching in my fingers, and fish it out.

Sweat broke out along my brow and over my back. I tried to swallow.

"Okay, okay, two hundred. For old time's sake. But that's it." She reexamined the necklace.

Something in my memory opened—*cl-tk!*—and I saw myself giving it to Ma; slipping it on her finger. Then I remembered what she'd said that morning she disappeared. "My little banana," she'd said, "no matter what happens, Ma always loves you." I picked up the ring with my pinky. It stuck at the first knuckle. The plastic surface was scratched.

"Eh?" Da Jie was getting impatient. "Take it or not?"

"Fine." I pictured Ma's face, her thin, beautiful face, and felt myself turn cold. I shivered. No—it's not. Can't be. What were the chances—one in ten million?

Da Jie stood and we shook. With my thumb, I circled the plastic gem around my finger.

"I'll even throw in the ring," Da Jie said. She smiled again, and the stress and fatigue, the loneliness of this life wrinkled into the bottom ridges of her eyes. Before I had a chance to say anything, she disappeared into another room.

She reappeared a few minutes later with a freshly lit cigarette and a paper bag filled with crisp bills. "Here's half," she said. It caught me off guard. As a rule, she never gave out more than a tenth until her guy examined the goods. She wasn't the type to take risks.

The surprise must have registered on my face. "Get a little something," she said, exhaling smoke into my eyes. "For your girl."

It was close to five when I arrived at the hotel. The chill was gone. I'd decided the ring didn't add up to anything—a million kids out there could've given their mothers a plastic ring like that. Besides,

Sheng's fat bitch was nothing like Ma. A hundred thousand dollars padded my pocket, and I was feverish with excitement. Da Jie had given me the hallway pass to a new life.

My shirt was dirty and damp with perspiration. I couldn't wait to shower. Laurel was with me, just upstairs. *This* is the shit, I thought. The lobby was empty, and when the doorman opened the door, I whistled, "Here Comes the Bride." There was a tingling in my chest: hope.

I took the elevator, and as it climbed upward, I thought about chance; about how Laurel and I had met, five years before. I'd been casing a brownstone down by NYU for a few days. I did this from the window seat of a coffee shop, dressed in a suit and tie, and carrying a jewelry case filled with tools. Laurel was there next to me in the window like clockwork. She arrived at twelve thirty-five and left at one-fifty. She bought the same thing every day: one corn muffin and a large black coffee. She kept to herself and read Shakespeare— *Hamlet, Othello, Romeo and Juliet.* I pegged her for a student—a snob at that—and fucking hated her. But one day I noticed her quartering the muffin, halving each of those pieces, then halving them again. She'd eat each sliver and chew it like a large, disgusting mouthful. This got to me: I thought of those times when I was ten or eleven and I'd cook up a pan of chicken livers. I'd tell myself—as Ma used to—that if I finished, I was good; it would be a sign that Ma was okay; she'd come back. But I never did eat all of it without gagging, sometimes chucking it back up. Anyway, I'm thinking along these lines when Laurel looked up and caught me staring. She glared. I wanted to smile and apologize—make some kind of joke— but something got to me. "You reminded me," I tried to explain, "I just thought about someone. . . ." This sad look came over her face, and she gave my arm a soft, reassuring squeeze. She understood. For a split second, we were connected—strangers and yet not—at the beginning of something, though we weren't sure what.

The hotel elevator arrived, the doors opening to the silent hallway. Our room was at the end. When I got there, I found Laurel in bed. A book lay open next to her. I set it aside.

"Seymour?" she asked, in a groggy voice.

"You should be asleep," I said. In the dark, I reached for my briefcase at the foot of the desk, felt out the combination with my fingers, and opened it. The lock's clasps knocked against leather. I slipped the gloves, gun, and cash into the case, then locked it.

"I was dreaming," she said.

"Grandma again?" I asked. Laurel had lost her grandmother back in junior high. Missed the old lady so much it'd made her sick. Said it was that anorexia thing; lost her appetite for close to two years.

"No, it was about your dad," she said, more awake now. She'd known my old man a few months before he died. "He was painting. You know—the one hanging in the hallway. Him on the white sofa."

"*Waiting,*" I said. It was an abstract, but I could tell the disfigured man on the couch was Dad next to a purplish-blue blur, which I took to be Ma, or at least his memories of her. I got onto the bed next to Laurel and kissed her forehead. She smelled of eucalyptus. Her dark hair lay sprawled out over the pillow, but she had the peaceful look of a child from a family with sound parents. She scrunched up her nose. "You smell like an ashtray," she said.

"Clients wanted to go clubbing after dinner."

She sat up and rubbed the sleep from her eyes. "So it went well?"

"Made a deal tonight. Big one. As big as it gets, anyway."

"Good for you. Didn't I say you'd break out of that slump sooner or later?" For years now, I'd kept her under the impression that the Asian economy was seriously affecting my business— something I didn't feel comfortable speaking too often about—and she was willing to allow for two- or three-week business trips without badgering me with questions.

I felt high. "How about we do a little shopping today?"

She kissed me on the cheek. The smell of sandalwood overcame me again. I thought about the robbery, wondered how something so simple could turn so nutty. There'd been all that had happened; all that could have happened. There was Sheng's face, the fleshy feel of his wife, and the tiers of fat along her thighs. My dick went hard.

I leaped out of bed. What kind of sick son of a bitch was I?

"What's wrong?" Laurel asked.

My heartbeat throbbed in my ears. I looked at her. What had I ever done to deserve such a good thing?

"Nothing," I said. I had the strange feeling that time between us was beginning to contract. "I need a shower."

"Hey, you crying?" She groped my face.

I caught hold of her hand and kissed it. "Just dirt and sweat. You know me—just your typical dirty dealer."

"Don't say that—you work hard for it all."

"Go back to sleep," I told her.

"You do." Reluctantly she lay back. I heard the airy sound of her head sinking into the pillow.

I got up, went to the bathroom, and shut myself inside. The counter was loaded with creams, eyeliners, lipsticks, powders, and an assortment of compacts. I turned on the shower and listened to it run. A pressure at the back of my eyes made it difficult to look in the mirror. I dug the plastic ring from my pocket, rubbed it between my fingers, then flipped it into the air.

"No," I called, but the ring landed face down, an almost impossible way to land given its rounded surface, and then I thought, Yes, it could have been her.

On the second toss, the ring landed on its side. See, of course it's not; couldn't have been. The mirror clouded, and slowly, all of me disappeared.

After the shower, I sat on a towel, hunched over on the toilet, staring at Laurel's facial astringent. It was pastel blue. My skin was pink from all the scrubbing, yet I still felt grimy, unclean. Steam fogged the mirror. I got to my feet and wiped it with the towel. The stroke arched from bottom left to top right. My forehead and eyes appeared in the glass, then disappeared beneath a new layer of steam. I brushed the towel over the mirror again, and this time the lower part of my face appeared. My lips turned down at the corners. They were surrounded by morning stubble.

I rubbed faster and faster, the incessant sweep of paintbrush over a canvas, then made quick strokes up and down. I scraped the plastic ring against the glass, and imagined the patter of paint dropping to the floor. I stabbed and stabbed.

The scent of sandalwood came at me again, and this time when I pictured the bloated face, I decided it couldn't have been her and yet for this very reason had to have been. "Bao ying," she'd said, and now I wondered if she'd been referring to herself. How much did a person have to pay for disappearing on a husband—on her child—and starting a new life? Did it cost a breast? Did it cause a robbery?

Had she paid her dues? I could feel the pressure of her flabby ass against my dick, see Sheng pleading on his knees. A sick, cold feeling rose up my back.

No, I thought, shaking it off. No, no, no. I dropped the ring into my travel kit, zipped it shut, and sat back on the toilet. I thought of my old man and the couch. Waiting.

"Seymour?" Laurel called from outside. The knob turned, and there she was in the doorway. Soap scum covered the mirror. Steam poured out into the dark room. Concern showed on her face. "What are you— What was that sound? Were you knocking?" She took my hand and led me to bed.

We spent the day window-shopping in Central. Eventually we found ourselves in the Landmark, a mall designed for the filthy rich. You had to be loaded to buy anything in the place, to exist there. In one of the men's shops, a salesman—a short Cantonese guy wearing a smart black suit and oval glasses—looked at me like I was a bad odor.

"That dress across the way," Laurel said, trying to distract me from Shorty with the attitude. Her hair was tied into a neat pony-tail. She pointed at a plain white dress in a shop window. "Wouldn't it look wonderful on me?"

"Yes." I let her lead me out of the store. I turned to stare Shorty in the face—give him the "We'll see who's boss" stare—but he was helping someone else.

Laurel found several dresses to try on. I told her I wanted to check out the tie store, and when she went into the dressing room, I slipped back across the hall into the men's shop. I approached an-other salesman and, in full view of Shorty, purchased a black sports jacket and slacks, a knit shirt, and a pair of black suede loafers. For the complete deal, I picked out a Hermès wallet and, for the hell of it, a platinum watch.

I paid in cash, then sauntered out of the store without turning back. In the women's store, Laurel was standing in front of a mir-ror, wearing a black dress with frilly stuff at the collar. As soon as she saw me, she turned. "Is that you?"

My hands dug into the pockets of my pants. "The new me."

She moved close, felt the fabric of the jacket between her thumb and fingers. From the expression on her face, I could tell she was figuring how much I'd spent, but she resisted whatever in-stincts were gnawing at her and smiled. "Nice," she said.

"Nice?" I said. "A guy gets himself a set of new duds and you say 'Nice'?"

"Oh, Seymour." She kissed me on the cheek. "You look hand-some."

"That's better," I said. "You look nice, too."

She blushed and turned to the mirror, flattened her palms over

her belly, and stepped back into the dressing room. I excused myself to the bathroom and went straight to a jewelry store. Laurel's
ring was waiting for me in the window.

"That one," I told the saleswoman, pointing at a clear, round
diamond.

"Lucky girl," she said. She explained the differences among diamonds, stressed the fact that this one was more than three karats
and as clear as the stone could possibly get—nearly flawless. It was
set in platinum. The rock came to seventy thousand U.S. dollars. I
hesitated. A voice in me went, Do it, man. Just do it. I forked over
the cash.

When I returned to the women's store, Laurel was trying on
the white dress. It was silk and embroidered with pink flowers.
"There you are," she said, studying herself in the mirror. The dress
showed off her chest and hips, but no leg. I could tell by the way
she checked over her shoulder at the open back of the garment
how much she liked it.

"Do I look fat?" she asked.

"No."

"But I am." She pointed to her waist. "Look—I'm such a
porker."

"You look fine. I swear."

"Blah, blah—" She looked in the mirror, her brows bent with
insecurity.

"Come on." I didn't want to go through this again. "You look
incredible, I swear. Now turn for me."

She circled, and swayed her hips from side to side.

"Get it," I told her.

"It's nice, but—" She flashed the tag. We were talking about a five-thousand-buck dress.

"My treat."

She searched my face as though she sensed something wasn't kosher.

"What? A guy can't get something for his girl?"

She fingered the tag. "Is it the business? 'Cause if things aren't going well right now, well, it's not like you've got to buy me expensive things."

"Laurel—"

"You could tell me if something was wrong, you know. I mean, I'm not going anywhere."

I laughed until my stomach hurt. "Business is fine. Didn't I say I made a deal last night?"

"Yeah, but . . . Oh, Seymour."

"Don't 'Oh, Seymour' me. You'll need it. I'm taking you out for dinner tonight. There's something I want to give you."

Her jaw fell open.

I smirked. "Get it already."

Her entire being lit up. She touched my cheek, whispered, "Who's my Romeo?" and disappeared into the dressing room.

After shopping, we returned to the hotel to wash up and get ready for dinner. Laurel leaned against the bathroom basin, close to the mirror, singing and drawing in eyeliner. She finished one eye and started on the other. She was wearing the white dress, with her hair loose over her shoulders. Her small tight ass poked out. *My ass*—it belonged to me now.

I sat on the bed, patting the ring box in my jacket pocket: She'll say yes, of course she'll say yes.

A voice inside me piped up: Oh, yeah?

Laurel continued singing. I got to my feet, walked to the bathroom for my travel kit, brought it back to the bed. I found the ring stuck on the cap of my toothpaste.

Just go ahead and watch, I thought, jamming the ring into my pants pocket.

Laurel stepped from the bathroom. She flipped her hair over her shoulders. A horizontal watermark ran across the front of the dress.

"You leaned against the sink," I said.

She gasped and returned to the bathroom. The hair dryer went on.

The phone rang, and I went to answer. It was Da Jie. When Laurel poked her head out of the bathroom, I indicated with a wave for her to shut the door. She closed it and continued with the dryer.

"Bad news," Da Jie said.

Something clenched inside me. *Shit.*

"Highest-quality junk jade you can get."

Everything went still. I could see it: Da Jie was on the couch, books spread open on her lap, her red pen tapping nervously against paper.

In the bathroom, the hair dryer continued to buzz. I opened

my briefcase. The clasps snapped against my thumbs. I located the gun and slipped it into my jacket pocket. "I'll be at the store in, say, half an hour." I figured I could hand the ring over as a down payment.

Da Jie sighed. "No, Seymour. The wife gave a description to the police."

Bitch. "She got me?"

"Got you better than if she'd been your own mother." Then she said, "Meet at Kowloon Star Ferry. Last boat." Da Jie was speaking in code, giving me a chance to run. Whether she was the one to put it there or not, there was already a red X on the page in front of her, and I was about to end up at the bottom of the harbor.

What the fuck was going on? A chill got me in the gut. She must have sensed something in my silence. "Sheng had a heart attack," she said.

Pain rammed clear through my Adam's apple. "Old man's dead?"

"Pronounced dead at the scene of the crime."

In a matter of minutes or hours, I might be, too. Before they could make any connections, I, like the necklace, had to be eliminated.

In the bathroom, the hair dryer shut off. Laurel came out and posed in the doorway.

"Eleven o'clock, then," I rasped into the phone before hanging up.

"How do I look?" Laurel asked.

I remembered the ring. This was my chance. "Needs a little something . . ." I reached into my jacket. "I was going to give this to you later, but . . ."

Laurel beamed. My throat clucked with each swallow.

Please, God. Help me this once. I swear I won't go back to doing that shit. *Please.* Is there a place where we could start over again? I pictured us together many years from now, our hair gray, our skin loose from age, Laurel still smelling of eucalyptus.

But my hand brushed against the gun. A voice inside me said, No. Laurel would never be safe with me now. The smell of sandalwood overwhelmed my sinuses. Bao ying. The price. Everything lost, everything found.

I'll be disappeared. Like Ma.

I took the purple ring from my pants pocket. "For you."

She glanced at the piece of plastic, then back at me. She looked puzzled, hurt.

"I gave this to my mom when I was a kid," I said, slipping it onto her finger.

"Oh." Her voice wavered.

"You know what she said? She said, 'No matter what happens, remember that I love you.'"

Laurel stared down at her hand. She seemed too thin, like the wind could knock her over. "Oh, happy dagger . . ." she said, her hands clasped to her heart. Her eyes turned shiny like polished marble. She bit her lip and smiled.

The diamond in my jacket weighed me down; it'd be going with me now.

"Turn for me," I said.

She turned a circle under my arm, flashing the plastic sapphire on her hand. "How do I look now?" she asked.

She looked the kind of beautiful you see when you know it's the last time.